Jon Wright was [...] Hampshire. In the [...] Modern History at C[...] Technology and the[...] University of Hull, where Philip Larkin was college Librarian. Despite spending much of his student grant on overdue fines for unread books, they never met. Since then he has worked in a number of different settings including old people's homes, day centres and a child protection team. He has also managed a Barnardo's child care project in Bradford. When not writing he now works as an emergency duty social worker in West Yorkshire, and his hobbies almost all involve contact with dangerous levels of cholesterol, intensive weight gain, and long bouts of sloth.

This is his second novel.

Also by Jon Wright:

Spitting Distance

Apron

Strings

Jon Wright

WARNER BOOKS

A *Warner* Book

First published in Great Britain in 1999
by Warner Books

A CIP catalogue record for this book
is available from the British Library.

ISBN 0 7515 2655 X

Typeset in Palatino by M Rules
Printed and bound in Great Britain by
Clays Ltd, St Ives plc

Warner Books
A Division of
Little, Brown and Company (UK)
Brettenham House
Lancaster Place
London WC2E 7EN

For Michael, Judith,
Elizabeth and Andrew.
As Gloria Gaynor says,
'I Will Survive'!

One

Clive Wrigley knew he was going to win the award. For years he'd felt he deserved it but was wise enough to know that, in his experience, people rarely got what they deserved. Being the best at what he did was not the reason he felt confident about winning; he knew it was going to be his because he had seen it in his dreams. This uncanny ability to foresee the future had teased him for months with misty visions of the glorious moment when he grabbed the award and celebrated the high point of a glittering career. He didn't usually understand these visions; they drifted into his dreams and then slipped away before he was awake and able to make any sense of them, recognising them again only when it was almost too late and they were happening in front of him, for real. But the latest insight into his future seemed pretty obvious, as visions go. He was going to get what he deserved, he was going to get the Listening Ear.

Clive was a family therapist, counselling those in pain and distress. Good counselling required the skills of listening, empathy, reflection and not falling asleep while the client was talking. Clive was good at all these things. People had shared their problems with him for as long as he could remember but he was well into his mid-twenties before he hit on the idea of getting paid for it. The rest had been a long, occasionally bumpy ride culminating in this night, the night when his achievements were finally going to be acknowledged. Certain of the result, he'd hired a dinner suit specially for the occasion and slipped into the silk-lined inner pocket an acceptance speech that was carefully honed until it perfectly blended humility with honesty and humour with solemnity.

His wife Grace wore a little black number, a new Prada dress, the price of which had added a long red number to her bank statement. The dress emphasised her natural elegance and gently subdued her more curvy bits. She was knocking back Martinis with the regularity of a metronome and was starting to enjoy herself at the expense of Clive's professional colleagues seated around them. He smiled at the people on their table and made futile attempts to reduce the impact of Grace's outbursts.

'When my wife says all therapists are nosy bastards who aren't happy unless they're knee deep in the other people's shit, what she actually means is . . .'

He laughed lightly as Grace launched another mortar attack on the assembled throng, a tell-tale pile of black olives left over from too many Martinis next to her on the table. 'My wife doesn't approve of our profession,' he said, faking a smile that was as sincere as a politician's in election year.

As if to prove his point, Grace turned to the frightened chubby woman on her left. 'Pass the Gestalt and pepper, or else me and my multiple personalities will kick your fat face in.'

From their table Clive could see the lectern on stage where sat the main award of the evening, the object of his dreams. Grace continued to infuriate and intimidate his colleagues while he gazed lovingly at the Listening Ear Award. It was given for excellence in Problem Solving Through Therapeutic Intervention, and was known in the vernacular of his profession as the Golden Lobe. It was the Holy Grail of counselling, and this year more than most he had his heart set on it.

His fixation with the award had nothing to do with its aesthetic qualities, far from it; it was a small loop of high-quality plastic moulding, 'a Jubilee clip with delusions of grandeur' was how Grace described it. Nor was it the financial value of the award that Clive craved; it was as worthless as it was tasteless. It was what the award represented that was important. Recognition. Recognition by his colleagues, his peers, his clients and, most importantly of all, Dr Amen Durkin, his bitter rival.

The cold coffee and warm chocolate mints had been served and the conversation in the hall had reached the required peak of boozy intensity when, instigated by the dimming of the lights, a hush swept across the room like a weather front. Then someone was on stage.

'Good evening, colleagues.' It was Professor Phil

Carmody, the youngest ever occupant of the Chair of Psychology and Clinical Analysis at Bradworth University. He was considered by many to be a genius in the mould of Freud for his work in the field of anal retention. Quite a few more, including many of those who allied themselves to the 'genius' school of thought, reckoned that when it came to things anal he was the biggest shit there was.

'Should he be up this late on a school night?' Grace asked, sending a breeze of neat gin wafting past Clive's nose as she spoke.

'We know why we are here,' Phil Carmody said, slowly and deliberately to build the tension.

'That's our job,' Clive said, loudly enough to be heard on stage.

Phil allowed a patronising smile to play around his lips. 'I disagree. Our job is to know *how* we got here, not *why*,' he said.

Clive saw several serious nods of agreement around the half-lit room. The cover of Phil Carmody's latest book came into his mind. Carmody was the master of the self-help manual, the most recent of which had a dark line down the centre of the cover from which curvaceous mounds of pink flesh rolled away on either side. The picture was taken from so close up that at first it looked like cleavage between pert breasts, which, by happy co-incidence pushed sales up by forty per cent. It was only after closer study, and perhaps a quick glance at the contents of the book, that it became clear it was not breast but buttock cleavage. Male buttock cleavage at that. The book was called *Holding Tight* and was sub-titled 'Anal Relaxation Techniques for the Busy Executive'. Clive had a copy at work which he used to swat flies. 'It relaxes me,' was his recommendation.

Phil wore a ponytail strangled at the roots by a coloured band, which kept bouncing forward over his shoulder like an excited squirrel. He may have been the youngest person to occupy such an exalted academic post, but he wasn't anywhere near young enough to realise that ponytails on men over thirty only ever made them look foolish. His deliberate pause still hung in the air.

'Get on with it, arse-face,' Grace shouted. Clive shushed her, but without daring to sound like he meant it.

Phil showed no sign of having heard Grace's heckle but his delivery sped up to a disabled snail's pace.

'Men and women from the world of inner healing, we are here to celebrate the best of our number. To show our gratitude for their efforts, for their unstinting and uncompromising work to improve the human spirit.' He paused to chase the offending ponytail away again. 'If the eyes are a mirror of the soul, then tonight the victor is a mirror of our profession. This prestigious award commends not just one person but all of us. It is a victory for everyone who deals with pain.'

Clive groaned and Grace helped herself to another horse trough of gin.

'And so to the shortlist.' He opened a golden envelope which looked like it had been borrowed for the occasion from a cheap television game show. *Answer this question correctly and you will win a car.*

'Barry C. Wainwright.' Polite applause like a gentle morning tide on a pebble beach washed around the hall.

Over the PA a disembodied voice, female and earthy, read from a sycophantic script. It dwelt on Barry's successful work as a stress counsellor, his books on the skill of negotiation in repairing relationships and his development of a chain of private clinics to work with 'the problem teenager within everyone'. The voice thoughtfully left out Barry's three messily broken marriages, his daughter's arrest for running a drugs ring at her public school, and his little indiscretion with the babysitter, her younger sister and the video camera.

'Shame,' Grace whispered to Clive, so loudly his ear buzzed, 'vulnerability might have won him a few more votes. The dirty old bastard.'

'Clive Wrigley.' The tide on the beach, while not quite a spring flood, at least washed in a few waves of polite applause. This died away before the earthy voice began again, glossing over Clive's partnership with Amen Durkin and dwelling instead on his ownership of the Listen To You family therapy and counselling practice.

'A man who is much respected,' the voice said, which Clive roughly translated as 'a bit dull and never knowingly killed anyone'. Clive strained his ears to catch any murmurs of agreement from around the room. The deafening silence confirmed that everyone still thought he was crazy to try to combine psychologists, counsellors and both the psychos (analysts and therapists) into one 'holistic' practice. After years of managing the operatic histrionics of professions in conflict he was inclined to agree. He'd even had mocking cards printed which he distributed around his colleagues. 'You don't have to be mad to work at Listen To You, but if you are there's bound to be someone who can sort you out.'

'And finally . . .' Phil was milking it now, winding the audience up for the biggest disclosure, 'Amen Durkin.'

The tide of applause now smashed against the sea wall and waves of support were thrown thirty feet into the air. It was like the sound of blood rushing through Clive's ears. It was loud, long and lovingly given. There wasn't a single voice of opposition, other than Clive's. 'Fucking quack,' he shouted, confident that no one would hear him above the adulation. He thought about his premonition, where he was the one holding the award, and this partially restored his dissipating confidence.

The gushing, earthy voice was back on air detailing Durkin's rise to greatness, his widely franchised Shrink-Fit practice, the glamorous clients, the daily afternoon television show *Amen in the Confessional* (in which a wide variety of fat, dysfunctional losers from a specially chosen audience of fat, dysfunctional losers would unburden themselves of their innermost guilt in the privacy of 3.2 million sitting rooms).

Clive chanted a mantra in his head to combat the insidious propaganda of the earthy voice. 'It's mine, it's mine, it's mine.' His Zen-like calm was interrupted by Phil Carmody.

'Fellow clinicians . . . dear colleagues . . . ladies . . . gentlemen . . . the . . . winner . . . is . . .' Phil's pauses, intended to underpin the tension, merely irritated Clive. The ponytail was on Phil's shoulder again, as if trying to get a sneak preview of the winner. Clive couldn't bear the tension any longer and he set off on his victory walk towards the stage.

He had taken several paces before he realised Phil's final pause had been followed by words that weren't in the script in his head. 'Amen Durkin.' The lights came on and Amen Durkin stood up at his table on the other side of the room shaking his head and mouthing with fake modesty that surely there'd been some mistake. Clive saw the familiar thinning silver hair, like a worn-out Brillo pad, the red-tinted glasses, the Falstaffian girth, the thin-lipped smile. The sight of Durkin being covered in glory did nothing to help arrest his momentum. He was nearly at the stage steps and he couldn't see any way out.

He wondered about going up on stage and denouncing the hypocrisy of such sickening mutual appreciation before spearing Durkin through the heart with the award just to prove his point. Panic was taking over from rational thought and his mind span out of control. Around him he could hear his fellow professionals sniggering as he continued on a collision course with public humiliation. He tried to pretend the whole thing was an ironic gesture but this was a room full of therapists and they knew the truth, or thought they did, which was just as bad.

He was just about to mount that first small step towards career suicide when he was saved by a green square of plastic, underlit by a warm yellow bulb, to the right of the stage. It announced 'Fire Exit' above a big green arrow which helpfully pointed the way to his salvation. He pushed through the door beneath as if his life depended on it.

Outside in the carpeted hall Clive tried to recover his composure. He could hear the earthy voice reading an elegy for Durkin over the hotel's state-of-the-art mini speaker system. Her gravelly tones told of his ambition to save the world. Or was it to own it? From his mirrored-glass Dockland premises (Leeds–Liverpool canal rather than Canary Wharf) of the Shrink-Fit head office, Durkin had developed his own exclusive brand of therapy (exclusive in the sense that it was the most expensive), offering a route to self-discovery for faces that were known in every sitting room in the country. A television veterinarian (recovering alcoholic), a fast-fading but still internationally famous footballer (reformed wife beater), and an ex-junior minister (deconstructed sex addict), all of whom happily came out in public to endorse his treatments. The ex-minister and the vet were at the awards, sitting at Durkin's table. The former happily watched the attractive cocktail waitresses in their neat black uniforms while the latter thirstily lusted after them for entirely different reasons. None of Clive's clients would be recognised in the sitting rooms of Britain. Indeed most of them would have struggled to be recognised in their own sitting rooms, which was usually the reason they came to see him in the first place.

He could hear Durkin, who was now on stage, presumably holding the Golden Lobe in his clammy grip and still gushing surprise.

'What can I . . . it's such a . . . how can I ever . . .'

'Don't say anything,' Clive suggested, but he knew that Durkin, just like himself, would have a well-written speech nestling in his inside pocket.

'My mother always said my heart was in the right place . . .' Durkin began, wishing to appear modest before going on to list, in detail, his many strengths.

'It's right next to your wallet, Shaman,' Grace shouted.

In his hideaway Clive heard her voice and smiled.

Grace stood up to throw some more well-chosen insults but the sudden rush of blood to her head was stemmed as all available space was occupied by gin and vermouth. Instead it swam back into her body. She sat down with the elegance of a sack of potatoes, feeling very dizzy and very sick.

Durkin smiled, he didn't mind being heckled because that indicated people were jealous, which merely affirmed his position at the very zenith of the heap. He sipped from a glass of mineral water left on the lectern.

'A good vintage.' It was a well-rehearsed joke, a clever link to the tale of his *Bad Times*; the self-loathing, the drinking, the drugs, the abusive relationships. (For the sake of a gripping narrative he wasn't going to mention that most of these could also be found near the top of his *Good Times* list.) Then he related a well-worn story about his lowest ebb and the point at which he had built his own Bridge Over The River Cried and things had begun to get better. Grace had heard this tale a million times at a thousand dull parties and called it his Dead Pets' Society story. She started to laugh loudly. Elsewhere in the room there were sniffs and dabbed eyes, which were usually a precursor to more adulatory applause.

It was then that Grace noticed her husband had gone missing. She stopped laughing and started to cry. Then she started to shout. The woman next to her visibly flinched at this explosion of raw emotions.

'Clive? Clive? Where the fuck are you? Come back. I think I'm going to be sick.'

The woman next to her looked on in horror. She would need all her skills in dealing with people in crisis to calm down this mad woman. She placed her hands in her lap to appear non-threatening, lowered her eyes in a supportive manner and spoke in her best off-the-peg reassuring voice.

'Can I help, my dear.'

'No, it's OK.' Grace pulled herself slowly to her feet. Her face was changing colour like a dance-floor light show.

'Are you sure?' The woman's tone suggested that Grace was completely wrong in her self-assessment.

'Yeah. I don't think I'm going to be sick.'

'Jolly good. Now may I suggest that when you get through this bout of self-loathing you might like to take a little time to reflect on what drove you to get in this condition?' She handed her a business card, the details of which swam around like so many black dots of frogspawn in front of Grace's weary eyes.

'I don't think I'm going to be sick, I know I am.'

Meanwhile Clive had decided that maybe his life wasn't completely over. If he'd dreamed about winning the Golden Lobe then surely one day it would happen. Satisfied with this poor rationalisation he went back to face his sneering colleagues. He pulled open the fire-exit door and walked into the hall. No one seemed to notice his re-emergence as every face in the room was turned in another direction.

He followed their gazes to the table where Grace was now standing. He narrowed his eyes against the gloom and had just begun to focus when he heard a slapping sound, as if someone had thrown a bucket of custard on to a concrete floor. Only it wasn't custard and it wasn't a floor.

As the howls of disgust spread through the crowded room, Clive turned and once again made for the fire exit.

From his safe enclave he heard the final applause as the evening came to a close. The noise almost drowned out the sound of Grace, who was now throwing up in the relative privacy of the euphemistically named Ladies' Cloakroom. The double doors swung open and his colleagues from the world of therapy washed past him, their chatter drunkenly incoherent. One or two slapped him on the shoulder and said 'bad luck' and 'at least you made the shortlist' and Clive graciously said something humble like 'Durkin is a two-faced tosser and I hope he has a terrible accident on the way home.'

Clive knew Durkin and what he was capable of. Once upon a time Durkin had even been his client. Clive's first job after qualifying had been with Durkin, who was already a well-established psychologist, working with wealthy couples in troubled marriages, wealthy alcoholics and wealthy businessmen looking for any justification to embark on their mid-life crises. Clive had quickly realised that there was a theme running through Durkin's work. Not health but wealth. At first Clive had tried to add a new dimension to the philosophy of the practice. He didn't presume to diagnose his clients, instead he listened to them and helped them diagnose themselves. 'No one knows what's wrong with you better than yourself' was his credo.

Durkin quickly saw the potential for adopting such an approach. 'The people we deal with like to think they have all the answers, that they are in control. They hate to be told the opposite. Your way they can answer the biggest question of all – "Who am I?" – themselves. We get more money for less work. Brilliant.'

'That's not exactly what I meant,' Clive tried to explain.

'Big picture, Clive. That's what I do. You worry about the small stuff, like principles; I'll take care of the big stuff, like profits.'

Soon they had the most profitable and fashionable counselling practice in the North. Durkin was so impressed with Clive's approach he referred his best client to him. Himself.

'I can't seem to respect myself. What do you think of me?' Durkin asked Clive during their sessions together. This question would inevitably follow his description of every personal failing and flaw, his extra-marital affairs, gambling, alcohol and drug abuse, and obsessionally buying every Chris De Burgh album he could get his hands on.

'This isn't about what I think, it's about what *you* think of yourself,' was Clive's stock answer.

'Which isn't very much.'

'Then that's what we've got to do. We've got to find a way to make you like yourself.'

'If only I was more like you . . .' was Durkin's wish.

Then one day he stopped wishing he was Clive. He stopped saying he hated himself and his self-abuse turned to self-praise.

'Hey, I'm OK!' he exclaimed.

'Good. That's good,' Clive said, a bit taken aback at this sudden change in attitude.

'I'm not like you,' Durkin said.

'This isn't about you being as good as me.'

'I know that now. I know that I'm better than you'll ever be.'

Durkin took full credit for his recovery, 'I knew it would take someone with prodigious skills and ability to save me,' he told the world. 'So I did it myself.'

Gradually Clive was relegated to the role of junior partner as Durkin's personality cult (or, to be strictly accurate, his lack-of-personality cult) took over. He became Amen the Shaman, a symbol of hope to the down and destitute – so long as they had a reasonably large private fortune. Durkin gathered status symbols like expensive loafers attract dog shit. A big car, a big yacht, a younger, thinner wife and the services of a well-known public relations consultant. He had it all.

With this picture of wealth and influence permanently shoved down his throat it was hardly surprising that when the opportunity of setting up his own practice in Bradworth arose Clive took it without hesitation. It seemed the only way he'd fulfil his vocation, his desire to become an example of excellence in his field. But best never came. He was known, but not on the scale of Durkin. He was successful, in a solid, unremarkable way, but he wasn't the best. That title seemed destined to remain with his former partner and one-time client, Amen Durkin.

'Bad luck, old man.' Durkin was in front of him, having broken away from a group of well-wishers and made his way to the corner of the foyer where Clive was trying to be obscured by a yucca plant. Durkin was smiling like a Cheshire cat that had been brainwashed by the Moonies.

'So you win again.' Clive now had Hot Chocolate in

his head, his pedantic memory recalling every tiny detail about 'So You Win Again'; its highest chart position (1), its record label (RAK), the fact that it shared the top ten with the Sex Pistols, Barbra Streisand and Boney M, whose song 'Ma Baker' was about a matriarch who earned her pin money by robbing banks.

'You could have had some of this, you know.'

'Some of what?'

'Success. You know, that thing you lie awake at night dreaming about.'

'The only thing I dream about is having my hands around your throat.'

'You know it made sense, me and you, together.' Durkin allowed a vacant expression to drift across his face, as if remembering happy days now gone for ever. 'We should talk.'

'About?'

'About getting together again. Obviously it would have to be a different sort of relationship. Less equal.'

'Get lost,' Clive said.

Durkin smiled warmly, punched Clive on the shoulder affectionately and leaned over to put his moist lips so close to Clive's face that he could feel their damp kiss.

'If it's the last thing I do I'll make you crawl on your knees,' Durkin whispered. Then he was gone, using both hands to wave farewell to the remaining sycophants as he made a presidential exit from the hotel. Clive watched him go. Into his head, unbidden, came the notion of karate. Karate, literally meaning 'empty hands'. Why did that remind him of Durkin? Because he wanted to kill him with his bare hands? He did of course, but it wasn't that.

Some minutes later the door to the Ladies' Cloakroom opened and Grace came out, her face now a pleasant shade of turquoise.

'Something I ate,' she said without conviction.

'Probably that raw bottle of gin,' Clive replied without rancour. 'Let's get out of here before we get thrown out.'

'Too late.'

It was the hotel under-manager, bristling with pomposity and eager to escort Grace and Clive off the premises. 'You ought to be ashamed of yourselves,' he berated them.

Clive thanked their escort for telling him how he should feel. He then told him to mind his own fucking business. Grace's hollow retch was a deliberate and successful attempt to force the under-manager to withdraw to a safe distance.

'Come on, let's leave this den of iniquity,' Clive said with as much dignity as he could muster which, given that he had Grace draped over one shoulder and a silver trail of her vomit running down the other, wasn't very much.

He was awake. The phone beside his bed was warbling viciously and had cut into his sleep. He opened one eye and looked suspiciously from under the snug and warm duvet at the radio alarm clock. It glowed fluorescent red in the dark room; the time was 3.33 a.m. He answered the phone, partly out of curiosity, partly out of concern that it might wake their two children sleeping in the next bedroom, but mostly because its imitation of a yodelling nightingale was really hurting his pissed brain.

'Clive. Is that you?' He felt a knocking in his head and an equally painful twinge in his groin. He shivered, it was early and the heating had yet to kick in. He switched the light on and noticed Grace's side of the bed was still empty and didn't look slept in. The clock changed to 3.34. Who the hell was ringing him at 3.34 in the morning to ask him if it was him?

'Yes, this is Clive.'

'You sound different.'

'It's the middle of the night, of course I sound different. Who is this?'

'It's Mammy.'

Clive thought about it. He didn't know anyone called Mammy. Suddenly Boney M were back in his head with 'Ma Baker'.

'Mammy who?' he asked. It didn't occur to him that it might be his Mammy because he had never called his Mammy anything other than Mother. To her face that was. Having established it was his mother his slowly awakening brain triggered its anxiety alarms.

'Where exactly are you?' he asked, crossing every part of his body, including an obscure pair of muscles that instantly increased the pain in his testicles tenfold.

'Saudi,' was her reassuring answer.

He sighed with so much relief Oxfam could have used it to end a minor famine.

'For a moment I thought you'd come home.' He was too tired to hide his obvious happiness at the news to the contrary.

'Not yet. We won't be with you until this afternoon.'

He let the time delay caused by the echo off the satellite hide the awkward pause. 'This afternoon? What do you mean by this afternoon? Hang on, what do you mean by we?'

'Me and your brother, Chrissy.' Another awkward pause.

'You and Christopher?'

'I can't stop, there's an Ay-rab who obviously got a machine gun for his birthday and he's hinting that I should get back on to the plane, pronto. All right, Aladdin, don't push! We arrive at Manchester around tea-time, I'll tell you all our exciting news then.' The phone clicked into a silence that was quickly swallowed up as the rushing of blood filled Clive's ears. Tea-time was, at that moment, less than fourteen hours away.

The pain in his groin was now a fully qualified throb with a special interest in sharp, jagged stabs. He couldn't stand it any more and threw back the duvet to explore the cause. He was horrified at the scene he exposed. He was still wearing his dinner-suit, just. His trousers were wrapped around his ankles and his boxer shorts bulged as if they contained a hernia that was destined to be remembered for posterity in the *Guinness Book of Records*. He gingerly slipped his baggy underwear down to reveal his penis, looking a bit worse for wear as it was firmly gripped by a tight yellow band. The Golden Lobe.

What was it doing wrapped around his tackle? How did it get into his possession? He looked around quickly, worried in case Durkin was also in the vicinity, ready to reclaim his prize. Then his mind began to clear. The end of the evening, Durkin going home empty-handed while the Golden Lobe rested on the lectern, forgotten. How could he leave it there, alone and unadored? The dream had come back into his head; he could make it happen.

He'd grabbed the Golden Lobe and shoved it in his coat. He hadn't been worried about stealing it when he was in the hold of swaggering drunkenness, but now that the hangover was waiting to flood his head with the cold, self-analytical light of day he felt different. He began a tussle with the object gripping his penis. The Golden Lobe, being made entirely of plastic, was easily bent and twisted but still took some persuasion to release its unfortunate, and by now roughly chafed, victim. As he struggled the bedroom door opened.

'So dreams can come true,' Grace said sarcastically, while stretching gingerly from the effort of sleeping on a cold bathroom floor in order to be within retching distance of the bidet.

'Only if you really want them to,' Clive said. 'I sort of borrowed it. I don't know what came over me.'

'You coming over that seems the more accurate description.'

'I was drunk. It was on the lectern. I just had to have it.'

'Does this mean you two will be moving out?' Grace asked, before falling face first on to the bed.

At this point the Golden Lobe came off with such force that it sailed out of Clive's hand and flew across the room, smashing into wall. It was such a mess it was inconceivable that he would be able to return it to its rightful owner. Not that he ever had any intention of doing such a thing. If he couldn't win the thing fairly and squarely then stealing it was a pleasing second best.

He gave his groin a generous covering of Vaseline to help nurse it back to health while Grace impersonated a heavily drugged dormouse. Into his memory came his mother and brother. It was seventeen years since they had gone to live in Australia and now both of them were going to walk back into his life. Within hours.

'Grace?'

'Ummph,' she answered, from at least two-thirds of the way into the sleep of the dead.

'You know how you've always wondered what my mother was like . . .'

Two

'Top stuff last night. Making the shortlist. Really top,' Larry said, his face perfectly straight while his voice was riveted at regular intervals with bolts of pure irony. He sat at the reception desk, the not-so-welcoming face of the Listen To You practice.

Even though Larry was only nineteen, and undeniably awful at all aspects of his job as office receptionist, his mesmerising ability to flatter and deceive meant that his position on the bottom rung of the company ladder at least was secure. One reason Clive kept him on the payroll was that it was nice to be liked, or at least have someone who was good at pretending to like him. The other reason was that having Larry around kept the rest of the staff off Clive's back. They moaned about Larry's lack of tact, lack of ability and lack of hygiene in the teenage-gland department, and this took their minds off other, more pressing issues, such as delayed pay rises, increasing work-loads or the hard toilet paper in the staff washroom.

Clive thanked Larry for his fulsome and entirely insincere commiserations and went into his office. He had a session with Mick Singleton, a client who was having communication problems with his wife.

Mick sat in the chair opposite and bit his nails. 'Do you know what she's done now?' he asked, rhetorically Clive hoped as he had no intention of replying. 'She's got the Merc, the gold one.' Mick had so many Mercedes, all at the very top of their specification, that he found it easier to distinguish them by colour. 'She emptied our joint account and then loaded the car with her jewellery, my Bang and Olufson stereo and Hercules—'

'Hercules? Is that the boy who cleans the pool?'

'No, it's my Newfoundland.' Mick looked very sad. 'Jesus I loved that dog.'

'Quite.' Clive was having to work hard not to look over his client's shoulder and out the window at the inspirational scene of the butcher's shop over the way.

'Then she drove off into the night to God knows where. That's the core of our problem, communication.'

'That you didn't ever discuss your feelings with her?'

'God no. I never got to tell her to fuck off.'

Clive gave his most reassuring smile, the one which could have induced calm in the most angst-ridden individual, and tried not to think about his hangover. It was going to be one of those days.

In fact it was a whole week's worth of those days all wrapped up in just a few short hours. During the session with Mick Singleton, blood-curdling screams emanated from the office next door. It was Marilyn Barker, one of Clive's more alternative colleagues, brought in to give the practice a more holistic feel. Marilyn undertook a range of extreme therapies and Thursdays was Rebirthing day. Some poor soul was role-playing their own birth, emerging fresh and new and unpolluted by the vagaries of life.

'Someone give her an epidural,' Clive said, before going over and banging on the wall.

Then there was the problem of his mother and brother. Last night he had broken the news to Grace that the woman she had never met but who had been a chip on Clive's shoulder for all of their married life was about to descend on them. Worse still, she had his spoiled elder brother in tow. Grace hadn't shown any emotion at the news, because she was fast asleep and didn't hear a word. 'At least I tried,' Clive kept reassuring himself. When she went ape-shit and started throwing things he would be able to cross his heart and swear to die that 'I did tell you', just before she clogged him round the head with something heavy.

He ate a prawn mayonnaise sandwich out of the clear plastic wrapper and looked around his office. It was a Freudian's lair, comforting in a cosy, womb-like way. It was furnished with a large black leather couch (which was completely unnecessary as clients were always firmly instructed to sit in the plain armchair), tall, thin lamp-stands that sprouted big round bulbs, and a forest of equally phallic carvings that he'd brought back in a container from a family therapy conference in Zimbabwe. Everything about the office was phallic, but Grace reckoned that by far the most phallic thing was

Clive. 'You're the biggest prick I know,' she joked. At least he thought she was joking.

The main drawback to Clive's office was the view, which overlooked the butcher's shop. Every day Clive had to suffer the horror of death and destruction outside his office which mirrored the pain and terror inside it. That and the smell of bacon cooking every morning, which since he had tried to become a better person by adopting vegetarianism was a temptation as great as any faced by Christ in his last days. He looked out now and saw the woman injecting pork pies with unset jelly, as she did at this time every day. It made him feel vaguely aroused watching the metal syringe prodding its daily ration of softly yielding pastry cases.

'Lucky sod,' he sighed.

There was a knock on the door and Mandy entered. Mandy was his twenty-one-year-old personal assistant and, second to a bacon butty, his biggest sexual fantasy. She was on the innocent side of maturity and still had faith, hope and a willingness to see the best in people in cash-and-carry quantities.

'I like her, she's smart. Too smart to let you shag her,' was Grace's judgement. She was right too, Mandy was smart. She was also gorgeous, with her tight sweaters, short pleated skirts and long legs. Especially to Clive, who had a gallon of dodgy hormones flooding his middle-aged body that convinced him that young women found dull, boring, married men with big stomachs and thinning hair drop-dead sexy.

Mandy was preoccupied in scribbling a message on her notepad so Clive took the opportunity to indulge in a reappraisal of her clean blond hair, pale face with the faintest hint of a peach bloom on her cheeks, astonishingly upright breasts and bare, long legs. It was somewhere in his late thirties that he had evolved into a heinous villain from a Gothic novel, dreaming of jumping on young women like Mandy and feasting on their innocence. He didn't dare, partly because he was afraid of an expensive claim for sexual harassment in the workplace but mostly because he knew his feelings for her youth and beauty wouldn't be reciprocated. There was a third reason, too. If Grace found out she would throw him from a very tall building, having first attached his testicles to the roof with a bungy rope.

'Mandy. Come in and sit down,' Clive said, unwittingly slipping into the mock jocularity he adopted whenever she was in his presence. Mandy may have been half his age and earned less than a fifth of his salary but he still couldn't help treating her like she was a goddess. If he'd had a pedestal handy he would have made a human ladder for her to walk up on to it. It was this feeling of being ill at ease with himself when surrounded by beautiful young people that caused Clive to spend a significant proportion of his income on trying to look younger and thinner. His lifeless hair had been prinked and pampered on a witness-protection programme and had been given a new identity as thick, luscious nut-brown locks with blond highlights. He selflessly put in many hours sitting in a comfortable black leather chair at an expensive hair salon, listening to Vivaldi while very thin teenage girls gave him cups of weak coffee and discussed hair care as if it was a cure for cancer. His huge expanse of skin was Bisto browned by a combination of foreign holidays and stolen moments on Grace's sunbed. 'You great balding jessie,' was Grace's opinion of his thirsty drinking from the soda fountain of youth.

He sighed with regret and reluctantly locked away his lust for Mandy in the specially prepared strong-room at the back of his mind.

'Mandy, what can I do for you?'

'I'm the personal assistant, Mr Wrigley, it should be the other way round.'

'What can you do for me?' Don't even attempt to answer that question, he warned himself.

'I've got the details on that flight you asked for.' She handed him the sheet of paper she had just been scribbling on. Her neat cubist handwriting was carefully laid out in the exact centre of the page.

'Thanks,' Clive said, as if he had just received a black spot edged in gold leaf from Blind Pew.

'That's OK. Were the awards exciting?'

'The award was very exciting,' Clive replied, fondly remembering his night of wanton sex for which he knew Grace was going to make him pay for the rest of his life. He looked at Mandy's note.

'Jesus fucking Christ!' he exploded. 'Excuse me, Mandy,' he added, noticing her look of injured innocence as she huffily pulled her pink sweater even tighter over her breasts, 'but the frigging plane gets here in less than half an hour.'

Clive was over an hour late when he finally arrived at the airport but he still jogged into the arrivals area as if trying to make up time. All the while he was testing a variety of excuses to use on his mother. He needn't have worried as no one was there. The widespread snowfall that weather forecasters had once again failed to spot had put paid to most arrivals.

He slowed his run to a more casual saunter and headed towards an empty counter occupied by a bored-looking woman in a vivid silk headscarf. She was reading a holiday brochure for mediterranean cruises.

'The four forty-two shuttle from Heathrow, I'm supposed to be meeting it. I'm a bit late.' Some understatement, he thought.

'Flight R101, Heathrow to Leeds Shuttle? No, you're not.'

He looked at his watch and then back at her. 'Over an hour, I think.'

'It hasn't left yet, sir. Heathrow's snowbound.'

'No it's not.' A jolly young man in a waistcoat that was worryingly similar to the woman's headscarf had joined them. 'I'm just off to tell the troops. The thaw's set in down there.'

Clive leaned heavily on the counter and rested his tired, aching head on his arms. The woman looked disgusted at this untidy behaviour but the jolly young man took pity on him.

'I'm going over to the café; they're providing free coffee until the state of emergency recedes. Do you want me to show you the way?'

Clive nodded wearily. He followed the jolly young man without a word.

The woman watched them both go. 'Thank you very much, sir,' she whispered bitterly. So much for the great British public, it didn't matter how many Consumer Care courses she went on, they were still pigs. 'They should be shot without mercy,' she mumbled, before returning to her holiday brochure.

Clive sat in the café, fenced off and hidden from view by a wicker statue that was supposed to represent the Polynesian Islands. As the snow began to fall on the outer limits of Leeds, Clive found it difficult to warm to the statue's message. Somewhere in the middle distance he could hear the piped music that whispered around the false ceilings and falser décor. Shanice was singing that she liked his smile (which Clive automatically recalled had reached number 2 in March 1992, being kept off the number 1 spot by the hysterics of Shakespears Sister, whose wailing wall of a lead singer was called Marcella Detroit, while Shanice's record was released on Motown, which was founded in the City of Detroit. Fact may be stranger than fiction, but in the world of pop music it was hardly ever as interesting).

The jolly young man set a free cup of black coffee in front of him and two small cartons of milk, which Clive knew would be impossible to open without staining his tie.

'Mind, it's hot,' he said, miming blowing on it. At least that's what Clive hoped he was miming, as the action had reminded him of his night of lust with the Golden Lobe.

'Have a nice wait,' the jolly young man added, a professional to his dyed roots.

Clive watched him walk over to the Hat Shop, and engage the shop girls in a joky discussion about the weather and their predicament.

He fell asleep on the table in the café. He wasn't sure

how long he'd been out when he was shaken awake by the sound of a plane landing. The shudder of jet engines massaged the concrete floor and walls around him. It felt like they were melting. Clive sat up and blinked in the bleached white of the lights hanging high above in the ceiling. It took him a few seconds to swim through the current of panic and fear before he realised where he was.

He got to the Arrivals lounge and heard the call from the customs gate in front of him.

'Clive? Clive. Cooooeeee! We're here.'

It was her, it had to be, no one else could 'Cooooeeee' like his mother. He turned to face her and saw not the demonic figure that had occupied his darker thoughts for so many years, but a short, fat, old woman who looked like an advertising agency's idea of everyone's sweet and harmless granny. Which showed just how much advertising agencies knew. It was Euterpe Wrigley. She was fatter than he remembered (which was pretty fat), her ankles were the same width as her thighs, and her chubby face hung from her neck like a slowly melting ice-cream. Her hair was like the flag of a newly independent African state, with hints of red, yellow and green and all shades in between.

Staggering along behind her, carrying and dragging three large suitcases which appeared to be doubling as lead weights, was Christopher Wrigley. He seemed about eighteen inches shorter than the last time Clive had seen him. His once thick black hair was now thinning grey, and his worn, chipped features were like a Roman statue that had suffered the ravages of time and had all the important bits broken off. Christopher was still wearing his sneering smile, which instantly reminded Clive of the old photos he had in a scrapbook somewhere. His mother, encumbered by nothing more than two hundred Rothmans and a litre bottle of duty-free vodka, was waving wildly.

Clive smiled unselfconsciously. It was the smile of separation healed by reunion. She was home and he couldn't help but feel pleased. 'Mother,' he called out.

From one hundred and thirty eight metres away Euterpe Wrigley began to yell.

'Sorry we're late. Some cunt of a darkie at Heathrow insisted on shoving her big black hand up my arse. And me Club Class.'

Clive suddenly became aware of everyone and everything around him, as if the people, the staff, the other passengers, even the bored-looking cleaners pushing their wide brooms along endless shiny corridors were laughing at him. He recognised the feelings of awkward embarrassment as they rushed in and smothered him, feelings he hadn't felt for years, certainly not since 1979 when she had left at the end of the Winter of Discontent and so made summer his time of glorious new-found freedom.

He walked towards his mother and brother, failing to notice the two shadowy figures who were on a collision course to join them in their family reunion. He was almost within touching distance of Euterpe and Christopher, indeed he had hold of the suitcase offered by his brother, when the two other figures stepped in and broke up the three corners of the impending Wrigley triangle.

'I'm Detective Inspector Good Cop.'

'And I'm Detective Sergeant Bad Cop,' they introduced themselves.

Clive knew it was unlikely the two men had just said
what he thought they'd said, but that was what it
sounded like.

'And you are under arrest.'

Clive looked at his mother and then his brother. All
three were trying to guess which of them the policemen
were referring to.

'Who is?'

'You all are.'

Three

'For fuck's sake, Gerhardie, just switch it on.' DI Good Cop shared a mocking grin with Clive. 'All I ask for is a loyal Watson and what do I get? Witless Willie here.' He jerked his thumb at his colleague who fiddled with the tape machine. DS Bad Cop pressed something that made a sound like breaking plastic and the tape machine whistled into life.

'I'm DI Mark Corby and this is DS Gerhardie. We are from the Bradworth Illegal Substance Unit. We're part of a joint investigation with our Customs and Excise colleagues based here at the Greater West Yorkshire Airport.' He spat out the word 'colleagues' as if describing a lower life-form. 'I just want to ask you a few questions about why you are here at the airport.' He sounded like someone from a 1960s door-to-door soap-powder campaign asking a simple question that could instantly win the lucky housewife five pounds.

'I'm here to meet my—' Clive began to volunteer his explanation, keen to be co-operative.

'Should the tape be going round, Guv?' DS Gerhardie whispered anxiously to his boss.

'Excuse me, Mr Wrigley.' The DI turned imperiously towards his colleague. 'For the benefit of the tape, my colleague has an advanced case of technofear. Of course it fucking should, you moron.'

'Only it isn't.'

'I don't believe this. Call a technician. I'm assuming you know how to work a phone.'

Clive coughed politely. 'I'm happy to continue without the tape if it will help clear this up. I don't even want a legal representative.' Clive hoped this waiving of his rights would give him an air of innocent confidence. DI Corby split him with a crossbow bolt of a stare.

'Get out your Biro, Detective Sergeant Gerhardie, find a sheet of statement paper and PAY ATTENTION.'

Despite DI Corby's politeness to him in contrast to his exasperation with his colleague, Clive still felt uncomfortable in the hot room. His lungs were tightening in readiness for an asthma attack, the kind that reached Krakatoan proportions, both east and west of Java.

Clive took a closer look at his interrogators as they searched for pen and paper. They were almost opposite in their appearance. DI Corby had a cheerfully youthful expression and a bunch of messy hair, which fell over his thin face like an untidy red waterfall. DS Gerhardie meanwhile had a round, melancholic face, and one glance into his eyes was enough to invoke a sense of futility and despair in the heart of even the most cheerful of burger-bar assistants. He had almost no hair on his head but had a beard that was nearly long enough to hide the old milk stains on his tie. The pair reminded Clive of the picture he had drawn as a child of a big round face with a beaming smile and bushy knot of hair, which could be turned upside down so that it became a big round face with an inordinately sad expression, no hair and a long straggly beard.

'Let me summarise what you have told us,' DI Corby said, after Clive had finished talking very slowly in order not to outpace DS Gerhardie's painfully slow handwriting. 'You are here to meet your family after an absence of some seventeen or so years. That's not a crime, is it, DS Gerhardie?' His assistant looked confused, as if he couldn't remember what did define criminal activity.

'Terrorism and drug smuggling, however, are.' DI Corby was still smiling.

Clive blinked slowly in the hope that the unfolding nightmare would have ended by the time he opened his eyes. It hadn't.

As DS Gerhardie resumed writing, DI Corby watched him closely, grimacing as his colleague's lips moved painfully: 'For . . . the . . . ben-e-fit . . . of . . . the . . . state-ment . . . Mr . . . Wrig-ley . . . blinked . . . slow-ly.' DI Corby grabbed the paper from under the heavy weight of DS Gerhardie's pen arm and read the last line. He ripped the paper into a million small squares and dropped them on his assistant's head, where they lay like industrial-strength dandruff. It seemed like a good time for Clive to make his reply.

'I don't know anything about drugs or terrorism.' Clive was hot and his lungs burned and his head hurt and he wanted a cigarette even though he hadn't smoked for sixteen years, and he could see he wasn't going to go anywhere until he had convinced these men of the truth. Or at least of something they could recognise as not being wholly untrue.

'So when did you last see her?' DI Corby asked.

'Heathrow Airport. Friday, 4th May 1979.'

'You haven't seen her since then?'

'No. It was the worst day of my life.'

'I guess so. Your mum going away.' DS Gerhardie looked like he might allow his emotions to spill over into tears and embarrass everyone.

Clive was actually thinking about the date. Margaret Thatcher had just become Prime Minister and 'Bright Eyes' by Art Garfunkel was number 1 in the singles chart for the fourth excruciating week. There was no accounting for taste. There was no accounting for his memory retrieving irrelevant pop trivia either. It was bad enough having hazy premonitions that made him predict the future, but worse he also remembered the past in pinpoint detail. He had a perfect mental record of everything that had ever happened to him, especially the bad bits, but for some reason he was particularly good on British Pop Charts since the mid-1960s. He knew every chart placing, every highest entry, every one-hit wonder. None of this had made his life any easier; in fact the only real benefit he'd gained from his photographic memory was to make quite an impact on the local pub quiz league.

'Something like that,' Clive eventually answered. His

breathing difficulties had become more severe, in that he was unable to continue breathing. He fumbled in the pocket of his coat, which hung over the back of the chair. The two policemen looked anxious, not about Clive's health, but that the notoriously idle Sergeant Freemantle might not have searched him properly for offensive weapons. Clive found what he was looking for and whipped it out in front of him. DS Gerhardie decided it was every man for himself and pushed back from the table so that he was a safe distance from any flashing weapon.

Clive puffed on the blue inhaler, oblivious to DS Gerhardie's sheepish looks as he wheeled his chair back from the furthest reaches of the small interview room. Clive breathed as deeply as he could to recover some sense of calm. The policemen waited for the right moment to start again. It never came so DI Corby started anyway. He scooped up a handful of his untidy hair and threw it over the top of his head like spilt salt.

'Tell me about why they left in the first place. Your mother and brother.'

'Christopher left for Australia in 1978, 19th August. There'd been some family problems, you don't need to know what.'

'We need to know everything,' DI Corby insisted.

'All right, it's no big deal. There was a row. Between me and Christopher. It was classic sibling rivalry stuff. Stupid really. Over a woman. Anyway he left without warning.'

'But with the woman?' DS Gerhardie sought clarification before committing his pen to a fresh sheet of paper.

'Yes. Mother blamed me of course. Soon after she sold up and followed him. I haven't seen either of them since. When I spoke to Mother this morning it was the first time since then. Even then I wasn't absolutely sure I hadn't dreamed the whole thing.' The looks from across the table assured him of the wakefulness of his experience.

DI Corby leaned forward and fixed Clive with his juggernaut stare, the kind that was impossible to meet head-on without feeling like a hedgehog during the evening rush-hour. Meanwhile DS Gerhardie was absently picking the fruits of his nose with his pen and eating them.

'You heard when today? This morning?' DI Corby wanted a little more accuracy.

'Yes. I came here to pick them up. She told me to. And even though I haven't seen her for over seventeen years I always do what my mother tells me.'

DS Gerhardie nodded approvingly. In his line of work it was a rare and satisfying event to find a boy who still obeyed his mum.

'And that's it, is it, then?' DI Corby asked briskly, as if readying to leave.

Clive brightened, he could almost smell the fresh air of freedom. 'Yes, that's it.' He reached to the back of his chair for his cashmere coat.

DS Gerhardie shuffled his papers together and began dreaming of a tasty fry-up for supper.

'Where the fuck do you think you're going?' DI Corby asked nonchalantly.

'Isn't that it?' Clive asked, already knowing that it wasn't, not by a long fucking chalk.

'That isn't it, not by a long fucking chalk,' spat DI

Corby. DS Gerhardie reluctantly picked up his pen and put all thoughts of bacon and eggs from his mind.

'Your mother has been arrested for having something . . . something she shouldn't have in her luggage. I can't say what yet,' DI Corby said, holding up a hand to stall Clive's inevitable question. 'That'll be for forensics to tell us, but it looks suspicious.'

'Extremely suspicious,' DS Gerhardie added, trying to extract the maximum effect from the statement, while struggling to remember how to spell 'suspicious'.

'Your brother was the one we've been watching but on searching the bags it turned up in Mrs Wrigley's case. The one you took from your brother.'

'What?'

'You were in possession of the suspect case,' DS Gerhardie pointed out helpfully.

'That's why you're here, isn't it? You're the go-between,' DI Corby accused him. DS Gerhardie played with the split ends of his scruffy beard while waiting for Clive's inevitable confession.

'What are you on about?'

'Your mum has told us everything. She says you came here to collect the suitcase, that you're the one behind the deal.'

'Jesus' Clive felt his lungs preparing for another collapse.

'When we interviewed her earlier she made a statement. Luckily that was still working.' Clive wasn't sure if DI Corby was pointing at the tape recorder or DS Gerhardie, or maybe even both. 'She said Christopher was innocent and you set the whole thing up.'

'Typical. I don't know why I'm so surprised. She

always did blame me when Christopher got in the shit. I know nothing about any of this and that's the truth.'

'If we had a pound for every one, eh, Willie?' DI Corby nudged DS Gerhardie who was almost asleep and jumped to attention a little too suddenly.

'So what happens now?' Clive asked.

'We wait until we get a forensic report and then we see. Meantime it's the five-star royalty suite for you.'

It was morning before the cell door rattled and clanked like a melodramatic ghost and wafted open. A shape stood in the doorway between Clive and freedom and he couldn't decide whether it was DI Corby, DS Gerhardie or a creature from his worst nightmare.

'OK. You're on your way,' the voice said, giving nothing away as to its identity.

'Me? Are you sure?' Clive was surprised at the news. During his lonely incarceration he had almost convinced himself of his guilt.

'Yep. Forensics came back clear. You're out of the frame. This time,' the voice added with a hefty pinch of malice.

'No bomb then? Or drugs?'

'She was taking the piss.'

Clive didn't think this sounded like something his mother was capable of. When it came to subtlety she brought to mind sledgehammers picking unfair fights with walnuts.

'Pardon?'

'Piss. Your mother had a case full of piss. She was exporting piss from Sydney. Not her own though. We checked.'

Clive recognised the tone of heartbroken disappointment in the voice. He'd heard enough of it in his work to be sure.

'I still don't—'

'Your mother had a case hidden within her case and in that case within a case was a small, self-contained refrigeration unit, and in that were several phials of yellow liquid. Our boys in forensics weren't sure if it was some kind of liquid drug or liquid explosive. Turns out it was liquid urine. And if it isn't drugs or bombs it isn't worth shit. The CPS believes people are entitled to their peccadilloes so long as they're legal. Me, I think they should do her for wasting police time. And if you don't get out of here inside the next five fucking minutes that's what I'm going to do to you. Once you've accidentally fallen down the stairs, that is.'

Clive took the hint, grabbed his coat, and four minutes and fifty-eight seconds later he emerged blinking into the blanched white light of a thawing winter dawn as it poured through the glass walls of Terminal 2 (internal flights). There, sipping complimentary coffee, waited Euterpe and Christopher Wrigley. He went over and sullenly indulged in the luxury of a reunion that this time wasn't gate-crashed by armed police.

From the balcony above, DI Corby and DS Gerhardie leaned on the highly polished chromium handrail, looking down on the Wrigley reunion below.

'Touching, isn't it, Willie?' DI Corby asked.

DS Gerhardie made no response so busy was he picking crumbs of toast from his straggly beard and eating them.

'I want you to keep a real close eye on them. Everything

they do. But for Christ's sake don't let them know you're watching them. Got it?'

'Yes, sir,' DS Gerhardie said, his tone betraying a huge lack of confidence in his ability to remain undercover.

'One fuck up and it will be the end of your glorious career. Understood?'

'Understood, sir,' DS Gerhardie acknowledged morosely. He knew that the extra work involved in close surveillance meant he wouldn't get to finish his new loft conversion before Easter, at best.

Four

Noilly Upchurch had an urgent appointment in Bradworth city centre and he had every intention of keeping it. He cut through the crowds of shoppers like the bow of a gunboat on a diplomatic mission, knocking aside both the frail and the hardy with equal vigour. His lank fair hair flopped over his pock-marked face like a shy bride's veil as he jogged purposefully towards his target. He wore a white waxed-paper suit, which made him stick out like a spare prick at a lesbian wedding. Or would have done but for the fact that it also made him look like a damaged victim of Care in the Community, which meant everyone did a Walter Raleigh and circumnavigated around him. By being threateningly visible he became almost invisible.

Outside Woolworth's he stopped and a partially-sighted elderly woman formed an orderly queue behind him.

'Is this the queue for the Evans outsize sale?' she asked in a friendly tone designed to put him off his guard and so allow her to sneak past and grab the best bargain in the store the moment the doors swung open.

Noilly turned to her without any obvious sign of malevolent intent. 'Fuck off,' he said, matter of factly. The elderly woman, who hadn't got elderly without knowing how to fuck off when told to do so, fucked off in search of another sale and someone her own size to do battle with.

A bounty hunter left alone in a sea of bargain hunters, Noilly looked around with letterbox eyes, taking in everything through his carefully narrowed field of vision. Satisfied with what he saw, or maybe didn't see, he took a sharp left and walked across the road towards Penny-Less, the discount store that made all other discount stores look like they were upmarket emporiums. Penny-Less prices were the lowest, slashed below anything offered by the competition. He didn't bother to pick up a plastic basket, as the shop notice politely requested, but brushed past packs of cheap nylons, gardening gloves and silver Christmas trees (slashed by a further 50 per cent all week!) and made his way to the door at the rear of the store.

He knew the way, he had rehearsed it many times in his head. He saw the notice that said 'Staff Only' but either didn't understand it or chose to ignore its central message. The door was unlocked as his mental checklist had told him it would be. He went down the empty corridor, its general seediness exposed by the unflinching brightness of the strip-lights, until he reached the last door on the left.

'Last door on the left,' he said in answer to a private conversation and shoved it open.

The tubby man in the spotless white shirt and acrylic tie (in the corporate hypothermia blue of the Penny-Less empire) looked up from the computer screen where he was plotting the next month's staff rota.

'Sorry, the public aren't allowed in here,' he said, cordially enough despite his impatience to get on with the chore of finding some poor bastard to do the ever-unpopular Friday evening shift.

'Donny Raymond?' Noilly asked, already knowing the answer as the man's harassed, podgy features matched those in the stolen holiday snap he had studied closely for weeks. Noilly put his hand into his paper-suit pocket and grasped the carpet knife that was snuggled up to his well-toned body as if it was a reassuringly cuddly teddy bear rather than the cold killing machine it actually was. There was an eerie click as he extended the blade in readiness.

'Yes. Do I know . . . ?' Donny saw the blade appear under his nose and stopped talking, moving, breathing; instead he adopted a state of fascinated, frozen watchfulness.

'No you don't. But your friend Mr Eltham does.'

'Graham? Shit.'

'That about sums it up.'

'Tell him it's over. I won't be seeing Michelle again. I swear.'

'I know. That's why I'm here.'

If Donny Raymond's acrylic tie, cotton shirt and

fleshy chest had been rolls of best Wilton carpet the knife couldn't have performed more effectively. Even Donny had to admire its handiwork as first his tie was cropped just below the knot, then his clean white shirt was slit asunder and finally the blade painlessly scored his skin. He would have been the first to admit that when it came to slashing things this knife was a cut above the rest, and that included Penny-Less.

Noilly stood back and looked at his work critically. 'Unuch' read the bloody inscription on Donny's torso. Noilly checked this with the word written in Biro on the back of his wrist.

'Bollocks,' he said, without meaning to be ironic. Everyone has a weakness, an Achilles' heel, and Noilly's was words. Whether it was spelling, pronunciation, grammar or general usage, they were always more than a match for him. Years of adult literacy evening classes had made no impression on his basic inability to string the right amount of letters together in the right order. He stepped forward and put the finishing touch to the canvas of Donny's pale skin.

'Eunuch.'

Donny looked down at the legend writ large and deep on his flabby chest. His blood gradually woke up to its new freedom and began to obscure Noilly's careful calligraphy. His ripped white shirt was soon bright red and the ragged ends flapped like the flag of a recently crushed revolution. He sat back in the chair, shocked and frightened but without registering any pain.

Noilly reached into another pocket of his suit and took out a small bottle, unscrewed the top and poured its black contents across Donny's fresh wounds.

'What's that?' Donny asked, fearing the worst without realising how terrible the worst was actually going to be.

'Permanent ink. Mr Eltham wanted you to have a reminder of your time with Michelle. Smile please.' From another pocket in his waxed-paper suit Noilly produced a small camera and took a photograph of his handiwork. This was for the portfolio he used for clients as proof of a job well done. It also helped impress potential clients as to his abilities, once they had stopped throwing up at the bloody images. He knew that complete customer satisfaction was the key element in any successful business enterprise these days. The camera's flash bounced around the room, throwing everything into stark relief and making Donny's blood glisten lusciously.

'This is your only warning, Donny. Next time it really is your bollocks. Mr Eltham has an idea to make a necklace for his wife. And remember, gob shut equals nice long life. Gob open equals future career as concrete support for new shopping mall. Got it? Nice to have met you, and you better hope we don't meet again.'

Leaving his victim in a state of glacier-like immobility at the sight of his own blood, Noilly calmly left the office and made his way back out into the shop. He didn't attempt to run because he knew he had nothing to fear for he was a wet-job expert, a man who could undertake a simple slotting or a complex razoring without difficulty or hesitation. He had seen fear close up in people's eyes and he knew it silenced them better than a whole roll of masking tape (which he had also used in his time), although not as well as death. From now on Donny's mouth would be closed tighter than a nervous clam on a fishmonger's slab. So he sauntered around Penny-Less like an ordinary customer, searching for something that wasn't complete crap. He failed miserably but did notice that the 65 per cent polyester shirts were only £8.99 for two, although the quality of the material made him think that even this was too high a price to pay. Luckily for Donny that he would be able to take full advantage of his staff discount to get a temporary replacement.

Even when he was outside the shop Noilly didn't panic. He knew there would be no posse, no vigilante group, no have-a-go hero on his trail. Right now Donny was probably locked in the men's washroom trying to clean himself up and working on an explanation that involved an errant tie and an out-of-control paper shredder with a remarkable vocabulary to satisfy the questions asked in the staff canteen.

Instead of running away Noilly went around the corner and into the Gents, where he had hidden his day clothes. He changed and then burned the paper suit in the toilet bowl. Happy there wasn't a trace of his previous incarnation remaining he went out and casually hailed a cab, which took him to another part of the city, one where shadows lurked all day long like lazy muggers beneath old and empty buildings.

He got out and overtipped the driver before jogging up a metal staircase and into a large textile mill which had long ago given up producing cloth, mainly because the world (thanks to places like Penny-Less) had been misled into believing that drip-dry nylon was next in line for the throne previously occupied by sliced bread, Cat's eyes and lava lamps.

He knocked on a narrow metal door and after a moment there was a subtle buzzing and it sprung open to admit him. Over the doorway in tiny letters not designed to attract attention, it stated that this was the Muscle Club. He went straight into the grubby changing room and took in a deep lungful of the sweaty stale air. As soon as its aroma of ammonia scorched his tonsils he felt at home. He took some well-worn sports gear from his locker and changed quickly. Two minutes later he was happily working up a sweat on an unrelentingly vengeful machine that imitated uphill skiing so well it was barely distinguishable from the real thing. There was no one else in the training room, which pleased Noilly Upchurch. He preferred his own company, where the conversation was brief and he could always follow it without too much difficulty or feeling too stupid.

After an hour of working out on a variety of machines that allowed him to go skiing up hills, rowing on rivers, jogging on roads and cross Channel swimming without ever having to venture out of the training room, he showered, dressed and made his way down a dark, gloomy corridor and into the small bar. Over the doorway a sign, handwritten in felt pen on a piece of paper Blu-tacked to the wall, read 'The Anabolic Arms-strictly members only'.

'Good to see you, sir.' The barman welcomed him as a regular customer but without using his name. He knew that with men like Noilly that would be an error. Formality was what most of his customers wanted; they didn't want to be asked things about themselves or to be addressed by their names. In Noilly's case this was doubly so, since his first name was something to be forgotten about at all costs.

His dad, *en route* for another day in the park drinking something caustic from a bottle hidden in a brown paper bag, had called in at the Register Office to name his newborn son. Unable to think of a name that summed up his hopes and ambitions, dreams and wishes for his young child, he reached for the comforting bottle inside his coat pocket. It was Noilly Prat which, although almost undrinkable unless smothered with something better tasting like lemon-scented Fairy Liquid, had the singular and crucial advantage of being very, very cheap. It also sounded exotic, foreign and mysterious. Mr Upchurch senior knew that would have suited the boy's mum, had she survived the trauma of giving birth to the great, big, ugly prune-headed bastard. So it was decided, as he wobbled threateningly over the seated figure of the timid and fearful registrar, Noilly Prat Upchurch. With a name like that his son would surely walk tall, or at least straight, which in comparison to his father's usual gait would be something of an improvement.

Noilly ordered a fruit juice, which had an indeterminate flavour (other than a treacle sweetness) but was supposed to be pineapple crush, and the barman left him alone and went back to counting mixers as if a sudden rush on ginger ale was imminent.

Noilly nursed his drink as he sat down in a corner that was darker than all the other extremely dark corners. He drank the ridiculously saccharine pineapple drink and listened to the bar radio, which was tuned ever so slightly past the station. Through the mild whistle of static the dull DJ was reading out a listener's love story over the top of a horribly lachrymose song. The song and the pineapple juice were perfect companions for Noilly's mood. He sipped his drink and wiped his eyes, grateful for the cloak of privacy the dingy bar gave him. He felt like this every time he fulfilled his contractual obligations, a longing for some other way to be, some other way to live that he couldn't quite aspire to, or that he somehow wasn't quite good enough to achieve. He needed help, he knew that, but he didn't know how, where or who to start seeking it from.

He looked at the low table in front of him. Covering up some of the many ring marks on its beer- and sweat-splashed patina was a discarded copy of yesterday's paper, *Bradworth Planet, Star and Universe*. He turned to the astrology page to see if the mystic, photographed wrapped in what looked like an old pair of curtains, had got any hints to help him find a way through his pain. She told him that he was on the verge of an important decision and he must put himself first when making it. This encouraged him a little, although it went on to suggest that now was also a good time to change his hairstyle and be daring with that hem-line.

He noticed a headline tucked away in a corner below the soothsayer. Squatting heavily on a short paragraph it read 'Bradworth Man Fails Again at Local Loony Awards'. When he had been in the Territorial Army Noilly's martial arts instructor, Sergeant Jacob, had told him that the longest journey started with the smallest step. That was just before the Military Police arrested the sergeant and cashiered him for his Maoist leanings. Noilly had a sense of his destiny packing its bags, putting on a warm coat and ringing for a taxi. It was time to change. He went over to the barman and borrowed the Yellow Pages.

After a couple of minutes he went back to the bar. 'Oi you,' he asked threateningly, 'how do you spell "therapist"?'

Five

Clive had a theory. He called it his theory of It-Takes-One-To-Denounce-One. It wasn't a new theory, it wasn't much more than an improved version of It-Takes-One-To-Know-One, which has long been one of the great insults of our time. Where it differed from the basic tenet of the original theory was that It-Takes-One-To-Denounce-One argued that individuals who declared a polar-like opposition to something were usually suppressing a rabid desire for it. Clive had evolved his hypothesis during years of observing and analysing people. He could cite dozens of examples of his theory. People who claimed that homosexuality was the work of the devil secretly wanted to grow a well-hung Zapata moustache and go disco dancing with the living embodiment of Michelangelo's David; Protestant theologians who denounced popery at every turn actually hankered after the swish of heavy golden robes, the heady whiff of incense, and a congregation so guilt-ridden they acquiesced to every demand; threateningly aggressive vegetarians, given half a chance, would gladly kill something fluffy for the merest sniff of lamb cutlets with fresh rosemary; self-appointed right-wing moral guardians were never happier than when they were alone with a fresh copy of *Big Jugs and Huge Arses* magazine and a box of man-size tissues.

Clive now had a new example that proved his theory, the assertion that abroad is better than home. Or, as in the particular instance of his mother, that Australia was better than England. Anyone who wittered on as much as his mother did about how good Australia was and so, conversely, how bad England was, must actually be suppressing a deeply felt passion for their former homeland. That was Clive's theory and when it came to suffering Euterpe's endless harangues about the depressing state that was England it went some way to easing his considerable pain. But only some way. For the rest of the time, even after a mere one hour in her company, he wanted to shut her up permanently.

Clive swung the car violently towards the pavement on Halcyon Terrace and braked so suddenly outside number 4 that Euterpe and Christopher were nearly throttled by their seatbelts.

'Welcome home,' Clive said, intending to be ironic.

'Australia's my home. Not this shit-hole full of Abos,' Euterpe said, choosing not to spot his irony.

'Asians actually. From Pakistan. He's a journalist.' Clive nodded in the direction of the family next door, who were piling into a Space Wagon in preparation for a walkabout around Tesco's.

'Same thing,' Euterpe snapped, the discussion now closed.

For the entire journey home Clive had been subjected to a dazzling litany of things that were better in Australia than in England, from the weather to the air quality, from the punctuality of the public transport to the efficiency of the sewage system. Clive had tried broaching the issue of the urine smuggling but he hadn't bargained on his mother's well-practised technique of blithely ignoring questions that she didn't want to answer. She simply refused to respond to his queries and instead put up an impenetrable smokescreen of biased opinions and observations.

Christopher didn't make things any easier. He acted as his mother's official echo, agreeing with everything she said and even throwing in the odd supportive statement to help prove her point. Clive had never thought of himself as much of a patriot but by the time the little car skidded to a halt outside his house and spewed its ungrateful load on to the street, he was ready to take up arms and spill his blood in defence of Queen, country and even, if given no other choice, the Welsh.

Given the horrors of the previous night followed by the awfulness of the journey home, Clive was pleased that Grace wasn't in. It was one of her college days at the Bradworth University of Modern Studies (so named by a vindictive Vice Chancellor who had been forced into early retirement and so subjected his treacherous former colleagues to the embarrassment of being known to the rest of the academic world as the BUMS). A serious bout of thirty-something self-doubt had caused Grace to return to college. Having retired from her career as a nurse in order to bring up their two adopted children, she had decided to try something completely new. Too late had she realised that the course in the Psychology of Business Management, picked at random from a glossy brochure full of laughing, happy students, was not so much intellectually stimulating as legalised euthanasia. Two years later she was still amazed that the Psychology of Business Management continued to be even more dull than it sounded.

She disliked being a mature student because she was surrounded by smart-arsed young people who treated her like she was an escapee from an old people's home. She spent most of her time sitting in the Sahara-dry lectures doodling in the margin of her notepad and wishing she'd chosen to study the Marine Biology of the Caribbean. The only pleasure she gained from the course was picking fights (usually verbal but physical when necessary) with her fellow students and lecturers. Grace enjoyed fighting. It was a subject she could have passed with First Class Honours.

She never needed much of an excuse not to go to college, citing head colds, period pains and the threat of heavy rain without fear or favour. Clive was thankful that today she had gone in as it gave him a few more hours before the shit became intimately acquainted with the fan. There were plenty of signs of Grace's recent presence around their home. The kitchen had her signature everywhere. The box of honey-roast cornflakes was still on the table bearing the legend 'Are you already a winner? You could have won £10,000 – instantly! See inside for details.' There were similar promises on bags of crisps, jars of coffee, yoghurts, bacon joints and even a box of tampons. Grace had grown impatient with waiting for the Psychology of Business Management to answer the problems of life and had decided to look elsewhere for a swifter solution. 'Some of the best things in my life are instant, such as sex with you,' she said when Clive challenged her about these obsessions.

He threw a bag of crisps at his guests. 'Help yourself to breakfast,' he said, hoping they wouldn't also be helping themselves to a winning ticket.

Clive had a bath to wash away the excesses of the grimy police cell, which democratically deposited crap on the bad and the blameless alike. He'd intended to spend the rest of the day catching up with his family and getting to know them, but one hour with them in his car was already bordering on an overdose and he intended to get as far away as he could.

'See you later,' he shouted down the hall, making a swifter withdrawal than a good Catholic.

'Where are you going?' his mother shouted above the dramatic scene being played out in full volume Nicam stereo on the television.

'To work, Mother. I'll try and get home a bit early.' Like about the year 2010.

'OK. Whenever,' she said.

He felt slightly irritated at this lazy acceptance of his rudeness. To put work before family was the kind of snub that would have once resulted in him being put across her knee, which hadn't happened since he was about twenty-one, but he expected something – a hint of annoyance, a sigh of disappointment, a straightforward 'Get your arse back in here'. But she seemed pleased that he was going out. He slammed the front door in something approaching a teenage tantrum and drove to work too quickly for the hazardous weather conditions.

'Thank God he's gone. The annoying little shit hasn't changed much, has he?' Euterpe said to Christopher, who was watching his brother drive away from his vantage point behind the net curtain.

'No, Ma. I just hope the fat tosser's got plenty of grub in. I'm starving.' He crossed over to the pine dresser and began a systematic search of the cupboards. If either DI Corby or DS Gerhardie had been watching him they would have recognised a professional at work.

Christopher didn't find any food in the cupboards so he moved his exploration to the drawers. He read with interest a recent Visa statement that showed a temptingly large discrepancy between the small amount owed and the huge borrowing limit allowed. He shoved it in his back pocket for closer inspection at a later date.

'I wasn't expecting you to come today,' Mandy said without a hint of the *double entendre* that Clive automatically read into her words.

'No. Quite. But I've things to do. Where's Larry?' It was a rhetorical question. He was sure Larry had proffered some ridiculous excuse for staying at home in the company of daytime telly, such as stress, induced by the pressure of coming up with unbelievable excuses for skiving off work so often. 'Any disasters I should know about?'

'Your mum's been on the phone; you're to ring her as soon as you get in. Not that your mum's a disaster.' Mandy's pale cheeks coloured with embarrassment. Clive couldn't help but find this arousing. 'In fact she sounded really sweet,' she added.

That's true enough, Clive thought; she made him feel sick.

Clive went into the sanctuary of his office and collapsed into the softly yielding leather of his trendy black chair. His desk was hidden by dozens of yellow stickers on which messages were optimistically left by his staff in the hope he would read them. Clive peeled them off, stuck them together in a pile and dropped them into his tall, thin litter bin. He knew there was only one message that he had to respond to. Unfortunately.

'What is it?' the voice on the other end of the phone demanded.

'Mother?' It was a fatuous question. Her adopted Australian accent was unmistakable.

'You took your time,' her tone demanded with menaces.

Clive found himself on the defensive, as usual. 'The traffic was bad,' he lied. He didn't want to tell her the truth, that he had spent the last hour looking out of the window at pork pies and dreaming about the Golden Lobe.

'Tell me where Disney lives,' his mother ordered. Clive thought about his sister, Disney. She had been living in a religious community for several years and he had kept in contact with her at key times, such as birthdays, Christmas and updates on their mother's progress. What he hadn't done, hadn't had time to do, was warn her about Euterpe and Christopher's return, which would inevitably bring a demand to see her. What would she say if he were to tell them where she was? Probably that he was a bastard quisling who had better watch out for a letter-bomb by return post. Like any good underling of a repressive regime Clive obeyed his orders without hesitation and gave Euterpe the details of Disney's whereabouts.

'Chris is going to fetch her.'

'Fetch her? Chris? Doesn't he want to rest for a couple of days? Get over the jet-lag and stuff?' Clive fired off questions like Magnus Magnusson on amphetamine.

'He'll be fine, he's not going until tomorrow and anyway, you'll be driving.'

'Me?' Clive exploded.

'Tomorrow's the weekend. Don't be so selfish. Or else.' Her voice was ominously quiet. Then she turned away from the phone and covered it with her fat palm. 'The useless lazy bastard will take you,' she could just about be heard saying.

'Hang on a minute, Mother—' Clive tried to interrupt her flow and failed.

'Must go, I want to ring Grace on her mobile and introduce myself.'

'No. Wait.'

'It's all right, Chris found the number in your address book,' she said in a tone that could be followed only by the immediate termination of the conversation.

'No, wait a minute, Mo—' The phone dutifully clicked and went horribly quiet. '—ther. Shit.' Clive frantically dialled Grace's mobile phone number but he was in such a state that he got it wrong and a bored-sounding man answered and then wouldn't get off the line, so desperate was he for a chat. Finally Clive got rid of him and redialled. The engaged tone mocked him like a playground full of ten-year-olds.

'Balls and bollocks!' At that moment tautology was the least of Clive's problems. He was for it, and he knew 'it' would be uglier than a cartilage injury in a Sunday League football match.

Three minutes later Clive heard the phone ring out in reception. Seconds later Mandy put the call through.

'Hello?' he asked timidly, fully expecting the worst.

'Clive?' If it was Grace at her worst then she sounded very different from what he was used to. Different as in sounding like a man.

'Who's that?'

'Ben. Ben Hopkins. I'm Grace's personal tutor at college.'

'Is everything all right?'

'Fine. The main budget's a bit tight but we've come to expect that these days.'

'I meant is everything all right with Grace?'

'Of course, stupid of me. Sorry. Yes, everything's fine. Well, with her that is. But she asked me to phone you to say she will be with you shortly and is looking forward to ripping your head off. I think I've relayed the message as accurately as I can. I hope that isn't bad news. Nice talking to you. Bye.' Clive could hear the relief in Ben Hopkins' voice as he rang off, grateful to have finished such an unpleasant task. Grace in her Boadicea mode was an awe-inspiring sight but not one that most men wanted to witness while still in the vicinity of her wheel blades.

She arrived twenty-three minutes later. She tore in. Her hennaed dark hair shone blood red under the office strip-lighting and her wildly flailing arms were like mini-hurricanes, ready to wreak terrible vengeance on the world in general and Clive's dangly bits in particular. The silhouette of her size 14 frame hardly made any impression in the doorway and yet she still managed to suggest a substantial physical presence.

'Hi!' Clive began brightly before all his confidence left him like clinically depressed lemmings off a cliff top. 'Did I mention that my mother was coming home?'

The punch wasn't very professional. It had little power and wasn't so much thrown as tossed underarm, but it was effective because it had the secret ingredient of any successful physical attack – surprise. Grace's ring-encrusted fist came up from the depths of her anger and broke the surface of Clive's line of vision only inches under his chin. Seconds later he was tasting fresh blood as it leaked from his raw gums. 'Obviously not,' he said to himself.

Grace put her hands on her hips and began one of her State of Their Relationship addresses.

'You don't think to tell me that your mother and brother are about to walk back into your life after God knows how many years.'

'Seventeen actually. It was 1979—' Clive risked an interruption in the cause of accuracy.

'Shut up while I'm ranting.'

'Sorry.'

'They arrive without warning . . .'

'Now they did actually phone . . . . I tried to tell—' Clive dared another interruption.

'Will you shut the fuck up. Without warning, tucked up neatly in our small terraced house.'

'I realise you're angry . . .' as the words left his mouth he knew he had made a bad choice in his approach. Grace could spot counselling patter at twenty paces, and this wouldn't improve her mood. She moved closer; Clive wisely remained flat against his desk.

'You can only guess at how pissing angry I am and even then your estimate will fall light years short. Why didn't you tell me, you bastard?' Clive didn't dare tell her that he hadn't dared tell her.

Grace stared straight at him. It was like looking at an oncoming train when chained to the track. She took a deep breath, shook her head slowly and turned back to the open door, which was still reverberating from her storming entrance. With the elegance of Columbo asking one last devastating question of the celebrity suspect she paused in the doorway and turned.

'She kept comparing me to the wonderful Julia.'

'That was the woman Christopher ran off with, my ex-fiancée—'

'I know who she is. Was.' Grace's tone was so cold it made Clive yearn for a jumper.

'Sorry,' he said again, knowing sorry wasn't good enough, no matter how many times he repeated it.

'Not good enough. Do something about it and quickly – or else you'll be sorry. Want an example of how sorry you'll be? How about having the mail-order catalogue as your only sexual partner for the next twenty years. Twenty years of folding down the corners of your favourite pages for ease of one-handed access. Poor Anthea Turner will have all the ink thumbed off her.

Again,' she added, to underline that she knew all about his grubby little hobbies that he had stupidly assumed were a well-kept secret.

'What can I do?' Clive asked pathetically.

'You're the counsellor. You sort her out.'

Beyond his open office door he could see Mandy at her desk, trying in vain to ignore the marital battle royal unfolding in front of her. Mandy didn't know what to say. Clive didn't know what to say. How he wished Grace was suffering from the same problem. He noticed that Mandy had a look of stern disapproval. Anthea Turner was obviously a positive role model, someone to admire but not in the way Clive admired her.

From her office on the other side of reception Marilyn Barker was watching the scene and Clive saw her smirking in a vindictive this-will-come-in-very-handy-at-some-later-date sort of way. Grace saw they had a captive and spellbound audience and took the opportunity to deliver her *coup de* Grace.

'Consider this a final warning, Clive Wrigley. If I have to take any further action it will be painful, bloody and fatal. Goodbye.' She walked out of the door and left behind a silence that was stonier than Southwold beach.

Clive turned to Mandy, who was still looking disgusted at the things men do. 'Get my mother on the phone. I'm going to kill the old trout.'

Six

The ignominy of having his most intimate acts exposed in front of his work colleagues seemed about as bad as things could get until Clive went home and was faced with more grapes of Grace's wrath. He had fully expected these to be as bitter as an early crop of lemons, so he was surprised that what he actually faced was a wall of silence that would have felt at home in any Buddhist retreat. In many ways this was worse than outright violence. Grace refused to acknowledge his very existence; she sat at the table and ate with Clive, but she didn't attempt to communicate with him. She coldly exchanged pleasantries with Euterpe and Christopher, but if the conversation threatened to involve or even mention her husband she changed the subject. Clive soon realised that it would be best all round if he didn't push his luck and instead blended into the background. Twelve years of marriage to Grace had helped him become rather good at this trick. A stranger walking into their front room might have had to look twice or even thrice before they spotted Clive, quietly reading the paper in the corner, safely camouflaged amongst the overgrown houseplants, like some forgotten Japanese soldier still in hiding long after the war had ended.

That night, sharing a bed with Grace but taking great care not to trespass anywhere near her, a transgression that would have provoked further physical pain, Clive had another dream. He was in a church attending a funeral, only it wasn't a funeral because there wasn't a coffin. But they were definitely burying someone, the dark suits, bored expressions and out-of-sync miming to the hymns told him that. Everyone he knew was there except for his mother, and yet he could sense her influence everywhere. It was as if they were all there because of her. Clive turned around and in the row behind him was DS Gerhardie, smiling like an Ecstasy tablet. He leaned forward and whispered, as discreetly as an ex-Page Three model with a salacious story to sell, that Clive was under arrest. Clive woke up sweating, fearful at both the events of the dream and the fact that his damp back was close to touching Grace. He quickly shifted over to his side of the bed. There was no sense in making things any more difficult for himself.

Grace didn't attempt to get up to sort out Dan and Hattie, their young children, who loudly demanded porridge, Coca-Cola and Penguin biscuits at five thirty a.m. Instead she diligently slept on through the heavy metal riff of their early-morning cacophony, or at least she pretended to long enough for Clive to get the message that it was *His Turn*, and probably would be for the rest of his life. Message received and understood, he went downstairs, dressed, washed and fed the children, dressed and washed them again, such was the devastation their untutored eating habits caused, and then settled down on the sofa while they jumped on his chest, imitating the random and sadistic violence of the early-morning cartoons on television.

So it was with some relief that Clive set off with Christopher shortly after seven on the long journey south to Newmarket, and the reclusive Disney. Clive was still tired and the thought of sharing a car with Christopher didn't exactly appeal but he had to admit that it was probably better than being at home in the path of hurricane Grace. Christopher spent the first few miles trying to sleep but then admitted defeat, turned on the radio and started to criticise Clive's driving.

As Clive's big brother, Christopher had always been first. He was the oldest child so he got first wear out of the clothes; they were then passed on to Disney, who gave them a more feminine shape before they fetched up in Clive's wardrobe, ensuring his sexuality was often the subject of a whisper campaign in the school playground. Christopher was the first to go to school, where he established the Wrigley reputation for arrogance and stupidity. He was a minor league bully, and subsequently failed all his exams. He was the first to get a job, which lasted three days before he got his mother to ring in sick for him. On a list of people who irritated Clive, his brother was easily first. He still thought that premature ejaculation was a sign of masculinity.

Clive looked at his brother's narrow, hungry features and sighed. He had a lot of questions which needed answers, but knew that the truth was a concept Christopher wouldn't recognise if it sat up and bit him.

'Are you going to tell me what all that shit at the airport was about? Why on earth would you smuggle piss?'

'It's was virgin's milk,' Christopher said, licking his lips.

Despite his foreboding Clive felt a tingle of interest buzz down his spine. 'What?'

'The milk of the virgin.' Christopher laboured the point by giving his lips another lascivious and gratuitous slow, wet lick.

'What the hell are you on about?' Clive asked.

'Liebfraumilch. Don't you know anything about wine?'

Clive's well-groomed middle-class pretensions were stung by this insult but before he could rally his defences Christopher continued.

'It's going to be the next big Aussie export. The world is tiring of Chardonnay, it wants something less classy and more sassy. The exuberance of youth rather than the stodginess of experience. Forget oak aged, this stuff is kept juvenile by genetically engineered additives.'

'What has that got to do with a suitcase full of chilled piss?'

'You'd be surprised. Liebfraumilch has very similar qualities to piss, such as storage needs, longevity, acidity . . .'

'Flavour,' Clive added pompously. He was still smarting from Christopher insulting his lack of knowledge about wine and was unable to stop his epicurean snobbery from elbowing its way in to the conversation like a bar-room bore.

'You could be lynched for saying that in the Bluebell Valley. They are about to become the biggest producers of German-style wines in the world. Even bigger than the Rhine. In the future when people think of cheap medium-sweet wine they won't think Blue Nun, they'll think Grape and Pillage.'

The charmingly named Grape and Pillage was the main brand name for the producers from the Bluebell Valley Vintners Co-operative. 'Chokers' was Christopher's nickname for them due to their sweet finish that was more effective at scarring the gullet than a chicken bone.

'I was making a dry run. Or maybe that should be medium-sweet run.' Christopher chuckled self-indulgently.

'Dry run for what?' Clive asked, ignoring the joke.

'We needed to see how Liebfraumilch would stand up to being transported over distance in a chilled and pressurised environment.'

'Why not use bottles?'

'Bottles!' Christopher dismissed the suggestion as if it was an insult to everything he held dear. 'That's so typical of narrow British minds. We're thinking much larger than bottles. We're thinking vats, reservoirs, oceans. I want Liebfraumilch on draught in every pub in the land. My vision is millions of teenagers buying Grape and Pillage by the half-pint. Mixed with blackcurrant.'

Clive was very glad that he hadn't inherited Christopher's eyesight. He wasn't sure if he believed Christopher, but he couldn't think of any other reason why a grown man would carry urine in his luggage other than one too disgusting to contemplate. Christopher didn't help his cause by insisting that Clive should trust him because he was 'family'. Clive concentrated on the road ahead and after a few miles of awkward silence he decided to ask the question he had so far shied away from.

'Why should I trust you? I trusted you with Julia,' he said, throwing caution to the winds and pouring the years of hurt and ire into one short, accusing sentence.

'Ah-ha!' Christopher bellowed like an under-rehearsed magician at a children's party. 'Now we get to it. That's what really grates on you, isn't it?'

'I don't know what you mean,' Clive lied unconvincingly.

'Come on. That's all you've wanted to know about since I got back, what happened to Julia? Why did I take her away from you? Have you seen that lorry?'

The red sports coupé had swerved out from behind a slowing bus and into the path of an oncoming articulated lorry. Clive quickly swerved back again, cutting in front of the bus. He didn't need to look in his rear-view mirror to know what the bus driver was calling him.

'Trust me, that lousy bitch wasn't right for either of us. All she ever did was moan. I spent every hour of every day trying to establish myself in a wonderful new country, chasing every opportunity, even going to prison for her, and the first chance she got she went off with someone else.' He didn't sound so much bitter as relieved.

'Pardon?' Clive knew there was something in Christopher's last sentence that didn't sit properly with his memory of events but he couldn't work out what it was.

'Didn't Mum tell you? No of course she didn't, bless her. I've been in prison.'

'Prison?' Clive gasped like a supporting actress about to be dispatched by the baddie in a cheap horror film. 'So you weren't missing for all those years?'

'Is that what she said? What a sweetheart. She's so proud.'

Christopher had seen the inside of quite a few prisons, it transpired. He told Clive his story. It was one that unashamedly glamorised his misspent life. It was with some reluctance and after much pressing that Christopher admitted he had only ever been in open prisons, the sort with a good library, quality food grown on the prison farm and regular unsupervised trips to the nearest shopping mall. He claimed that none of the stays were his fault.

'Was it my fault if I sold land that I didn't exactly own or sold merchandise that didn't actually exist? It was all a question of perception.'

'You perceived yourself as innocent while the police perceived you as a criminal?'

'Bang on, little bruv. As far as I was concerned I was just taking care of business.'

Christopher did quite a few stretches in prison and Euterpe kept an eye on things until he got out. Then during his last internment he was sent to an open prison in the Bluebell Valley and put on the vineyard detail. With his usual eye for the main chance he made himself indispensable to Bluebell Valley Vintners Co-operative. He learned the limits of the law and surfed along them like something from a Beach Boys' song. He now knew so much about the wine trade that if he fell in shit he'd come up smelling of fruit blossom, peaches and freshly cut grass with a clean citrus finish. No change there, then. Clive thought.

'I've looked after Mum all these years. You ought to thank me for that.'

Clive concentrated instead on overtaking an estate car in which a mother, father and three children were happily singing songs like the worst kind of family cliché. He reminded himself to thank Christopher sometime, preferably with something brick-like.

'Who was it she went off with?'

'Who?'

'Julia.'

'No one you know.'

'That makes a change. Was it someone you knew?' Clive was pleased to notice that his brother's thin lined face showed distinct signs of discomfort.

'If you must know, it was my probation officer.'

Clive's tears of joy threatened his ability to see the road ahead.

'I haven't seen or heard from her since, and I don't want to.'

'Any kids?'

'Good God no.' Christopher paused and gave his thin lips a sly lick. 'You and Grace adopted your two, didn't you?'

Clive hesitated. His stock answer was complicated and involved a detailed breakdown of demographics, the declining sperm count in Western males, and Third World hunger. 'Yes,' he said, thinking better of it.

'I guess there's a problem down there. I could help with that.' Christopher nodded towards Clive's groin.

'How dare you.' Clive clenched his fists on the steering wheel until his knuckles were translucent.

'I mean Bluebell Valley. We've developed a profitable little sideline in fertility treatment. In fact we've just about got conception covered. We can get people pissed so they can get off with each other and get pregnant, and those that can't we can fix with a test tube. I could arrange for you to have tests.'

Clive ignored the suggestion, shuffling uncomfortably in the bucket seat of the Celica.

Christopher was enjoying his younger brother's embarrassment. 'I'm sure it's not all your fault, she is a bit sour, isn't she? That can't help when it comes to poking the fireplace, if you know what I mean.'

Sadly Clive was left in no doubt what Christopher meant.

'You really are a walking charm school. Allow me to point out, you stupid great idiot, that you are talking about my wife, and she's "a bit sour" because she's just had a couple of very demanding strangers descend on her without a moment's notice.' Clive bristled like an old paint brush deprived of white spirit for too long.

'Pardon me for seeking a heartening reunion with my loving family. What is it with you? Why don't you like me and Ma?'

'I don't like either of you because I'm not a slimy, creepy, two-faced, arrogant, spoilt shit-head. I don't flatter to deceive, I don't lie and cheat, I don't spend all my time making poor excuses for the things that I've done to people. In other words I'm not like you. Or her for that matter.' That about summed it up, he thought, satisfied with an answer that was as pithy as any he could have hoped for.

'You really are a whinging Pom.'

'I've no intention of trading insults with a small-time crook with nothing but shit for brains.'

'Shut your mouth, dag face . . .'

'You bastard idle jail-bird tosser . . .'

This would have continued until one of them went crying to Mother (usually Christopher) but for the intervention of the radio. From all four of the Celica's speakers the insistently nostalgic radio station played a familiar refrain which managed to stop Clive and Christopher mid-thump, something that even a professional referee would have found tricky.

> Sweet sweet lips, that kissed me goodnight,
> Loving eyes that sparkled so bright,
> Mother Love, Mother Love, Mother Love,
> I miss you now you are with God above.

Clive looked at his brother, who was looking right back at him. There was a meaningful exchange, one of understanding, maybe even a little forgiveness. Christopher began laughing, Clive joined him. Then they started to sing in reasonably close harmony.

> Apron strings . . . apron strings . . . apron strings . . .

The words to 'Mother Love' had played a part in the lives of almost everyone over the age of forty. Why? Clive's photographic memory was willing and able to provide the answer. The year was 1967, the Summer of Love. Everyone was dropping out, dropping acid and adopting paisley as their badge of courage. Change seemed to be in the air. So what was the song that Britain associated with that era? 'All You Need Is Love' by The Beatles, its repetitive chorus in perfect harmony with the ethos of a generation? Or 'See Emily Play' by Pink Floyd, occupying a space somewhere between weird and catchy? Or 'San Francisco (Be Sure To Wear Some Flowers In Your Hair)' by Scott McKenzie, the hippie message interpreted as a cabaret standard? No, the song that surprisingly captured the Nation's *Zeitgeist* and then nearly throttled it was 'Mother Love' by The Family Affair. A bunch of sickly sweet children singing a song of devotion to their mother. As the accidental archivist for the career of The Family Affair, Clive remembered every trivial detail of the song. It had a sweeping harp intro, angelic lead vocal (by Christopher), heavenly choir in the middle eight, and a chorus warbled by tone-deaf juveniles (Clive and Disney), whose sole aim was to add extra sweetness to an already well-stocked reservoir of saccharin.

'Look at us. We haven't changed a bit. The Family Affair, still fighting after all these years,' Clive said.

They listened to their song, 'Mother Love', and Clive punched Christopher again, this time with a smattering of affection.

'Well I was fighting,' Christopher said. 'I thought you were just waving your handbag.' Clive's smile took on the rigidity of a recently deceased cadaver. He tightened up his right fist and prepared for round two.

*

The radio waves wafted their middle-of-the-road message all over the nation, bringing succour to those who deliberately sought them out, and frustration to those who accidentally tuned in expecting to get the news and weather. In Bradworth the waves found a willing receiver to amplify them in full stereo around the permanent darkness of the Anabolic Arms. In the farthest, darkest corner of the bar, Noilly Upchurch, recently returned from another well-executed execution, was listening to the broadcast and crying.

> *Those child-bearing hips, that made my birth*
> *   right,*
> *That sad, weary smile always a wonderful sight,*
> *Mother Love, Mother Love, Mother Love,*
> *Dear sweet Jesus, when you see her please give*
> *   her a hug.*

He felt the tears rolling over his cheeks and down to his dumper-truck chin, where they jumped off like Olympic diving champions, completing a triple somersault with half-backward twist before landing gracefully on his heaving chest. He loved this song more than any of the other weepy, sentimental songs that formed the core of his musical bad taste. It was his favourite song of all time, the one he would forsake all others for to take to his desert island. Not for the first time he was grateful for the anonymity the bar gave him. Blubbing like a baby might be all right for most end-of-the-millennium men, but for those who earned their livelihood from being harder than the crust on a service-station sandwich it wasn't a good thing to indulge in too publicly.

He fumbled in his pocket to find the bit of paper that had two phone numbers on it. This time he would do something about it.

Clive and Christopher were looking up at the sign that hung like a guillotine above them. 'Nostrum Hall. Spiritual Home of the Followers of His Holiness The Brahmin Rajneesh. (Note: hitchhikers, anyone in receipt of welfare benefits and those without visible means of support will be denied access to this community.) The love of the Brahmin Rajneesh (and, therefore, God) always goes with you.'

Clive drove through the imposing gates, designed in a century when the upper classes knew how to make everyone else feel lower class. 'Will you look at that!' He had no words to describe the impressive canvas that lay before them. Despite the muddy brown emptiness of the winter scene, the drive through the perfectly executed landscape of open pasture, woodland and formal gardens still took the brothers' breath away. The wintry lack of leaves and flowers only emphasised how perfect the whole design was. Two hundred years after someone with nothing better to do had dreamed it up it still stood as a notable testament to that idle dream.

'Fucking magnificent,' Clive said, deciding that swearing was the only appropriate response when there were no other words to hand. They drove through the frightening beauty of nature tamed. Rounding the rural idyll of a well-behaved beech copse, which had long ago replaced the ugly, dirty and unkempt village and its equally untidy inhabitants, they got their first sight of the glorious eighteenth-century red-brick treasure that was Nostrum Hall. The spiritual home of all the followers of Brahmin Rajneesh. So long as they weren't on welfare benefits or hitchhiking.

'Bollocks.' Again Clive was deprived of anything more apposite to say.

'She's fallen on her feet, our Disney.'

'Or her knees.' Clive felt it only proper to respect the spiritual nature of their sister's relationship with the place.

In front of the house a number of people were engaged in quiet discussion or lost in private contemplation. They all wore the distinctive red and green clothing of the followers of Brahmin Rajneesh, which led them to be known to outsiders as 'The Red and Green People'. Whenever a few of them gathered together, as outside the hall at that moment, they looked like a 1950s 3D film viewed without the glasses. The stubborn refusal of the colours in their clothes to co-ordinate or co-operate in any way gave Christopher and Clive instant headaches.

A tanned, sprightly man with dyed brown hair looked over to them. He was trying to look late forties but his well-worn green eyes put him closer to sixty-five. He was on the front steps talking to several young women who were laughing at something he had just said. He politely excused himself and limped over to the car. Clive and Christopher jumped out and shuffled about like guilty gate-crashers at a party. Clive couldn't help but notice that the man had an unashamedly huge erection in his puke-green cotton hipsters.

'Morning, friends, glory in the love of Brahmin Rajneesh. Can I help you?'

'Hi. We're here to see Disney Wrigley, we're her brothers,' Christopher said.

'Brothers in the blood-relation sense,' Clive added, nervous about any misunderstanding that might somehow commit him to a lifetime of wearing a hair shirt and sleeping in a stone cell.

'Disney? Disney. Sorry, friends, I don't recognise the name.'

'She's forty-four, mousy hair, six feet tall. The last time I saw her she was wearing a safety pin through her right eyebrow, had short spiky blue hair and a T-shirt with "Fuck the Police" written across it. But then it was 1978. She may have changed a bit since then,' Christopher said.

'I think you must mean Sunray. She's the only woman that old we have here.' Clive wandered what this ageing man could mean by the phrase 'that old'.

'Come, join me, we will go and find her. That's a nasty bruise you have there,' he said to Christopher, 'have you been in a fight recently?'

He motioned for them to walk beside him and led them into the tasteful splendour of the main hallway. They were surrounded by wooden panelling of a quality and quantity that had it been a recent addition would have so severely threatened the living conditions of several Amazonian tribes, Sting would have happily flown in for the benefit concert.

'I'm Soleil, by the way. Please have a seat.'

Clive and Christopher sat down somewhat self-consciously on a bright red and green leather Chesterfield.

'Can I get you a drink?'

The brothers looked at each other uncomfortably,

unsure what he meant by 'drink'. Carrot juice, soured goat's milk or something equally worthy that tasted like shit, probably.

'Such as?'

'Whatever. Gin, vodka, cider, lager, three kinds of bitter.'

'You have alcohol?' Clive asked.

'We have a fully stocked bar with a licence to open regular hours. Name your poison.'

'Do you have any medium-sweet white wine? Australian?' Christopher asked.

'We have our own label, imported specially. Should I get you a bottle?' They both nodded obediently.

Soleil went away to get their drinks and Clive looked around at the opulence that filled every square inch of his vision.

'Some place, isn't it?' he said.

'I never thought Disney had it in her. What is all this?'

Clive explained as much as knew about the Brahmin Rajneesh, which was gleaned from the innermost recesses of his own prejudices rather than any empirical study of the community. The Brahmin Rajneesh had established his religious sect ten years previously and his woolly Eastern mysticism attracted many rich, disillusioned Westerners to his cause. He was a prophet who made reassuringly deep (and completely impenetrable) statements claiming to explain the meaning of life. Harmless stuff really, taken seriously only by late-developing adolescents, people in early mid-life crisis and those who suffered from almost total colour-blindness.

'Here's your wine, friends. That'll be eight pounds exactly.'

'What?'

'Eight pounds. For the wine. Oh, I'm sorry, did you think it was free? Dear me no. The Brahmin believes in financial security, he says it begets spiritual security.'

'I bet he does,' Clive said as he paid up, noticing that Christopher didn't offer his share.

'Sunray will join us after her Circle group ends.'

'Is that like the Women's Circle?' Clive asked ingenuously.

'It's where acolytes sit in a circle and listen to our spiritual leader the Brahmin Rajneesh. His speeches are beamed in by satellite live from his home in Poona. It's an emotionally enriching experience that refreshes even the most dispirited of souls.'

'A bit like Heineken?' Clive joked. Soleil ignored him.

'Your sister will be a while, she has much to refresh. Would you like to take a look around at our community?' Soleil's offer was sprinkled with so much religious zeal even Clive found it difficult to refuse.

Christopher jumped at the chance like a new convert. 'That would be great. I feel a great spiritual peace in this place.'

Clive's memory of Christopher was that he would once have had a job spelling spiritual peace, and now he was feeling it, greatly. Exile in Australia had made a difference to Christopher, Clive decided. He was always an irritating bastard but now he was an articulate irritating bastard.

Soleil led them around the estate of Nostrum Hall, calling in at a variety of beautifully converted outbuildings to show the daily routine of the Brahmin's faithful acolytes. The print shop had industry standard desk-top publishing and full-colour laser reproduction yet despite all the modern technology the people working in there were still a bit inky, and they all had hooded eyes from the constant squinting for any sign of a fuzzy edge. Everyone in the room wore red and green. Clive felt his headache coming back. Soleil introduced the visitors and gave the women working in the print shop a cheeky grin for no reason Clive could see, other than he was a dirty old man.

On the way to the next well-equipped and beautifully refurbished building Christopher asked a question.

'Are you the top banana around here?'

'We are a non-hierarchical organisation, friend. I am as everyone else.'

'One of the bunch,' Clive joked.

'But there's got to be someone to look after things for the Rajneesh in his absence, surely? Someone he can rely on.' Christopher winked at Soleil conspiratorially.

'I suppose I do take a lead role in the day-to-day matters, on worldly issues only, of course.' Soleil raised his eyes to the heavens, possibly wondering if he was about to be struck dead for such blasphemy.

'Sort of God's area representative for Newmarket?' Clive's tone was sarcastic but Soleil didn't seem to notice or care.

'What did you do before all this?' Christopher asked, sounding very sincere.

'In my old life I was the Reverend Harry Brompton, Emeritus Chaplain of Beaumont College. You may have heard of me,' he said a trifle pompously. He looked a little deflated when Clive and Christopher shook their heads. 'I've lived and worked here since my retirement. I get an annuity from the college that pays the fees. The Rajneesh is my life now, and this is my destiny.'

'Is this one of those communities where everyone's into free love?' Christopher asked, failing to camouflage the smutty innuendo that was shot through his question like letters in Blackpool rock.

'That would be too simplistic a description. Some people are here to test out a commitment to celibacy, whereas others prefer to explore the freedom that promiscuity gives.'

It was clear to Clive which was Soleil's preference.

'Celibacy, eh?' Christopher sounded intrigued by the notion.

'Above all we love one another through our shared love of the Brahmin Rajneesh and God. We are not bound by the restrictive bonds of an unsure and intrinsically corrupt post-Christian society.'

'So you can shag who you like, then?' Clive asked.

'A question from someone who isn't enlightened cannot be properly answered. It is not the question that is the barrier, it is the mind of the questioner. The Brahmin Rajneesh said that.'

'I kind of guessed he might,' Clive smirked.

'Your earth sister, Sunray, for example. She is a strong adherent to the idea of celibacy.' Soleil sounded disappointed by this, as if he had personally experienced the sharp elbow of this commitment.

Christopher gave Clive a warning look. Clive recognised that his brother was up to something, the sort of something that had led him down many paths before and always to the same place, a place where even the pyjamas had arrows printed on them.

Next was the community shop, which, amongst other things, stocked alcohol, cigarettes and a few fresh vegetables.

'At least there's no meat,' Clive noted with enough smug approval to prove his own It-Takes-One-To-Denounce-One theory.

'The Brahmin has suggested we don't have it on site. But there's a burger place down the road in Newmarket, and Cambridge has some of the finest restaurants in the land, so we can nip out whenever the bean sprout en croûte gets a bit too much.'

'It's nice to see such dedication in an intrinsically corrupt post-Christian society,' Clive said, contumely. Christopher gave him a dum-dum nudge that exploded under his lower ribs and bruised everything within a twelve-inch radius. By happy coincidence the next stop was the community's own health centre.

'We have two full-time doctors on call, a nurse, a physiotherapist, masseur and of course a beautician. Should I ask someone to help stop your nose bleeding?'

Once he and Christopher had finished fighting in the car, Clive had shoved a cone of rolled-up toilet paper into the leaking nostril, and then forgotten all about it. He examined it. Satisfied the worst of the flow was stemmed he politely shrugged off the offer.

Soleil continued with his sales pitch. 'We also have a maternity unit and a small theatre to enable us to tackle minor surgery. Things like breast implants, liposuction and facelifts.'

'You're kidding?' Clive asked.

'No. We believe that it is a spiritual duty to look our best when presenting ourselves to the glory of God. I've recently had my cheeks tightened,' he said, winking so hard that Clive half-expected Soleil's cheeks to pull so tight there'd be a split all the way down to his arse.

'With all these gorgeous chicks around I'm surprised you're not on the job all the time, bugger celibacy,' Christopher said, enviously wiping a drool of saliva from the corner of his mouth with his sleeve.

They arrived back at the main hallway where something approaching a commotion was in progress. Dozens of men and women in the standard red and green fancy dress were hugging one another and yelping like sports commentators. From one of the garish leather sofas sprang a tall woman in a blood red blouse and long, well-tailored pale green trousers who threw herself in Clive's general direction and hugged him tightly.

'Clive! What brings you here?'

'Disney. To see you of course. How are you? You look great.'

'That's because I'm on the perfect diet; swallowing pride and arrogance isn't fattening.'

'Right,' Clive said, struggling to grab the jelly-like logic of Disney's words.

'This is brilliant,' she said. 'Today is really brilliant. You've come at a momentous . . . moment. A real chaos into cosmos thing, you know? We've just had wonderful news on the satellite link. It's time to spread our golden wings. We're all going to Payback Falls.' It was Disney as he remembered her, as ridiculously enigmatic and ultimately pointless as a Led Zeppelin album cover.

'Slow down, Disney. Who have you got to pay back?'

'No, Payback Falls. It's in America. Minnesota actually. And not so much of the Disney, if you please, I have left my previous life behind. Thanks to the Brahmin Rajneesh my name is now Sunray. Hello, Chris. I thought you were in Australia?' She welcomed her other brother as if he was a used-car salesman who had just tried to convince her that she needed a rusty heap with no brakes and the smell of rotting haddock coming from the heating vents.

'Hello, Sunray,' he said, smoothly enough to make Disney's frozen smile show just the smallest trace of defrosting. He exuded more charm than could be found in the basket of an old gypsy woman. 'How are you? It's brilliant to see you. You look great.'

'Thanks.'

'What's all this about going to America?' Clive asked.

'The Brahmin's broadcast today was a revelation. He's had a vision. Our Lord has chosen him to set up a new commune for the next millennium. We are to sell up and move everything to Minnesota, to Payback Falls. It's a small town that's ripe for spiritual renewal. It also happens to have huge expanses of cheap real estate which the Brahmin's been quietly buying up for months. He's transporting his large collection of Impressionist paintings to a purpose-built gallery so all the followers will be able to enjoy their beauty. Such a generous guy. We go in two weeks. It's so brilliant I want to cry. But why are you here?'

'I'd start crying now if I were you,' Clive suggested sympathetically.

'I'd better leave you to your . . . family concerns,'

Soleil said. 'It sounds like I've got a lot of work to do. Thanks to the Brahmin for his mercy, generosity and leadership.' Soleil limped off towards the staircase, his erection eagerly leading the way to the next millennium.

'It's time you came home.'

'Pardon me?'

'Home, it's time to come home,' Christopher pressed his point.

'This is my home. For the next few weeks anyway. Then Minnesota will be my home,' Disney said with as much firmness as she could, which was akin to a particularly crumbly Wensleydale. Clive had no choice but to interrupt their debate.

'Christopher, when you say "home", do you by any chance mean my home?' He had just counted up the number of bedrooms in his comfortable terraced house (two and a barely serviceable box room) and divided it by the total number of people who now appeared to require sanctuary there (seven) and didn't like the answer he had arrived at.

'This here,' Christopher waved his hands around at the fine décor of their surroundings, 'is a beautiful place, a loving place, a spiritual place. What's more it is your home, I see that and I'm happy for you. I'm sure Minnesota will also be a happy home. But I mean "come home" in the family sense, in the roots sense, in the home-is-where-the-heart-is sense.'

'What he's trying to tell you in his smarmy way is that Mother is waiting at my house to see you. And if we go back without you we're dead.'

'She's here? In England? Sugar.' She clutched at the

well-worn wooden beads around her neck as if they were the only lifebelt in a stormy sea.

''Fraid so,' Clive tried to comfort her.

'You must come. It's important we heal our rifts and achieve a spiritual peace.' Christopher was sounding more like Soleil every minute.

'I don't know. There's a lot of planning to do if I'm to go to Minnesota within the Rajneesh's tight time schedule. I might be able to come up for one night, perhaps.'

'Tonight,' Christopher said firmly.

'No. I couldn't. There's lots to do here and I'm still not sure if I've forgiven . . . her.' She couldn't say *Mother* and Clive knew how she felt, it being an impediment to free speech from which he too suffered.

Disney's relationship with her mother had always been difficult and she had wasted huge stretches of her life trying to untangle her feelings about it, first through a series of random sexual encounters and then through a series of random religious encounters. 'From sex to sects', as Clive succinctly put it. Disney had never been able to handle her mother, falling apart whenever she was confronted by the towering personality of a parent who made Joan Crawford look like Bambi's mum. The new, improved Disney was the result of a lifetime learning how to banish demons and assert her true self. The trouble was it was all theory, and theory had a habit when tested of running off like a frightened rabbit and skulking in the undergrowth until the big bad thing went away.

'I don't know if I'm strong enough, despite all the time and all the work I've done here.' She thought about all the self-improvement courses she had done at

Nostrum Hall: positive self-imaging; assertiveness of the soul; mind and body shaping; first-level food hygiene certificate. 'If I did come with you it would be on one condition.'

'Name it' Christopher said. Clive remembered that another thing about Christopher that pissed him off was the annoying way he promised things that he had no intention or ability to deliver.

'You must promise to let me come back here when I ask. No arguments. No exceptions. Can you do that?'

'Of course he can,' Christopher answered before Clive could raise any objection.

Disney thought about it. 'It would be an opportunity to close things properly before embarking on the new. The Rajneesh would approve of that.'

'Even if there was nothing in it for him?' Clive asked quietly. She linked her hands together, as if praying for guidance. Unluckily for her, spiritual guidance in the shape of Christopher was closer to hand than even a live satellite link to Poona could provide.

'Go and pack. Quickly! Clive, you help fetch her cases while I have a quick word with our friend Soleil. Don't look like at me like that, little bruv, trust me. We're going to be a big, happy family once again.'

'Once again?' Clive and Disney queried in unison, the concept of being a big happy family not being one they had come across before.

On the way home they felt duty-bound to reminisce about their childhood as singing superstars.

'Do you remember Gerbil?' Disney asked.

'Gerry Williams. The sound engineer who wrote and

recorded "Mother Love". Great guy.' Christopher happily recalled the distant memory.

Clive had another memory of Gerbil; a man of such immense dimness he made the candle on a birthday cake look like a magnesium flare.

'I was eighteen when we recorded "Mother Love",' Christopher said, for no apparent reason other than to prolong the enjoyment of remembering a happy moment.

'He died in a car crash just before we were due to record the follow-up,' Clive remembered with crystal clarity.

'Broke Mum's heart. That was the reason why we never made another record.' Christopher sounded full of regret at the implications of lost love.

'That and the fact we were crap,' Clive said truthfully.

'We were ahead of our time. We could have become the British Osmonds.'

'Lucky for Britain we didn't,' Clive sneered.

Christopher wrinkled his forehead with the effort of thought. 'In fact we had a hit record long before the Osmonds, so in Britain we were actually the Osmonds before the Osmonds were the Osmonds.' He noticed Disney and Clive giving him their sympathetic psychiatric-nurse looks. 'What I mean is, we were the first family group. We beat the Jackson Five by at least a couple of years. The Osmonds are really an American version of The Family Affair.'

'That must be like an albatross around their scraggy Mormon necks, forever to be known as the American version of The Family Affair,' Clive said. In Christopher's perverted logic lay the reason why their brotherly relationship would never progress beyond a state of open civil war; they had less in common than the divided fans of Celtic and Rangers.

'Anyway,' Disney said impatiently, annoyed at the interruption to her story, 'he took Mother to an exhibition of my art class at school and she bought two pictures.'

'How thoughtful,' Christopher said.

'Both of them by Barbara Lavery.' Disney didn't try to hide the wetness around her eyes. 'I hated Barbara Lavery and I really hated her chocolate-box pictures. And do you know what Mother said? She wanted to buy something she could live with, not something that looked like a leak from my menstrual cycle.'

'Your pictures always were a bit grim,' said Christopher, proving that everyone is indeed a critic.

'Did anyone notice that car,' Clive asked suddenly, pointing to his rear-view mirror at the green Vauxhall Vectra disappearing into the flat Cambridgeshire countryside.

'I noticed the driver was sticking his finger in his ear and then eating it,' Disney said, showing an uncharacteristic level of observation.

'Exactly,' Clive said.

Back at Nostrum Hall the Emeritus Chaplain of Beaumont College once again stood on the front steps and welcomed a visitor.

'Hello, friend. From the look of your expression you need the cheer that only the love of the Brahmin Rajneesh can give you.'

'Shut up, you bloody Scientologist nutter. I want to

ask you a few questions about them that have just left.'
DS Gerhardie showed Soleil his badge and was pleased
to notice that the man's tanned face paled to a light
shade of fawn. Below Soleil's waist his permanent erection collapsed faster than a prosecution by the Serious
Fraud Squad.

'I've got to get to Do It All before they close to get
some blinds for my velux windows, so don't even think
of fucking me about.'

Seven

On Saturday afternoons Amen Durkin led his Men-At-Pause encounter group. There were eleven members of the group. The chief excuse they used to slip away from their crazy lives to attend the sessions was 'to watch the football', which led them to give the group the unofficial name 'Mad United'. Despite having famous faces the members remained anonymous within the confines of Mad United. They didn't want anyone to know they were having therapy, at least not until a cure was in sight and they could write a book on their experiences (usually called *Back from Hell* or something similar) and do the chat-show circuit to promote it. Instead everyone had a nickname, usually conferred on them by the rest of the group. A heavy coffee drinker was called 'Maxwell', someone who jokingly confessed to an addiction for curries was known as 'Rogon Josh', and the newest member, who Durkin had just introduced, was immediately named 'Super Sub' as he made their number up to twelve.

He was a young man, the youngest in the group by ten years or more. Despite his obvious lack of celebrity he still exhibited the right attributes for a quick entry into Durkin's élite group by proffering thick bundles of high-denomination money. He was wearing a big green anorak with a hood that fell over his head and made him look like a medieval monk. It also allowed him a level of privacy usually only offered by a ten-foot wall.

'Today we are going to exercise demons,' Durkin announced dramatically.

'Don't you mean exorcise?' asked Maxwell.

Durkin looked around the celebrity circle in the comfortable seminar room at the head office of his Shrink-Fit empire.

'No. If you truly want to understand what drives you then you have to explore your inner demons, come to know them and make them work for you, not against you. Do not eradicate them. I believe the core of any addiction is the desire for secrecy.'

'Last week you said it was denial.'

'Did I? Well denial and secrecy are much the same thing.' Durkin brushed aside Maxwell's query; after all it didn't do to take too seriously a man who, for recreational purposes, liked to put carbolic soap up his bottom.

'Secrets. Everyone in this group has to expose their biggest secret before we can move forward. The secret that presses your particular self-destruct button. Remember, today you must expose yourself, and there are no transcontextual rules to worry about. So who's up first? Rogon Josh?'

Rogon Josh paled at the offer. 'I'd rather not, Amen, There are so many things I could choose. I need time to think.' Rogon Josh was already far away, fondly remembering all the terrible secrets in his past.

'Why don't you go first?' Super Sub asked Durkin, who was taken aback by this telling interruption from the newest member.

'Yes. OK. Why not? My secret addiction is envy. I will do absolutely anything to get even with someone I'm envious of.'

The group looked at their guru in some surprise.

'I once envied someone, a colleague.' He paused. 'An ex-colleague now, I'm glad to say. We worked together for many years, I taught him everything I knew and yet there was always something about him that I wanted but couldn't have. Of course I didn't admit to being envious, it was my secret. But I worked hard to get bigger and better than him and didn't give up until I'd surpassed him. Yet I never felt properly satisfied despite my success. I still can't forgive him for that. I don't think I ever will.' Durkin noticed a lot of heads nodding in agreement, success for most of these people had been driven by envy and revenge. 'I got better, in both senses of the word. Better in that I recovered, and better in that I am now more powerful than the snivelling shit I used to envy.'

The group looked at each other, shocked by Durkin's venom.

'I left him in the shade and that's where he remains to this day. Obscured and obscure.'

'Sounds to me like his shadow is still falling across your life,' the new man said innocently.

Durkin face briefly flushed with anger but he quickly controlled himself. 'Wrong. I have exercised and exorcised him. The other night I beat him out of sight at a national awards ceremony. It's not just me that knows I'm better than he is, the rest of my profession has acknowledged it too. I have nothing to envy now, it's him who is envious of me. That is true success.' Despite his best efforts Durkin sounded as if he was some way short of being convinced.

'Beating someone doesn't make you better than them,' Super Sub said with quiet strength.

Durkin was silent for quite a while before nodding his agreement. 'A good point well made,' he said softly. 'Maybe I haven't truly exorcised him. I might still have a secret place where envy thrives.' He looked at the newcomer. 'Thank you, friend, you have shown me that the journey to self-awareness is often longer than it looks on the map.' He made a mental note to charge the new man double for his troublesome interference and to put him on a behavioural modification programme that involved a lot of electricity.

He smiled at him. 'I wonder if you'd like to go next. Share your darkest inner demon with the group?' Durkin gave a sly look at his clipboard in search of revenge for the newcomer's effrontery. 'Earlier you told me you had a problem with an addiction to mindless violence.'

Super Sub looked at Durkin, and he didn't like what he saw. 'I told you that in confidence.'

'Secrets again. You'll never be cured if you hang on to secrecy. Don't be a coward all your life.'

'If I were you I should watch my back. No one calls me a coward and gets away with it.' With that Super Sub stood up and swept proudly from the room. The rest of Mad United weren't too concerned, each of them remembered a time when they too had stormed out of a session under Durkin's intrusive and sometimes insensitive probing.

'Shall I go after him?' Maxwell asked.

'Leave him,' Durkin ordered, running his fingers through his thin silvery hair. His red glasses glinted threateningly. 'Time to stop pissing about boys. Rogon Josh, what are you going to own up to this week, the cocaine or the rent boys?'

It began as nothing more than a slightly pretentious dinner to celebrate the Wrigley family reunion but it quickly turned into The Four Course Menu of the Apocalypse.

'Thank God you're home.' Grace welcomed Clive's return from Nostrum Hall by expertly digging her long, painted fingernails into the soft and sensitive skin on the underside of his forearm. It was clear from her demeanour – the pencil-sharp stare, the rampant red hair, the lines of harassment around her eyes that looked like the London A–Z – that Grace was pleased to see him only because it gave her a victim to vent her anger on. He knew he was soon going to wish he was still hundreds of miles away hugging Red and Green People.

In the sitting room Disney was already facing the music. Which in Euterpe's case was of the Wagner's *Ring Cycle* (unabridged version) variety. Christopher added his own selection of reassuring noises to help the chilly reunion along.

'Darling, you look so much shabbier than I remember. Didn't I always say that red and green should never be seen?' Euterpe mocked through pursed purple lips.

'Unless worn by the Queen,' Christopher chipped in and gave his best imbecile's grin, which compared favourably with anything John Mills pulled in *Ryan's Daughter*.

'This isn't meant to be fashion, Mother. These are the robes of my church,' Disney explained while looking at the floor and shuffling nervously.

'Looks more like the curtains to me. You never did have any taste, in men as well as clothes. But at least you've not become a tub of lard like Clive. Isn't he a fat bastard? Anyway, it's been too long.'

'Too long,' agreed Christopher, failing to reflect the feelings of Disney, for whom it obviously hadn't been long enough.

In the kitchen Clive was preparing an appropriate feast for his newly united family. Cooking was one of the few things he was able to indulge in without fear that he would be discovered as a fraud. In everything else he always suspected that it was only a matter of time before the thin veneer of his abilities was uncovered. His attempts to be a successful businessman, a professional therapist, a good husband all felt about as secure as a fast-cooling soufflé. But cooking allowed him freedom to express himself as he wished, to be wild and creative, to be impulsive and daring, and who cared if it failed. At home in his kitchen he could cook whatever he wanted, however he liked, without the parameters of disapproval, or the threat of a malpractice case hemming him in.

Tonight there was another good reason to celebrate this freedom – the geographical position of the kitchen. Even though the terraced house was quite small, the kitchen was about as far away from the rest of the rooms as it was possible to get. It was as effective a retreat from his family as Nostrum Hall was from the evils of the world for followers of the Brahmin Rajneesh, and the decor was a lot less harsh on the eyes.

In the kitchen he was free, or he would have been except for Grace holding his collar tightly as she hauled him backwards across the worktops. His collar cut deeply into his neck and nearly garrotted him, his heels made little indented tracks in the Cozi-Cottage cushion flooring (or Middle-Class Lino, as Grace called it), and he narrowly avoided a painful collision with the corner of the scrubbed pine table where Dan and Hattie were playing Operation. As he came to a halt next to the game it buzzed and the patient's red nose lit up to indicate that a delicate piece of surgery had just gone horribly wrong. Dan and Hattie found the jarring buzz so gratifying that the patient was as safe in their hands as a dying man in the care of Burke and Hare.

'Your mother is, without any shadow of doubt, the devil incarnate. In fact I'd rather have the devil in my home, he'd eat a lot less and he wouldn't castigate me every five minutes for not plumping the cushions.' Her tone was ironic rather than vengeful, but she was clearly someone in the middle of a crisis that had his mother at its core. Clive didn't want to ask what, exactly, had happened as he was sure that the answer would not be pleasant, but he saw it was his marital duty to do so.

'What's up?' He felt Grace's grip loosen so he took the opportunity to free himself and pick up a fish slice, which could be pressed into action as a defensive weapon should the need arise.

'What's up? Let me count the ways. She insinuates that I'm nothing short of a lazy slut when it comes to housework. Then she tells me I should be looking after her. She says the children need discipline, but when I tell them off she says I'm a sadistic, vicious bitch. Of course it goes without saying that Dan and Hattie think she's wonderful and do whatever she tells them, but I suspect that may have something to do with the endless supply of Smarties she's got in her handbag.'

I hope that's it too, Clive thought to himself, rubbing his thigh at the memory of his mother's highly individual and often devilish ways of making children behave.

'But the worst is the constant unfavourable comparisons she makes between me and everyone else. "Julia never spoke to me in that tone"; "Christopher always does that for me without needing to be asked"; "In Australia the old people are treated like royalty". Apparently even Ned bloody Kelly always made sure his mother-in-law got the clean duvet when she was in town.'

Clive saw the problem, but knew it would take X-ray vision to see a solution. Ever the good professional he began to waffle.

'Relationships with in-laws can be problematic . . .' Clive poured gallons of his own blend of soothing oil on the stormy waters, noticing too late that it was actually untreated crude oil and this was an area of outstanding natural beauty where many species, such as his happy marriage, were under threat of immediate extinction.

'You can say that again, only don't or else I'll bash you. Do you know how long she's planning to stay?'

'I hadn't really explored that with her as yet,' Clive gabbled.

'She's talking about twenty-five weeks, minimum. That's half a year with the blue-rinse Antichrist in my home.'

Clive blanched. 'How long?'

'Apparently she's here for some deeply personal reason, one she can't bring herself to share with her "bad-seed daughter-in-law", and she won't go home until the mission is complete.'

'I'll suggest putting her up in a hotel. A nice one, one with great views.'

'Preferably of Land's End. Or maybe Sellafield,' Grace said, perking up noticeably.

'Then we could all enjoy her stay even more.' Clive accentuated the almost negligible positive.

Grace looped an arm around his waist. The action reminded Clive that his wife wasn't always the hard-as-nails modern woman she liked to appear, although her more tender moments occurred about as often as a visit from Halley's Comet. The almost permanent barrage of her heavy artillery made it was easy to forget how vulnerable she could be.

'I just don't want her to come between us. It's like we're on either side of a wall. One built by that fat, interfering old toad.'

Clive kissed her on the forehead. 'I know.'

'Talk to her. You're a counsellor, you're supposed to

know what to do.' She let the innuendo that actually he hadn't got a clue what to do hang in the steamy air of the kitchen.

'I'll try. I promise. When the time is right.' Clive tried to sound confident about the task ahead.

Grace jabbed a sharp, pointed finger at him with the ferocious intent of a voodoo witch doctor. 'You've got a week or I kill the evil cow.'

There was the sound of spitting and squealing as Dan tried to remove a funny bone, not from the cartoon character patient with a red bulb for a nose but from Ginger the family cat. If anything the noise of a displeased cat was even more enjoyable than the game's buzzer and the children immediately began a course of very intrusive surgery on the irritated pet. As they chased the cat and tried to corner it behind the kitchen door, showing a level of skill normally associated with Border collies, Disney came storming in to the room making a similar spitting noise to that of Ginger.

'Five minutes and that woman has already tested my faith,' she screamed. 'She can't accept that I have grown up and am now in control of my own life.'

'Have you two fallen out already?' Clive asked, wickedly.

'What do you think? By the way, she wants to know when the food will be ready, and if it's going to be long can I make her a sandwich and a cup of tea?'

As usual he had to prepare two meals, one with prime cuts of meat in a range of rich tastes and textures, and a boring vegetarian option, full of fibre and tasting like particularly nutritious minced cardboard. Clive's pleasure was vicarious, lovingly preparing meat dishes that he would never eat. His enjoyment of the meal was always second hand. His pleasure was the plaudits and fulsome praise of others. Clive wasn't a vegetarian out of love for the animal world, his view was that anything that tasted good deserved to be eaten even if it did have a face, but because it gave him the nice feeling inside that self-denial always gives. It was just a shame that it never got close to the joy offered by a medium-rare Châteaubriand with a Bordelaise sauce.

For a first course, or 'starters' as Euterpe insisted on calling it, Clive had decided on red mullet for his guests, with a chickpea dip for him. He cleaned the mullet and made sure that he left the livers intact as the recipe ordered. The Saturday evening sports programme on the radio told of crises in the world of throwing, hitting and kicking balls that made the one unfolding in his terraced house sound insignificant. A Spaniard with a speech impediment for a surname had faced the humiliation of missing the cut at the Billyo Motors International Golf Open in North Korea.

'Poor bastard,' Clive said absent mindedly. 'How will he ever cope with the stigma?' He didn't dwell on the misfortunes of a distant golfer for long. He reasoned that people who liked golf deserved everything they got. Except for Durkin. He liked golf and he didn't get anything near what he deserved.

The Wrigley family sat around the large oak table that greedily filled the small cupboard Clive and Grace had optimistically designated as a dining room. They were grappling with a duo of knotty problems, boning red mullet and getting to know one another after so long.

'Pulling one thing apart while putting another thing back together,' Clive said, to a general air of apathy.

'Do you mind me mentioning something, Clive?' Euterpe asked, before seamlessly moving on so that he had no time to object. 'It's just a little household tip, simple but effective. If you line the toilet bowl and water surface with tissue when you want to go . . .' she gave a begrudging nod in the general direction of Dan and Hattie, similar to the one Snow White's Stepmother reserved for those special family occasions, '. . . go poo poo, you'll find it wraps around those big smelly shits of yours and stops them grazing the porcelain when flushed. It'll do until Grace finds out how the toilet brush works.'

Clive looked up at his mother with her recently dyed head of dazzling honey blond hair and found he was paralysed, unable to speak thanks to her rudeness and his mouth being full of chickpea cement.

'I have something to say if no one objects,' Grace said to no one in particular, putting down her knife and fork as she did so. Clive relaxed slightly, if Grace was unarmed this would mean she couldn't do any immediate physical harm.

'Something to say?' Euterpe licked her lips and then turned as if to an invisible audience beyond the dining-room wall. 'At least that's one thing you seem to be good at.'

'Now look—'

'Time for a toast.' Clive jumped up and started to pour the Riesling like a drunken footballer showing off in front of several Miss Worlds.

'Good idea,' Grace said, raising her glass. Clive made sure he only partially filled it so as to keep her sober for as long as possible. 'You tie her up and I'll put another log on the fire.'

'To the family,' Clive cheered.

'The family,' a few begrudging voices mumbled back at him.

'That's not in the brainwashed cult-religion sense,' Euterpe said to Disney.

Disney tried hard not to burst into tears. 'A child brought up in the love of God is seldom brought up in court,' she said, with feeling. Then she did burst into tears.

Christopher gave an ironic laugh and then, noticing the devastation that was unfolding around the table, tried to smother it. Clive knew it was time to do something. He prepared to run from the room but Grace grabbed his arm with her razor-wire nails and re-opened his earlier wounds.

'What I want to know is, what are you doing here, exactly?' Grace asked Euterpe, who was pulling fish bones from her mouth like a cartoon cat. Still in Grace's grip, Clive found himself wishing that the fish bone might lodge in her throat and put an end to their misery once and for all. It didn't.

'Yes, why have you come back after all this time?' Disney asked, looking up from tear-stained sleeves.

Euterpe looked at Clive, who was trying to calculate how many seconds it would take to get to his car and drive off into the safety of the night.

'Is that what you want to know too, Clive?' She fixed him with a driller-killer of a stare, one he knew from a million dressing-downs over the years.

'I suppose it would be interesting to know . . .'

'Very well. It just so happens that there are a few

reasons why I've chosen now to come back and reunite my family. But right now I'm pigging starving so maybe we can get our stomachs on the outside of this poncey crap before I give you an answer.'

'I'll bring in the main course,' Clive said, doing what he did best, which was what he was told.

Out in the kitchen someone had phoned up the radio programme to bemoan the fact that his football team was looking a dead certainty for relegation.

'It's a disaster, David. A totally tragic disaster of epic proportions.'

Clive thought he could hear the swish of David's head, nodding in agreement.

'Certainly is, Mark. Of epic proportions.'

Clive picked up his seven-inch professional kitchen knife, a seventh wedding anniversary present from Grace that was meant as a threat to any itching he might have been feeling in the faithfulness department, and threw it straight at the radio.

'Why don't you go fuck yourself, David?' Clive said, with uncharacteristic ferocity, as the radio fizzed and crackled before going terminally silent.

'Grace, why is it that modern tarts like you are so bloody neurotic? This is a happy family occasion for Christ's sake.' Christopher was cheerfully doing his bit for good family relations as Clive entered the room with the main course, beef olives. He almost turned round and went straight back to the safety of the kitchen but somewhere deep in his shaken subconscious something stirred. He couldn't quite put his finger on what it was but then it stepped into the light like Orson Welles in *The Third Man* and he was surprised to recognise it as chivalry.

'Shut up all of you and enjoy the meal,' he said. Christopher was about to open his mouth again but Clive knew that his foot wouldn't be far behind. 'No, Christopher, enough. Feet for dancing, mouth for eating. You too, Mother.' He hoped Grace would appreciate this intervention but she was too busy pouring herself an unhealthily large glass of wine and knocking it back in one.

A couple of minutes of thankful peace passed, broken only by Euterpe sucking at her meat and Dan and Hattie rowing over who had the biggest portions. Then Euterpe put down her knife and fork and fixed a gimlet-eyed stare on Grace.

'The things that I have come to say,' she began slowly and with considerable menace, 'are things that shouldn't be said in front of those who don't belong to this family.' She also shot a look at Dan and Hattie that would have made King Herod envious.

'What the fuck do you mean by that?' Grace thrust her wine glass in the direction of her mother-in-law, an action that made the dregs in the bottom splash Euterpe's face like an advert for aftershave.

'You are so cruel to me,' Euterpe cried, tears appearing in the corner of her eyes, drawn there as a Pavlovian response to her injured little-girl voice. 'Why don't any of you tell her to stop?' she asked.

'Pudding anyone?' Clive asked valiantly.

'In many ways I'm glad I'm dying. I won't have to suffer the shame of being part of this family.'

Clive opened his mouth and then closed it again.

Disney scratched at her wild hair until it was a pretty good imitation of a haystack the morning after the great hurricane of October 1987. Grace stared straight at Euterpe. Dan and Hattie took the opportunity to steal some wine from the grown-ups' glasses. Only Christopher carried on undisturbed, licking his plate and then looking hungrily at Disney's.

'Great grub. Do you want all yours, Dizzy?' Not receiving an answer from his sister, who was held perfectly still by the reverberating silence, he grabbed her plate and flicked the remains of the meal on to his.

'Dying?' Clive asked in a breathless whisper.

'Dying?' Disney repeated, just as quietly.

'Pudding. And then I'll tell you all about it,' Euterpe said, handing Clive her empty plate.

'I'll just get it.' Clive pointed weakly towards the kitchen and made his exit.

Clive found he had a real appetite for the chocolate tort because it had all the richness and calories he had longed for throughout the meal. That was the great thing about puddings if you were a vegetarian – there was usually very little meat or fish in them. He returned to the dining room to find that Grace had, thankfully, left the group to put a now-drunken Dan and Hattie to bed.

'Come on, Ma, what's all this about you dying? You seem fitter than a butcher's dog to me,' Christopher said, jokily.

'Chrissy my love,' Euterpe said, spitting full-fat crème fraîche over everyone, 'I'm not sure now is the time, on such a happy occasion.'

Clive looked at his mother closely but could detect

no sign of sarcasm. 'Now would seem as good as any,' he said.

'If you're sure I won't ruin the atmosphere?' she asked in her butter-wouldn't-melt voice. Clive looked around at all his guests and felt confident that the atmosphere could not be ruined any further.

'Very well. I'm an old woman, no, don't try and deny it,' she said, raising a hand to stop the flood of denials that showed no sign of emerging from anyone's lips, 'and I need to make my peace with my children. I need to be sure that we are all square before I die and that there's nothing left hanging in mid-air.'

I quite like the idea of you hanging in mid-air, Clive thought, wistfully. But he didn't speak, for his mother's promise of resolution had galvanised everyone's attention. He had started to sweat; Disney was refusing eye contact like a nervous teenager; and Christopher had a greedy look in his eyes, as if calculating life-insurance payouts.

'You're really dying?' Disney asked suspiciously.

'I am not long for this world.'

Disney looked quickly at Clive; Christopher choked on his tort.

'She's dying,' Christopher blubbed, the message finally sinking in.

'Please, no tears,' she said, faintly. Clive recognised the melodramatic tone his mother always adopted when giving bad news. He called it her Dying Swan Act. The Pavlovian tears were back on duty again, glistening in the candle-light.

'What's wrong with you?' Clive asked. Disney and Christopher exchanged 'and exactly how long have you got' looks. Christopher even glanced hopefully at his watch.

'I have a suspicious nodule.'

There are some things that make people laugh even though they know they shouldn't. It's probably because they know they shouldn't be laughing that makes them so funny. 'Nodules' was such an example of something people ought not to laugh at but did. Add to that the suggestion that the nodule in question was suspicious and you had a Marx Brothers back-catalogue of things people shouldn't laugh at. Which is why everyone around the table, apart from Euterpe, exploded like a meringue under a steam hammer. Linen napkins were wedged into mouths, knuckles were almost bitten off, shoes were suddenly examined in more detail than by the quality assurance department at the manufacturers. But none of these measures were able to hide the fact that the entire Wrigley family was laughing at their mother's announcement of a possibly fatal condition. To her credit Euterpe said nothing. Instead she stored it in her memory and privately swore vengeance on every one of the ungrateful little bastards at some point in the future, which given her current life expectancy would be sooner rather than later.

'That is why I am here. I have come to make my peace with you.'

Clive figured this shouldn't take too long. With any luck she'd be on a plane bound for home before the end of next week.

'I have a final wish for each of you, which I intend to achieve before I go anywhere. I also have a wish for the family as a whole.'

'What?' the three Wrigley siblings blurted out with well-choreographed timing. But Euterpe wasn't to be hurried.

'I had intended to spend some time amongst you to break the news gently, but let's face facts, who wants to stay in this shit-hole with a bunch of selfish bastards like you? I want to get back to the Bluebell Valley and get on with the rest of whatever is left of my life.'

'So what's your last wish for me?' Disney asked impatiently.

'Little Miss Empty Head, manners always were your weak point. One of many weak points actually. Such a shame that your sham religion doesn't appear to have shored up your crumbly little mind.'

Disney tried to regroup her rapidly deserting assertiveness for one last assault on Fort Euterpe. 'I hope it's a simple wish because I won't be around for long. I'm going to Payback Falls.' Disney sounded like someone who already had an inkling that she wasn't going anywhere near Payback Falls.

'Your dozy little idea of heaven on earth. I'm afraid you won't get to waste any more time on that stupid scheme. My wish for you is this: I need you to come back to Australia to help as my medical condition worsens.'

'You *need* me?' Disney sounded slightly flattered at the request.

'No, I need your nursing skills. Sadly that means you coming too. It's a cross I shall have to bear with my usual good grace.'

Disney's mouth locked open in a gesture of stunned capitulation to the matriarchal force that was flattening all before it. She had one last card to play. 'I won't be going anywhere without the approval of Soleil.'

'Who's he when he's at home?' Euterpe asked mockingly.

'He's my spiritual guide at Nostrum Hall. I don't do anything without his say-so, and I know he'll say no to this. The Brahmin Rajneesh has instructed him that no one is to be left behind in the great move westwards.'

Euterpe showed no sign of being upset at Disney's refusal to acquiesce, she just gave her her 'We'll see' look.

'What's mine then?' Clive asked, feeling the sweat of anxiety gather in the fat folds between his stomach and chest.

'My wish for you is to get a proper wife and family and stop messing around with that sour-faced bitch and her fraudulent brood. I want a grandchild I can call my own. With Wrigley blood in its veins. Unfortunately I think you're the only Wrigley likely to provide it.' She shot a look of dissatisfaction at Christopher. It was the first one Clive had ever seen go in his big brother's direction.

'You're mad. Totally mad.' Clive shook his head in disbelief.

'We'll see,' the look on her face said for a second time.

'I hardly dare ask,' Christopher laughed.

'As my favourite child my wish for you is the hardest. I have to spend the rest of my time on this earth thinking of myself and no one else.'

Clive gave Disney a half-smile; 'What's new' it said.

'I was going to leave my savings to you, Christopher, but as you seem incapable of managing the contents of a piggy bank I've decided to keep them for myself. It's time you made a go of one of your hare-brained business schemes. Smuggling piss through customs and leaving me to take the blame was the last straw. I'm leaving you on your own from now on. Sorry, my darling.'

Christopher was still smiling, in the manner of a recently beheaded chicken that has just set off on a six mile jog.

Euterpe refilled her glass. 'So let's raise our glasses to the Wrigley family. Back together again for the last time. I hope.' She drank the wine and then threw her glass at Clive's coal-effect gas fire. The shards of glass went all over the hearth rug.

Grace chose this moment to re-enter the fray, having finally got Dan and Hattie to sleep. Christopher stood up to object to something but thought better of it and crashed back down.

'Still alive, Mother-in-law?' Grace sounded disappointed.

'What's your last wish for all of us?' Clive hardly dared to ask but he thought it better to know the whole truth, no matter how awful.

'What's all this?' Grace snapped. Clive blushed.

'Tell you later,' he promised, knowing it was lie, as whatever he told her would be a much-watered-down version of the original.

'Oh yes, my wish for all of you. A bit of fun really. I want The Family Affair to play a reunion concert. It will be a lasting memorial to me.'

'The Family Affair back together?' No one was quite sure who actually articulated the question, as it was one that they were all asking themselves.

Christopher was vaguely excited at the prospect as it provided some kind of cushion to the news that any future inheritance had been denied him. If there were any profits to be made, then he would make sure he had first pick. Disney looked sick at the thought of all the horrors of her childhood coming back to haunt her again. Clive was shaking his head slowly. The Family Affair back together. It was like hearing conscription had been re-introduced and he was next up for a short hair-cut and exhaustive basic training. Except this was far worse. His mother had been a bigger psychopath than any drill sergeant when she had controlled The Family Affair during their dazzling, dreadful and doomed career. As the central figure of a briefly famous singing group she had dominated their every waking thought and quite a few of their sleeping ones too. She had taken them out of school, away from their friends and sur-roundings, and put them into a new world. It was a world that demanded unquestioning obedience and one where children should be seen and not heard. But every adult involved with the group depended on them adher-ing to this criteria so Euterpe moulded them and her regime was severe and utterly without mercy.

'Fuck that for a lark,' Clive said, trying to sound like a man putting his foot down. Euterpe trod on it.

'I've already been in touch with Monty Gliver, our old record producer. He's semi-retired now, but he runs the Summer Show on Cromer Pavilion for a bit of a hobby. He's putting the acts together for this year's summer season and wants us to headline Saturday nights. That's if he can't get someone from *Neighbours*. I'm now on the look-out for a choreographer.' It was the

Euterpe they dimly remembered from their childhood, in charge, unstoppable and ruthlessly pursuing her ambitions.

Back in his kitchen Clive couldn't believe how far the evening had descended into hell. He arranged Elizabeth Shaw mints on a Royal Doulton plate, unconsciously shaping them into a swastika. He had hoped that the evening would be an opportunity to set some boundaries with his mother, preferably of the great big electrified kind, to protect himself and his family. But instead she had taken the initiative and thrown hand-grenade surprises at all of them. Suddenly they were her little children again, scared to challenge her, impotent in the face of her threats, willing victims in her demonic plans. They now stood on the brink of death, disaster and, much worse, public humiliation at the end of a Norfolk pier.

Eight

Unusually for a Monday morning Clive was keen to get to work. The chance to worry about other people's problems, no matter how dull or irritating, seemed infinitely preferable to worrying about his own. The idea of ordinary problems seemed quite attractive when compared to the Gothic horror of his own familial situation. Going to work was an opportunity to get away from the claustrophobia of sharing a house with his mother, and he took it willingly.

The euphoria he felt at escaping from the nuclear fallout of Halcyon Terrace lasted most of the day until he saw the strange-looking man waiting in reception. There was something about the long flapping fringe, hiding all but the vaguest hint of a face, that registered doubt, concern and a small whisper of fear in Clive's mind. Such a fringe could have hidden a lot of things, but in

Clive's experience as a psychological expert of some note it usually hid a physiognomy that had been honed in the field of battle, be it on a foreign field or the Dog and Muzzle on a Saturday night. In Noilly Upchurch's case it was both.

Mandy smiled at Clive and pointed to the agitated figure who waited impatiently in the waiting room.

'New referral, Mr Wrigley. Name of Noilly Upchurch.' Mandy gave him an exasperated look and mouthed, 'He doesn't have an appointment.'

Clive smiled back, switching the smile off when his attention fell on Noilly.

A Sinker. Clive could tell straight away. He knew he was looking at someone who was a maelstrom of raw emotions wrapped in a tormented body, and that was enough to make his heart sink. There was usually very little he could do to help the sinkers, short of buying them their own electric chair, but he was professional enough to smile brightly and get on with it. After all, he reminded himself, quickly finding a thread of a silver lining in an otherwise ebony-black cloud of a Monday afternoon, they all pay the rent.

'Follow me, please,' he said, feeling oddly vulnerable as he turned his back on the dangerous-looking man in the camouflage jacket.

'First things first,' he began, having pointed Noilly towards the seat opposite. 'I'll explain exactly how these things work. We have an hour for this session, no more, no less. If we run out of things to talk about or simply don't want to take things any further then we shall sit in silence. Silence can be very therapeutic, even cathartic on occasions. Anything you choose to share with me is confidential. You can talk about anything you like. My job is to try and reflect back what you say so you can try and make sense of it. Then you can begin to put right the things in your life that are bothering you. OK so far?'

Clive watched his client closely. Any misunderstanding about why they were here could prove fatal for their relationship later. Things might become so bad that the unthinkable might happen and he might not get paid. Noilly nodded, or at least his head bobbed about like a coracle rounding Cape Horn, which Clive took as a sign of understanding.

'Then let's begin. That's an interesting name.' Clive managed to restrain the smile that was as keen as Gene Kelly in a thunderstorm to dance across his face.

'I don't want to talk about that,' Noilly said firmly.

Clive knew it was pointless, and possibly fatal, to pursue it, but he had a professional hunch that Noilly would need to talk about it before his healing could begin. But for now what the client wanted the client got.

'Very well, what do you want to talk about?'

'I want to talk about my spelling.' He looked straight at Clive with a razor-blade sharpness. There were no obvious spelling mistakes in Noilly's body language. It said clearly and coherently, 'Don't fuck with me'. Clive didn't think it would be advisable to give him leaflets for adult literacy classes either.

'If that's all that's bothering you there are other ways of dealing with it. Cheaper ways.' Clive was always honest with his clients. His knowledge of psychology had taught him that honesty was always the best policy, especially when honesty also ensured the customer kept coming back. Telling a client they didn't have to continue with their treatment if they couldn't afford it was a sure way to make them even more determined to see it through. Noilly wriggled about like a two-year-old who'd just forgotten all he'd learned about toilet training.

'Money is not my problem.'

'So what is?'

'Before I . . .' He stopped, nervously took a breath and started again. 'Before I can tell you anything, I need to know I can rely on you to . . .' he waved around at the phallic forest in the room, '. . . to be reliable.'

Bad spelling and tautology, Clive mused in the privacy of his own head.

'Can you promise that whatever I say will be confidential?'

Clive went into his spiel about how confidentiality was the most sacred aspect of their relationship. He didn't mention that experience had taught him that a secret, especially one held by someone who demanded confidentiality, was usually something they actually wanted to tell the world, one person at a time. Noilly looked out from under his feathered fringe, which reminded Clive of a particularly ugly bassist in a long-forgotten Glam Rock band from the early 1970s (long forgotten by everyone but a few sad, overweight, middle-aged women still wearing tatty tartan scarves and Clive, who could still whistle the chorus from their follow-up single, which bombed so badly it could have been twinned with Dresden). It was a Mount Rushmore of a face, rough and uneven, and made forever ugly by teenage landmines of vile yellow-hearted acne that had exploded many years before. From this brief glimpse of his features Noilly didn't look like a man who was convinced by what he was being told. This surprised Clive who prided himself on his ability to get most people to trust him.

'I've had a bad experience with another counsellor. He didn't respect confidentiality,' Noilly explained.

'Sounds like Durkin,' Clive joked quietly to himself. Under the fringe Noilly's hard stare changed from rock to diamond.

'I like you. You're smart. I'd like to tell you what I do for a living.' It was a tentative offer made from behind his safety curtain of hair.

Clive smiled, he grabbed the offer before it could be withdrawn. 'Tell me whatever you like.'

'Right.' Noilly went silent while he composed himself. From next door a piercing scream rent the air. It sounded like a thousand cats being neutered without the benefit of a local anaesthetic. Noilly jumped up and turned from side to side, trying to identify the source of the agony. He reminded Clive of the Action Man doll from his youth. (Not a doll, his memory insisted, a marionette. It was a far more masculine description.)

'Sorry. It's Monday,' Clive said matter of factly and then threw one of his Hush Puppies at the wall. It was so light it barely made a sound as it bounced back at him. 'It's Primal Scream day. My colleague Marilyn helps a group of women explore the core of their anger. I'm not privy to the details of the sessions but I've a funny feeling men crop up pretty regularly as source material.'

Noilly nodded as if he understood, even though it was plain he didn't. For the next few minutes the wails continued. Eventually there was a still, exhausted silence. Once the silence had become established and was obviously going to continue Clive resumed.

'You were saying something about your work.'

'I'm a professional cleaner. I clean things up.'

'Really?' Clive asked.

'I clean up messes, other people's messes,' Noilly went on slowly.

'I understand what cleaners do.'

'No you don't,' Noilly said firmly and without any room for dissent.

'Then explain it to me,' Clive said cheerfully, wriggling his ample backside into the leather chair to find some extra comfort for what was obviously going to be a long obsessional tale of floor polish, vinegar on windows and the occupational hazard of housemaid's knee.

But Noilly shook his head. 'No. That's just it. I want to tell you but I can't because I need to know I can trust you.' Noilly swept his hair away and looked at Clive. Clive felt like he was looking down the double barrels of a sawn-off shotgun. 'I need you to prove that I can trust you,' Noilly said.

Unaware of the deep hole he was about to plunge into Clive took a steadying breath. 'So what do I need to do?'

'I want to clean for you.'

Clive waved at his office. 'Fine, great, go ahead. You'll find all the necessary in the cupboard at the back of reception.'

Noilly wasn't listening, he was searching for something from one of the many zippered pockets that glinted all over his camouflage jacket, like early-morning slug trails in a flower-bed. Finding what he wanted he turned back to Clive.

'This address, tonight at six. Then we'll see if I can really trust you.' Noilly put a small piece of card on Clive's desk. On it appeared to be the entrails of a blue-blooded spider which had died a quick death under a steamroller.

Clive tried to read the handwriting. 'Bi Keens Rood?'

'Eighty-one Queen's Road. The one on the outskirts of town.'

'I don't make house calls,' Clive said, unable to keep the pompous tone from hacking into his voice.

'This isn't a house call. Just park out in the street. Whatever you do, don't go in. Six o'clock. Sharp. I promise it will be to your benefit.' He stood up so suddenly that Clive thought an attack was being launched from behind the fringed curtain, and he ducked back into the safety of his chair to avoid the blow. By the time he'd realised his mistake his bizarre new client was on the other side of a softly, almost inaudibly closing door.

Clive raced after him. There was someone in reception but it wasn't Noilly.

'Christopher? What are you doing here?'

'Hiya, bruv. Thought I'd check out your empire. Not bad.' He gave Mandy a lascivious look. She blushed and looked away.

'Not now, Christopher. Bit busy. Mandy, did Mr Upchurch make another appointment?'

'No. I don't have an address for him either. He insisted it was out of the question. Is that all right?' Mandy asked, looking up from the computer where a hundred names with a hundred different neuroses blinked out from the blue screen.

'Sure, he's given me an address. Eighty-one Queen's Road. I'm meeting him there tonight at six.' Mandy dutifully tapped the details into the computer.

'Problems?' Christopher asked, as usual sticking his nose in where it wasn't welcome.

Clive ignored him. 'I'll remind him he must make appointments,' Clive said, looking at Christopher as if he too should take the hint. 'I'll make sure he pays in advance too.'

'He did, he left this,' Mandy said, holding up a bundle of money.

'Jesus. How much is there?' Christopher asked, excited by the sight of money in much the same way as Clive was about accidental glimpses of Mandy's underwear.

'Twelve hundred pounds, roughly. That's quite a bit on account,' Mandy said. Clive looked at her and briefly considered asking her to be a bit on his account. The widening schism with Grace was seriously affecting his ability to distinguish between fact and fantasy. He shook his head vigorously to clear the obscene picture-postcard image from his mind.

'Put the money in the safe. I have a funny feeling about him.'

'Me too. I know his sort and they usually spell trouble,' Christopher chipped in.

'In his case with two Bs,' Clive said, smiling as the same quizzical look appeared on Christopher's and Mandy's faces.

A few hours later Clive was driving towards Queen's Road. The Bradworth outer ring road was an amusement park ride that cut through the socio-economic strata of the city. He began in a forest of low tower blocks, constructed in the late 1960s and given reverential names like Kennedy House, Einstein Towers and Bomber Harris View. They stood self-consciously in open squares of grass devoid of any life or ornament other than huge regular piles of brown soil that looked like the spoils of urban moles. They were actually lumps of dogshit thrown off the balconies of the flats by dog owners who wouldn't dare walk their pets out on the grass, such was their fear of walking down three flights of badly lit stairs.

This uncompromising modernist landscape finally gave way to a mish-mash of Victorian mills of once-fantastic, almost cathedral-like grandeur, which now had the look of dereliction in their boarded and broken windows. Then new buildings appeared, as if thrown up by a volcanic activity that spewed out corrugated-metal sheeting. These boxes housed businesses set up by what appeared to be a tribe of dyslexic garage owners who revelled in names like 'Enjin-u-luv' and 'Fics-it-Qik'. One sign that briefly raised the general educational standards of the area bragged that its personal car valeting service offered 'The Best Hand Job in Town'.

Clive accelerated out of this unlovely place and entered the outskirts of bed-sit land, where the front doors had long boards boasting dozens of doorbells, indicating warrens of self-contained hutches, each with enough space to swing a cat, providing it was a tailless Manx variety. Here students from the BUMS college lodged cheek by jowl with prostitutes, drug-users and veterans of the now-closed local mental hospitals.

Clive's foot stamped down even further on the accelerator and moved into an area of vast detached private dwellings with big, spreading gardens, occupied by the upper echelons of Bradworth society. Through the centre of this area ran the elegant, quiet, tree-lined thoroughfare of Queen's Road.

Queen's Road was a washed-out sepia tint thanks to the orange street-lamps in the early-evening darkness. The area was one of Victorian splendour, which had once housed the rich mill owners and merchants of the region. In the early 1980s it had nearly been relegated down the social strata into the lowest league of student bed-sits but had been saved when the fast developing phone-banking industry discovered how cheap the local land was and bought up vast tracts to build their telephonic nerve centres. With this vibrant new industry came hundreds of status-hungry senior managers who quickly saw the unrealised potential an area like Queen's Road offered. Houses were stripped out and refurbished as authentic family homes for the discerning middle classes. Authentic was the watchword in this transformation. Authentic Victorian decor, authentic gardens laid out to original Gertrude Jekyl plans, authentic wine bars and bistros instead of the old pubs and fish and chip shops, and authentic private security firms and closed-circuit television on every second sycamore tree. The cars too were authentic top-of-the-range status symbols and they reflected the new-found affluence of the area that made even Clive's smart red sports car as ordinary as a standard Ford Escort with a fluffy Garfield stuck to the passenger window.

He stopped outside the huge detached villa which

lurked, almost hidden yet somehow impressively obvious, in the darkened, well-tended grounds, and tried to understand how this place fitted with Noilly Upchurch. There was a bronze Toyota Lexus in the drive, flash in an understated 'it might look dull but it cost a fucking fortune' sort of way. Its registration plate read: F4 EUD.

'Feud,' Clive laughed admiringly. 'I ought to get that for Mother.'

From the house, which Clive reckoned would boast seven or eight bedrooms, two reception rooms and enough toilets and bathrooms to keep him and his mother happily apart for years, he heard talking. At the double front doors a man was turning away. Standing inside the door was a woman; she didn't seem to recognise her visitor and he was apologising profusely for some misunderstanding.

'My client must have given me the wrong address,' the man mumbled. The woman gave him a farewell wave and closed the big doors behind her. The man went to unlock the driver's door of the Lexus. He turned and absently looked up the drive to where Clive was parked.

'Oh fucking Christ,' Clive whispered. He looked back at the man. Then quickly at the number plate on the Lexus. It didn't say Feud at all. It was supposed to say something else, at least that was what the man had intended, pretentiousness blinding good sense. It was supposed to read FREUD.

The man at the car was now smiling stupidly at Clive, the way one does when meeting someone familiar in unfamiliar surroundings. Before he could say anything his attention was caught by something to his left. Clive's open-mouthed attention went with him to the rhodo-dendrons, which in two months' time would be a striking blaze of red but now stood alongside the sweep-ing gravel drive as colourful as an old army blanket. From out of these stepped another figure, apparently dressed as a bottle of milk. It was Noilly Upchurch. It was like something out of his premonitions: Clive had no idea what was happening but he did have a horrible notion of what was going to happen.

He wanted to shout, he wanted to get out of his car and run over to the two figures and intervene, he wanted to drive off quickly and put as much distance between himself and the scene as he could. But he couldn't. Instead he sat like a deadhead couch potato and watched the plot that was about to be broadcast for his benefit.

He saw Noilly walk up to the man without pause or hesitation and pull out a long pistol that looked so ridiculous he fully expected it to shoot out a flag with 'Bang!' written on it. Noilly held the gun up to the man's forehead. Suddenly Clive was released from the hold of fear's gravity. He threw open the car door and rocked his overweight body back and forth until he fell forward and began his own peculiar version of running. This activity seemed to break the concentration of Noilly, or at least to attract his attention away from the terrible deed he was about to commit. He turned to look at the fat man wobbling in his direction.

'No!'

Clive heard the voice of a terrified animal shouting in his ear, and then he realised that it was his voice and he was the frightened animal.

'No!' he shouted again.

He was fast approaching the violent vignette when Noilly did an unspeakable thing. He winked at him. Then he smiled and lowered the gun to the man's right knee, pulled the trigger and there was a quiet explosion. No flag came out but something else did, so fast that Clive didn't see it. Nor did the man by the Lexus. The bullet hit his leg, as Noilly had intended, and then it went right through and on until it hit the granite gravel on the drive and spat back for a another bite at its victim. Like the younger, dumber brother of JFK's magic bullet it entered the leg for the second time just below the back of the knee. In a perfectly choreographed response, and still smiling stupidly, Amen Durkin slid slowly and with some grace down the driver's door of his Lexus and lay in a neat pile, bleeding all over the nice clean driveway.

Clive expected something else to happen, police sirens, the firm grip of the authorities seizing him by the collar, a women's scream (he was a traditionalist), but instead there was a silence that belonged in the sound-proof booth of a quiz show. Noilly, who had played this scene too many times to expect anything other than an anticlimax, put the gun inside his white suit and walked towards Clive, who was now in a wash of sweat. Clive wondered briefly if this was where he got his, if there was a bullet in that chamber with his name scratched on it, and if so would Noilly have spelt it correctly?

As Noilly got up close he gave Clive another heavy wink. 'Bock bock bock,' he said. The impersonation of a chicken chilled Clive to the core.

Then Noilly was gone.

Twenty seconds later, after wiping the residue of

sweat from his eyes and blinking hard at the collapsed Durkin in front of him to make sure it had really happened, Clive began to run again. He heard the gravel surrendering to his heavy weight as he pounded up the drive. He wished he had Grace's mobile phone, except that she never trusted him with it because he was so crap with technology, usually sitting down and flattening the life out of it.

'Here use mine,' Durkin said, rolling over and handing him a slim phone the size of a Mars bar. 'I'm sure you never carry one.'

Smug bastard, Clive wanted to say but a combination of fear and relief made him sensitive to Durkin's predicament. He rang for an ambulance and then he knelt over his rival in a pose that, had Rodin used it as inspiration for a sculpture, would have been named *The Carer*.

'I owe you for this,' Durkin said, in a tone that was best described as ambiguous.

'What?' Clive asked

'You saved my life. If it hadn't been for you . . .'

Guilt, fatter than Robert Maxwell before his last midnight swim, sat heavily on Clive's shoulders. He slumped under the weight and made a weak excuse to leave his wounded charge and go back to the road to watch for the ambulance.

Clive waited in the foyer of Bradworth General Infirmary for two hours, killing time by looking around the parade of shops that had been opened to help ease the money worries of the local Health Trust. He studied all the books, daily papers and soft-core pornographic magazines in the newsagent, bought some basic provisions from the grocers and gave careful consideration to the Lycra maternity wear in the Mums and Tots shop. All the time he was reviewing in his head what he had witnessed. Look at it from any angle and it came out the same, his mystery client had been intent on killing his business rival apparently for Clive's benefit.

'Bock bock bock,' Noilly had said as he left the scene of the crime. Intimating that it wasn't Clive's kindness or tolerance that had saved Durkin's life, it was his yellow-bellied, cowardy custard cowardice. If he'd said nothing Durkin would have been shot dead. For a brief second he'd had the power of life and death over someone he'd always wanted to have the power of life and death over. The feeling was so electric and exciting that it scared him witless. He paused mid-witless, while browsing round the Interflora florist where he was wondering if it was the done thing to buy a man flowers, and fell backwards into the loving arms of DS Gerhardie.

'Evening, sir,' DS Gerhardie said, showing as much insolence as a civil servant dare, which was heaps.

'Are you following me?' Clive asked, stepping forward out of his shadow's kindly embrace.

'I'm here to investigate a shooting incident. It occurred in an area where I had seen you only minutes before.' DS Gerhardie sounded cocky, but what he didn't mention was that he had given up tailing him thanks to a wallpaper sale at Texas Homecare.

'Are you saying this is something to do with me?'

'No. Are you admitting it is?'

Clive felt panic start to block off the oxygen supply to

his blood. He took a deep breath to steady himself while DS Gerhardie prepared another question designed to knock him sideways.

'I'm here to help,' Clive said quickly, hoping his feigned good intentions wouldn't sound unconvincing.

'Me too. I want to find out exactly who shot him. Care to join me in visiting the victim? And I wouldn't want you to think you have a choice because you fucking well don't.'

Clive bowed his head and fell in alongside DS Gerhardie, setting a personal best to keep up with him as they made their way to the intensive care department.

'That man saved my life, sergeant. He is to be hailed as a hero,' Durkin said, beaming at his hero. On the pillow under Durkin's head read the legend 'Bradworth General Infirmary – a healthy partnership with Turner's Breweries'. His red-tinted glasses hid his eyes ominously.

'I have some way to go to be fully convinced of that, sir,' DS Gerhardie replied, indicating that a journey to the other end of the universe would be required to get even faintly close to total conviction. 'Perhaps we could begin with why you were there,' he asked Durkin with icy politeness.

'An ex-client had asked to meet me there, sergeant. I can say no more because of the confidentiality of my profession. For which I make no apologies.' Durkin was being far too pompous for someone who had recently suffered a near-death experience. Clive remembered what it was that had caused him to walk out on Durkin all those years ago. The old windbag loved playing the crowd and it wasn't enough that he was the centre of attention, he needed to be the single focal point through which everything had to pass.

Like the arsehole that he is, Clive thought to himself. Now that someone had tried to shoot Durkin it meant that he was the ultimate centre of attention for the man who had tried to kill him. Or the man behind the man who had tried to kill him. Despite the initial feelings of relief that Durkin hadn't been shot dead in front of him, Clive was now wishing his former partner terrible harm. His guilty daydream was interrupted by a tense silence of the kind that usually follows an awkward question.

'Sorry, miles away. What was that?'

'Maybe you should have been miles away but I asked what you were doing in Queen's Road, sir.' DS Gerhardie made the word 'sir' sting like a darning needle in the eye.

'Short-cut home, I take it when the traffic is heavy.' Clive had been rehearsing this for two hours and was quite pleased at the way it came out, which was somewhere between nervous nonchalance and over-rehearsed glibness.

'Mr Durkin, the woman in the house where the incident occurred says she had never met you before. And you told her someone was supposed to be meeting you there.' Gerhardie sounded like he was giving a statement to a judge and jury, even consulting his notes to give the whole thing an air of authenticity, despite the fact that he was actually consulting a rough sketch of the central-heating pipes in his loft.

'There we go again, sergeant, scuppered by confidentiality. My hands are tied, I can neither confirm nor deny what the woman at the address says.'

'So are you saying the woman at the house is lying to me?'

'In my business there are no liars, sergeant, merely the self-delusional.'

'Thank you both.' DS Gerhardie didn't sound like he meant it. He turned and left the small room with its beeping monitors and clear bags dripping fluid. Clive was about to say something to Durkin as DS Gerhardie quietly came back into the room and stood behind them, his shadow spreading across the hospital bed like a stain.

'Just one more thing, gentlemen.' Durkin and Clive both jumped at the intervention. DS Gerhardie wore his usual down-turned mouth around which his beard sprawled like a lazy cat.

'If you two are fucking me around you'll know about it. G'night all.'

He saluted with his middle finger, turned and left the room.

'Nice chap, is he a friend of yours?' Durkin asked, using all his considerable professional skills to notice that a history existed between Clive and DS Gerhardie.

'Not so much a friend as my own private stalker. How does it feel?' Clive nodded at Durkin's knee.

'It feels great. Bloody hurts, for sure, but it could have been far, far worse. That's what helps me keep the pain in perspective.'

Clive sighed. Durkin was well on the way to having his name entered into a new edition of *Fox's Book of Martyrs*, and somewhere quite near the top of the list.

'I have you to thank for saving me. I shall never, ever forget this, old chap.'

'It was nothing.'

'There is one other thing that I don't think I'll ever forget.' Durkin sounded worryingly like DS Gerhardie, all probing insinuation and implication. Clive kept his face perfectly still.

'You said "no".'

'Pardon?' Just act stupid, Clive reassured himself, you're good at that.

'When you were running up like a particularly impressive bodyguard you shouted "No". Not "Look out" or "Run for your life". You said "No".'

'These things come out. Heat of the moment. You know.'

'Of course I do.' Durkin smiled as he spoke.

The silence that followed spoke enough volumes to furnish a mobile library. More was to come, Clive knew that much.

'Except. If you'd said "Look out" you'd have been talking to me, the victim I mean. To say "no" suggests you were talking to him, the assassin. Now that's what I call curious. It was almost as if you knew him. Which is really funny because I'm damn sure I do. I'm tired now and I need to sleep but we'll talk later. Yes, we'll talk later.'

Durkin dismissed Clive with a regal wave and closed his eyes. A cloud that was much darker than all the other black clouds was sweeping in and blotting out Clive's once-bright firmament. He considered grabbing the pillow that claimed a healthy partnership with Turner's Breweries and shoving it over Durkin's face to finish the job, but the thought soon passed and as he left he gave the armed policeman on guard outside the room a polite nod. He wanted to go home and never ever come back to this place again.

Clive got home just after ten. He got out of his car and walked through the garden gate. The wind rustled through a bundle of tall shrubs in the garden and reminded him of the terrifying emergence of Noilly Upchurch from the rhododendrons in Queen's Road. Clive stopped and strained his eyes against the darkness for any sign of a man dressed as Alec Guinness in *The Man in the White Suit*. He began to have one of his sweats.

He found the door key in his pocket and ran up to the heavy front door like an asthmatic hippo. He burst in and locked the door behind him and then walked backwards down the hall as if the long barrel of Noilly's gun was about to smash its way through the smoked-glass panel and give him his deliverance. He wasn't aware of the gun barrel coming up behind him from the opposite direction until it was too late and it was on intimate terms with his vertebrae, between seventeen and eighteen.

'Bang!'

Christopher was extremely gratified with Clive's response when he poked the metal fountain pen into the small of his brother's back and shouted 'Bang!' Clive had a major asthmatic attack and had to be rushed to Bradworth General Infirmary – Accident and Emergency Department. Clive lay in a cubicle for three hours waiting for a house doctor to tell him what he already knew. Eventually Christopher emerged through the curtains carrying an old magazine on caravanning.

'Why did you have to do that?'

'Sorry, bruv, I didn't think you'd take it so badly. You're really out of condition, aren't you?'

'I've had a terrible day.'

'I bet,' Christopher said knowingly, without shifting his attention from an article extolling the joys of caravanning in the Gower Peninsula.

Clive reran his bad day in his head, like an old Pathé newsreel. 'Give me one of your cigs,' he demanded of Christopher.

'You don't smoke.'

'I don't, didn't, but I do now. Just give me one.'

Christopher handed him a bent packet of duty-free Chesterfields with three cigarettes in. Clive took one.

'You do realise that a) this is a hospital and they don't go big on smoking, and b) in your condition it will probably kill you,' Christopher said, his pompous tone strangling any hint of genuine concern for his brother's health.

'Well, a) I don't fucking care, and b) I should be so fucking lucky.'

'I should be so lucky. Kylie. Gorgeous chick. Aussie of course.'

'Number 1 for two weeks, February 1988, written and produced by Stock, Aitken and Waterman. There was an Australian version which substituted the title and chorus with "I can see her nipples".' Clive's memory responded like a Pavlovian Dog to the visit of an Avon Lady.

'You can still do that memory thing then. Hasn't anyone ever told you how irritating it is?'

'Sure. 14th June 1981, five-oh-six p.m. 31st December 1985, ten thirty-three p.m. 16th August . . .'

'Very sharp, kid brother. You could cut your own throat on that wit. With luck.'

Clive didn't die as a result of his sharp wit, or the cigarette, such was the way his luck was going. After inhaling a whole Chesterfield he then spent a night inhaling steroids before being declared fit and ready to be released from the hospital.

'You can return to the bosom of your family,' the staff nurse said, a Hattie Jacques look-alike despite his black beard and moustache.

'Nest of vipers would be more accurate,' Clive remarked, to no one in particular.

Then Grace arrived and he was forced to put his recovery on hold.

'I warned you,' she said, ripping the curtain to one side and exposing his naked body as he slowly and painfully got back into his clothes. Luckily the rest of the ward was too ill to take much notice.

'I know. My blue inhaler was at work. I'd taken the brown one as usual but I'd forgotten the emergency dose.' Clive noticed that Grace's hair was redder than usual. This was such a bad portent that the Ancient Romans would have slaughtered several generations of their first born in order to counteract its effect.

'I meant that I warned you about your miserable family and their nasty, evil ways.'

'Listen, Mother needs to get this "last wish" off her chest and then she'll be gone. No more problems. Be patient. That's what I'm doing.' He laughed at the joke, expecting Grace to join in.

'I wasn't talking about your mother. I was talking

about Her.' Grace spat out 'Her' and then left as swiftly as she had arrived.

A few minutes later he heard the unmistakable sound of Grace's Ford Mondeo being slammed into first gear and pointed at the quivering figure of the hospital car park attendant. Clive felt anxiety filling his lungs where the air used to be. Then they collapsed in on themselves for the second time in twenty-four hours. His face contorted under the effort of attempting to force enough decent air through his piss-hole thin airways to try to meet the required quotient of oxygen in the blood. He woke up with a mask clamped over his face and Durkin sitting next to his bed reading a newspaper and eating from the bowl of Israeli strawberries the staff nurse had left to add colour to the room.

'Hallo, old man. Awake at last. How do you feel?' His tone suggested that he'd soon be feeling far worse.

'Great,' Clive smiled weakly, his voice echoing in the green plastic mask.

'We're in the paper, look.' He swished the newspaper in front of Clive's eyes so quickly he couldn't read anything. 'This will be very good for business. Very good indeed. It'll be worth ten more Golden Lobes.' He gave Clive an accusing look, which Clive had to admit was really quite good.

'I bet.'

'Save me having to fix the vote, eh!' Durkin laughed heartily. 'We'll chat when you are up and about and I'm back in the old trick cyclist's saddle. We've a lot to discuss.'

'Have we?'

'Oh yes. We need to discuss how I can help you.'

'Help me?'

'Yes. Time you thought about downsizing. And I'm just the man to help your wishes come true. It'll need some major compromises, but you'll soon get used to making them. Ta ta for now.'

Clive felt the familiar dull ache in his chest as he watched Durkin hobble out of the room. He tried hard to go back to sleep. In the event it didn't prove too difficult as his body was tired from the twelve-hour struggle to find a breath and sleep found him a willing victim.

When he woke up and realised he was going to live, unfortunately, it was late afternoon. He wasn't sure which afternoon it was late into, his best guess would have been three weeks after his first attack, but it was actually only Tuesday. It was less than twenty-four hours after he had gone to meet Noilly and had witnessed the shooting of Durkin. Sitting next to his bed this time, eating the guava slices that the staff nurse refreshed the private rooms with after lunch, was Disney.

'I think you'd better come home. There's all sorts of bad stuff going down,' she said, popping the final slice of guava into her mouth, picking up her red-and-green duffel bag and rising to leave.

N i n e

Clive nearly had another speedy return to hospital thanks to his sister's driving, which left his jerry-built lungs feeling ready to fall in on themselves again.

'Remind me to show you where the brake is,' he said as he gingerly walked up to the front door. 'I can't believe anyone can subject a poor innocent engine to that level of abuse.'

Clive was aware the door had been opened, he assumed by Grace, but he was so busy giving Disney his advanced driver tips that he had stepped over the threshold before realising it was someone else.

'Hiya, mate,' the new person greeted him, her guttural twang sounding like a Duane Eddy solo.

Clive gave her a long hard look.

'Julia?'

She was bigger than he remembered. When he was

in his twenties and they were a couple he described her
as statuesque. That was partly because he was more
romantic then, and partly because it was the only
description he could come up with that wouldn't have
been deeply insulting. Like Brick Shit-house. Or Back
Of a Bus. Or Side of a Barn. But now she was even
bigger. Side of a Barn, Back Of a Bus, Brick Shit-house
bigger. Sure they were all bigger; each of the interven-
ing decades had added several inches to his waistband,
but with him it was good old-fashioned middle-age fat.
Julia had grown without restriction in all directions in a
curiously muscular way. Through the thin cotton
sleeves of her blouse (what was it about people coming
over from Australia in February that they didn't think
to dress for a British winter?) he could see undulating
mounds of firmed sinew trying to escape. She obviously worked out, or took a Boots' counter full of
steroids, or both. Bigness was a subjective concept, he
realised that, but she met all the established criteria.
Her lips refused to follow the standard delineated lines
and instead spread over her face like runny jam.
Muscles sprouted from places where they had no business sprouting. Her teeth burst out of her mouth like
king-sized gravestones and clacked together like
number 9 knitting needles as she masticated on a large
banana. An unnerving by-product of her chemically
enhanced lines was the abundance of bodily waste that
poured forth undammed from every orifice. She had
crusty sleep on her eyelids, dried spittle around the
edge of her giant mouth, and encrusted salt waste
around her nostrils. She had big white-blond hair that
looked like it had been sun-bleached to death on a diet

of surf, sand and extra thick toilet bleach. She also looked older, which was understandable as they were all older, but time had carved its passing into her face as if it were a coral reef.

Look at it any way he tried, Julia had made bigness a personal crusade and she had achieved a total victory. Once she had been the love of his life, before she had discovered brotherly love and Christopher had swept her off her feet and on to another continent. But now she was something else. She was the new Julia. To assimilate smoothly and quickly into her newly adopted country she had taken on every characteristic of the stereotypical Australian. She had become crass, loud, boozy, rude, crude and lewd, barely rising to the lowest common denominator in her attempt to become a cultural chameleon. All she needed was a daft green hat with corks around the rim and a can of ice cold lager and the image would have been complete. She was twelve thousand miles and eighteen years away from the quiet, shy young woman who had left him, apologetically, for his brother.

'Come here and give me a bloody great tongue job, mate.'

Surprise depriving him of the chance to put up any resistance she easily managed to turn the threat into reality. Her big tongue was like a fat slug, dripping in saliva and banana slime. It scared Clive at first before its very effrontery began to offer a hint of illicit sexual excitement. But then he smelt mothballs, a smell that was like a musty wardrobe in a rarely used spare bedroom, and it shrivelled his ardour quicker than a bucket of cold water. She had ignored the first rule of travel. Never buy counterfeit perfume, no matter how cheap; it always smelt of mothballs.

'What the fuck are you doing here?' he said in a friendly enough tone considering the horrible revenge he had wished on her for the last seventeen years.

'This is my wish for you,' Euterpe emerged from the darkness down the hall, the narrator of the scene. 'My dying wish for you.' She gave Julia a saucy wink and linked arms with her. Clive wanted to ask his mother who she wishing death on, her or him. But an innate insistence on being polite in front of guests, drummed into him early on by the Ginger Baker of all mothers, forced him to hold his tongue.

'She's a sweetie your ma. She insisted on flying me over to see you. I want you to know I'm going to pay you back just as soon as I get a job.'

There were so many questions going around in his mind that it seemed a trifle petty to question her about this, but for some reason it was the one thing that stood out above all others.

'Pay *me* back?'

'I used your Visa card to pay for her ticket. I knew you wouldn't mind. It was Christopher's idea,' said Euterpe, Cupid of the Underworld.

'Remind me to thank him sometime,' Clive said, leaning heavily against the hall wall.

'Julia's going to do the choreography for The Family Affair reunion,' Euterpe gushed.

Clive was seized by a half-forgotten fear. 'Where's Grace?'

'That bitch? She's sulking upstairs,' Euterpe said, barely moving her pursed lips.

'I thought you were married to a probation officer?' Clive asked Julia, his whole world whirling around in his head, out of control.

'We didn't last the probationary period. But hey! Look at you. Don't be shy, come on in.' She pulled him down the hallway towards the sitting room. 'There'll be enough time to hang around in my front passage later!' Julia nudged him under the ribs, and snorted a laugh so dirty it should have worn a Parental Guidance sticker. As he doubled up in pain from her nudge, she followed up with a solid bash to the shoulder and he felt the fillings in his teeth work loose.

He stood up straight to find Grace was standing at the bottom of the stairs. From the acidic look on her face Clive could see that she was in the kind of sulk that resulted in Archdukes being assassinated in Sarajevo.

'Happy darling?' she asked, before turning and going straight back upstairs. Clive went to follow but was knocked off course by a second blow to his shoulder.

'Weird bit of clit that one. Christ, I've missed you, you crazy bastard. We always had such a laugh, didn't we, mate?' She cackled at the memories. Try as hard as he liked Clive couldn't recall any.

It seemed odd to be welcomed into his own house by a woman he hadn't seen for eighteen years and yet who had made herself so at home that he felt like a visitor. It was an uncomfortable feeling not eased by her yobbish demeanour. When he had first known her she had been a sweet girl with a polite manner and vowels flattened by the driving northern rain. But now the only thing she seemed to have in common with that innocent girl of his youth was an unhealthy interest in consuming his food. She was already peeling another banana.

'I'm hungry. Do you fancy a bacon butty? I'll cook it. But first I must change my sanny. Twenty-four hours on that plane and phew! You wouldn't want to do any yodelling down there. Don't panic, mate, I'll soon be off the blob and ready for action!' She winked, knowingly.

Clive watched the big, hungry, foul-mouthed monster in front of him. It was like watching a video nasty. She had rustled up several inch-thick bacon sandwiches and four cans of beer, which she opened, passing only one to him.

'Give your tonsils a hand job with that and you'll be all right.'

'Oh God, when will this torture end?' Clive asked aloud. Not for some time, the knock on the front door replied.

Clive ran to answer it, hoping for something to take his mind off the agony of his life. On the doorstep stood a slight Asian woman, long greying hair showing under the plain dark headscarf she wore loosely over her head. Her eyes were black holes that sucked everything in to their centre, yet somehow allowing a friendly sparkle to escape.

'Mahinder?' Clive held out his hand and she took it, lightly.

'Do I know you?'

'Clive. Clive Wrigley. I ran a training course for Social Services last year. "Listening To The Anger Within". You were on it.'

'Oh yes.' She pulled her limp hand away quickly.

'What the hell are you doing here? If you want to

listen to some anger you've called at just the right moment.' He smiled weakly at his joke. Mahinder's smile was without any humour, frozen to her face.

'No, that's not why I'm here.' Out of habit she flashed her identity card. It showed a face surprised as the flash-gun exploded and it bore very little resemblance to the real person in front of him.

'We've had an allegation. Can I come in?'

Clive ushered her through to the sitting room. Grace had come down again and was trying to settle Dan and Hattie in front of a video; Clive wasn't sure if it was *Driller Killer* or *Nightmare on Elm Street*, or if it really mattered. Euterpe was pretending to read the *People's Friend*. Julia smiled at Mahinder and held out a bacon sandwich.

'No I don't think so,' Mahinder said, embarrassed at the offer.

'You sure, sweetheart? You look like you could do with a bit of pork.'

'I don't eat pork.'

'Who said anything about eating it!' Julia's smutty laugh assaulted their ears with its suggestive peals.

To Clive's relief she went off in search of another quick snack. Half a pig presumably.

Mahinder tried to set the scene. 'I work with the Emergency Response Team. We've had a call. Anonymous. The caller alleged that you have been abusing your children.'

'What?' Clive's lungs began to strangle his chest. 'Who said this?'

'I'm afraid I'm not at liberty to say. The suggestion was one of neglect. The caller said the children were underfed, poorly clothed and locked outside in all weathers.' As she spoke she looked at the two well-fed, well-cared-for children watching extreme video violence in front of her. 'Although they both look fine to me.'

'I can't believe someone would make such an allegation. It's just not true.' Grace was clenching her fists and desperately holding back tears.

Into the embarrassed silence came Euterpe's chilling voice. 'It's not an allegation, it's fact.'

'You did this?' Grace's voice was flat with shock.

Euterpe dismissed her with a wave of the hand. 'Don't believe this happy scene. These children are not safe here and I'd swear to that in any court in the land. She can't cope. She only knows how to be violent. She needs locking up.' Euterpe's finger was pointing at Grace like a rifle.

There was a stunned silence, as if no one could quite believe Euterpe's treachery and were searching for the hidden irony. Then she was talking again.

'They're not hers, that's why. Or his. They're someone else's little bastards. That's why that bitch doesn't really love them. She can't. That's why she's so vicious. Look at their legs. Black and blue.'

Mahinder looked at Clive, who shook his head in disbelief.

'Come here kids,' he asked softly.

Dan and Hattie groaned.

'Do we have to, Daddy? That man's about to get his face sliced off.'

'Come on, it won't take a minute.' He leaned over Dan and rolled up his trousers to above the knees.

Halfway between the knee and the thigh was a strange

bruise, made up of two interlocking half-crescents. It reminded Clive of the logo used by Coco Chanel. For a brief second he worried about a possible infringement of copyright and then he was distracted by Mahinder, who was writing something in her notepad. Upside down he saw the words 'finger marks'.

'How did you get this?' he asked Dan. Dan looked at Hattie, who looked worried. Both seemed on the verge of very loud tears.

'She did it,' Euterpe said, pointing at Grace. 'Hattie's got one just the same.'

'You fucking liar.' Grace leaped from her chair and threw herself at Euterpe, putting her hands around her mother-in-law's throat in one smooth movement and squeezing. Clive noticed that Euterpe made no attempt to defend herself, instead she sat perfectly still and smiled while Grace half killed her. It took him, Mahinder and Julia to pull Grace off her intended victim. Dan nudged Hattie, both children happy to be missing a film rampage as this real-life version was staged in their sitting room.

'There'll have to be a case conference,' Mahinder told Clive, as they held the sitting-room door closed while Grace ranted and raved out in the hall. 'And I need to ring my boss about the children having a full medical.'

'She's lying. My mother,' he said.

'I'm bloody well not.' Euterpe was red in the face from her assault and sipping too much of Clive's vintage port in an attempt to revive herself. 'You saw for yourself, danger to life and limb that one. Very unpredictable.' She put her finger to the side of her head and waved it round in a circular motion to indicate madness.

'The evidence is convincing enough for me to have concerns,' Mahinder agreed. From the other side of the door came the sound of a hammer being smashed against the antique pine panels.

'Grace isn't violent, she's just headstrong. And she . . .' Clive pointed at his mother, 'is the world's most convincing liar. Aren't you?' He hoped Euterpe might break down and confess under the strain of accusation but instead she poured herself another schooner, or possibly oil tanker of port and picked up the *People's Friend*.

Clive walked Mahinder to her car and begged her to reconsider what she kept referring to as 'a classic case of abuse'. Having failed to convince her he knew he was left with only one choice, he would have to reveal his innermost secret. He unzipped his trousers and slipped them down to his ankles.

'What the . . .?' Mahinder looked away, and then back again just in case Clive did anything more offensive while her attention was elsewhere. He didn't, although his ragged boxer shorts were pretty offensive.

She got into her car, locked the door behind her and began dialling on her mobile phone. 'I'm calling the police,' she mouthed through the glass.

Clive started to point at his genitals. She closed her eyes and spoke into the phone urgently.

'You'll be waiting hours. You can never get a policeman when you want one,' Clive said, as he reluctantly hopped back towards the house holding his trousers by the waistband.

*

Always the exception that proved the rule, a policeman was already there. DS Gerhardie was leaning at a dangerous angle so he could peer through the window into the front room of Clive's house.

'What the fuck are you doing?' Clive's shout surprised DS Gerhardie and he lost his balance, falling over in a heap on the front border.

'Listen, pal, I can do what the bollocks I like. I'm the law.'

'You're a bloody Peeping Tom.'

DS Gerhardie looked at Clive's gaping-open trousers. 'I'm in the right place then, aren't I.'

'This isn't as bad as it looks.'

At that moment Mahinder saw DS Gerhardie, who she vaguely remembered from a joint visit they had made when he had arrested the wrong person, in the wrong house, in the wrong street. She threw open the car door.

'Help. Sergeant. That man's just exposed himself to me.'

'If anything it just started to look worse,' DS Gerhardie said dryly. For the first time in a long time an arrest was falling into his lap without requiring any effort on his behalf whatsoever.

Clive, his trousers done up again and his arms firmly behind his back thanks to the grip of DS Gerhardie, was marched back into the house. Mahinder followed at a safe distance.

'If you'll just let me explain,' he said as he was rudely ushered into the front room. Euterpe was no longer there. Nor was Grace.

'Please. Just let me take my trousers down, quickly,' he implored. Mahinder gave a disgusted grunt and went back into the hall looking for any sign of the children. Clive took his opportunity, threw off DS Gerhardie and whipped down his trousers.

'Look, there.'

'I prefer Y-fronts myself. Roomy yet supportive.'

'No. I mean on the inside of my thigh.'

Time was a great healer but it was usually a crap plastic surgeon. The wounds had long ago grown scar tissue across them but they were still visible. Wrinkled and white and standing out against the surrounding acres of fawn, freckled skin on Clive's thigh were two little crescents interwoven. The work of Psychoco Chanel.

'That was her. My mother. That's her "punishment spot". Every time I did anything to upset her, like getting her the wrong brand of fags from the corner shop, she'd find the punishment spot and top it up. Where the two nails crossed it never properly healed. It still hurts if I so much as brush it with my fingers, but I suppose that's just pyschosomatic.'

At this moment Mahinder came back into the room.

'Do you see now?' he said, pointing to the mark.

'Maybe. I can certainly see that Grace has taken the children and disappeared.' She gave DS Gerhardie a seen-it-all-before look.

Clive searched the house and found that several suitcases and a few wardrobes of Grace's belongings had also disappeared. And her car.

'Good riddance,' Euterpe said, coming downstairs

with a copy of *The Lady*. 'One day you'll thank me, Clive. You'll see.'

'What are you trying to do to me?' Clive had finally got rid of DS Gerhardie and Mahinder and now had revenge in mind.

Euterpe looked at him indulgently. 'She's the one for you, Julia I mean. You let her go once but not again. I won't allow it. She's fit, healthy and can bear you children. *Your* children, not some adopted monsters.' Euterpe winked at him. 'She's a trained dancer too. That means great legs, very flexible.'

Unlike her two sons, Euterpe had never lost Julia. She wanted her as a daughter-in-law whether her sons did or not. She had all the right attributes, such as a complete absence of assertiveness and the malleability of Plasticine. When Julia left Christopher, Euterpe took action. She kept in touch, even met up occasionally, sticking her own brand of carbon-fibre spanners in the works of whatever relationship Julia was currently in, usually damaging it beyond repair. Eventually, when Julia was at her most vulnerable, having been recently deserted, Euterpe moved in for the kill. A job working with The Family Affair and having her own reunion with the Wrigley brother of her choice were offers too good to refuse.

Clive would have liked to go to bed early, given his stay in hospital, the shock of finding Julia in his home, the visit from Social Services, the public revelation of his childhood injuries and the exit of Grace and the children, but he didn't dare. To do so might mean sharing a bed with Julia, which would make the trials of the day seem very tame. He had seen her go into his bedroom several times, to get changed, to put on some more make-up (presumably with a spade), and to change her sanitary towel again. He wasn't sure if she was planning to sleep there but he had a horrible feeling that she was. Disney had staked a claim to Dan and Hattie's room the moment she found out Grace had gone, so he didn't have many options left.

He waited until Julia made her excuses and went up to bed, giving him a meaningful look as she closed the sitting-room door. Christopher and Euterpe turned to him and smiled encouragingly but he pretended to be deeply absorbed in the late-night science-fiction film on the television. Then they went to bed and he was left alone. He sank into a fitful sleep on the sofa, which was too short, too sharp and, with no blankets or covers, altogether too cold a shock to his shattered system. Even so it was an infinitely better solution than the Attack of the Fifty-foot Woman, who lay in wait upstairs.

'Night night,' he said to the cat as it slept on his chest and offered a small respite from the night-time chill.

He woke up feeling cold. His fingers were an Oxford shade of blue and his nose was a torrent in the gusting Arctic draft of his sitting room. Clive lay awake until dawn and did something he hadn't done for seventeen years. He started to bite his nails. He had resumed smoking and now he was biting his nails again.

'I'll be eating meat next,' he said, the longing already lodged in his stomach. 'But until then I'll make do with eating myself,' he told the cat, who slept on, reassured by the news.

Ten

The next week went by slowly for Clive, reduced to a crawl by the absence of Grace and the children. Grace left a message on the answer machine at work, which Larry took great delight in relaying to him. The wording was Grace at her most succinct. 'We're at Monica's. Tell anyone and I'll kill you.'

Clive's life was more than just a sorry state, it was a teenager's bedroom of a sorry state, a Sellafield safety record of a sorry state, a happy-families-politician-discovered-enjoying-an-exotic-cocktail-in-a-gay-bar sorry state. He decided to try to regain some control of the runaway train his love life had become.

He approached Julia to clear the air between them, in the hope he could persuade her to leave, preferably before his weekly food bill hit four figures. He held the basket of dirty laundry while Julia methodically sorted it into whites, colours and gentle wash. She lovingly held up his underwear to the light and said that it was a real treat to be with a man who didn't have streaks in his knickers.

'That's what I want to talk to you about,' Clive said, feeling like a melodramatic detective rounding up a group of suspects in order to announce who had murdered their hated employer/uncle/man-who-once-ruined-their-father.

'Jeez, that's what I always liked about you, we have so much in common.'

'Not about my laundry, Julia. I want to talk about this idea you have that you're somehow "with me". You're not. I'm not with you either. We're not with each other, full-stop. I'm with Grace.'

'But you're not with Grace.'

Clive had to acknowledge the accuracy of her synopsis. 'Not at the moment, maybe, but I will be again soon.' He tried to sound convincing, but inside he knew that things had already sailed past Bad and were expected to make Worse by nightfall.

He gave up trying to regain control of his life and went outside for some air. That was when he found that it wasn't only his wife that was missing, so was his red Celica GT. Not so much stolen as borrowed, although he didn't realise the subtle distinction until later when he discovered it was in the less-than-reliable hands of Christopher. Cut Christopher's less-than-reliable hands off (as practised under some of the world's less tolerant regimes) and he would have had Taken Without The Owners Consent written through his DNA like a watermark. When the car was returned that night it had an additional three hundred miles on the clock and an almost empty petrol tank. Christopher refused to say where he had been.

'It's all a bit hush hush, purely reconnaissance at this stage, so I can't say too much. But this is a solid-gold blue-chip business opportunity and I'll be seeing you all right when it comes off. Believe me.' With that he took the cordless phone upstairs for the rest of the evening.

Clive's convalescence meant he was confined to his home, which wasn't the most relaxing of environments, what with Julia vying for his attention, and the endless arguments between Disney and Euterpe and him and Christopher. Even outside there was no respite. While walking along Halcyon Terrace for some fresh air he noticed a group of young children who were enjoying an unexpected day off school thanks to a dodgy heating boiler. They were gathered around a parked car and laughing at something inside. Clive walked over to the scene.

'He's fucking dead, I tell you,' a boy, obviously the leader of the group, was saying.

'Is he fuck. He's in a coma or summat, I can see his gob moving. Look, he's dribbling the mucky bastard,' disagreed another, making a tentative bid for leadership in doing so.

The boys parted as Clive walked up to the car. Fast asleep, or possibly in a deep coma as he had been reading a copy of *The Complete Home Handyman* by TV's own Jeff 'you can't overdo the dado' Evans, was DS Gerhardie. Crisps and crumbs nested in his beard, indicating that he had been there sometime watching Clive's house, and watching Clive.

By the end of the week Clive couldn't stand his house arrest any more and so he went back to work. He wasn't fit but it was the only way to keep his car out of Christopher's greedy clutches, his arse out of Julia's and his collar out of DS Gerhardie's.

It was the following Monday before Noilly walked back into his office. Clive reflected how it was only ten days since his mother had arrived back in Britain and yet how different his life was. It was the difference between a classic dish such as Coquille St Jacques, made with fresh scallops, a bouillabaisse sauce and a light buttery pastry crown, and the same classic dish that had passed through the digestive system, been dumped into a chemical toilet, flushed to the local sewage farm and spent the week stuck to the side of an ancient and rusty effluent unit. It wasn't a great feeling.

Noilly entered the offices of Listen To You with his usual business-like confidence, even though he wasn't on business, luckily for Clive.

On a brief sabbatical from almost permanent sick-leave Larry greeted him with the sort of enthusiasm a foxhunt reserved for a group of eco-activists. 'What do you want?' he snarled, unable to hide the gnawing withdrawal symptoms for lying in late and watching television.

'I have an appointment to see Mr Wrigley,' Noilly said assuredly, considering it wasn't true. Larry didn't quibble with Noilly's lack of an appointment. There was something about this lean, fit, muscle machine that Larry recognised as the mark of someone he shouldn't mess with.

'Take a seat in there. If you don't mind. Please.' Larry politely and carefully pointed towards the waiting room, as if any sudden movement might cause Noilly to grab his forefinger and bite it off before French kissing it back to him. Job done, Larry quickly turned his attention away from the scary visitor and busied himself with illicitly loading a football game on to the office computer.

Noilly sat and looked around. There were tasteful prints of lakes and waterlilies, which he didn't know were by Monet, thanks to his lack of education at a bad school that failed him in almost every lesson other than bullying and physical violence. This lack of knowledge didn't stop him finding them calming.

'Mr Upchurch, please come through,' Clive urgently ushered him into the safety of his office, this time taking great care to let him go in ahead so as not to offer his back as a target.

Clive sat down and was faced with Noilly's fringe looking straight back at him, like a vindictive English sheepdog.

'Don't you ever make appointments?'

'Appointments mean people know when to expect you and that gives them an edge. If there's any edge to be had, then I'm having it.'

'Frankly, when it comes to edge, I think you've gone over it.'

'Really. Gone to the police, have you?' Noilly's tone was mocking, he knew that Clive would have done no such thing.

'No need, they came to me.' Clive practically screamed at Noilly as he told the story of DS Gerhardie almost tailing him to Queen's Road. 'What the fuck were you doing?'

'Couldn't you tell? I was trying to kill Amen Durkin. Except you stopped him from getting his just deserts.'

'What?'

'From what I can tell, and believe me I've done my research, he hates you as much as you hate him. For the record you're a much better counsellor than he'll ever be.'

In vain Clive tried to freeze the warm glow that Noilly's flattery had inadvertently fanned across his face. 'That's as maybe but it's no reason to top him,' he said.

'It's as good as any. I'm sure he means you harm,' Noilly stated flatly.

'Wait a minute. Go back a bit. What was that you said about the desert? What has this got to do with deserts?' Clive thought he could see a nod of discomfort from behind the protective curtain of the fringe.

'Isn't that how you say it?'

'What?'

'Desert. As in "Just Deserts".'

Clive started to understand. 'That's what you meant about having trouble with words. Spelling and pronunciation.'

Noilly pulled the hair curtain to one side and Clive saw one and a half very scary eyes staring at him. Noilly thought for a second and then, feeling more confident, tucked the hair behind his ears and left his eyes on view.

'You are like me. You're good at what you do. I'm good at what I do to.'

'Which is going round killing people. So we can't be that much alike.'

'Maybe not, but you can see into me and I think I can see into you.'

'You reckon? I suppose you also reckon that the only good rival is a dead rival.'

'But I didn't kill him. Thanks to you.' Noilly looked like he was about to do his chicken impersonation again. 'Anyway it was a freebie. Next time it'll be full price.'

Clive felt his breathing start to falter and decided to go for a calmer approach.

'No one was seriously hurt, and Durkin is, even now, garnering great prestige out of the incident. Every pretty female psychology student will be queuing around the block to sleep with him, the lucky bastard. The problem is that I think he knows you, and suspects I was involved. Not that I was,' Clive added nervously.

'Oh yes you were. You told me to do it. That's my line if anything awkward should happen, like a visit from the police. ' Noilly's hair had fallen across his face again and his eyes appeared from behind the curtain like fish coming up for air. He scooped it back behind his ears and scanned the room before settling his gaze like Dr No's laser on Clive's bollocks. 'I was Durkin's client, so he does know who I am.'

'What?' Clive's breathing tightened again.

'Don't worry, he doesn't have my personal details any more than you do, and he hasn't turned me in yet, has he?'

'But what if he does? There'll be an identity parade.'

'Then I'll have to rain on it.' Probably with a semi-automatic, was the suggestion in his tone.

'How can you kill and maim people so easily?' Clive asked.

Because he was a damaged soul was the quick answer. But this being counselling, there was no such thing as a quick answer, even for a mad, vicious bastard like Noilly Upchurch. There was only the slow, one-visit-a-week-for-twenty-seven-years-until-you'd-forgotten-the-question-anyway answer. Clive rationalised the situation. His client hadn't actually killed Durkin, but he might conceivably kill Clive if he tried to turn him in, or worse refused to see him. In the meantime it was seventy quid an hour paid upfront in cash, and who knows, he might actually help the poor bastard. It would be blood money yes, but at least it was Durkin's blood, which was fine by him.

Clive laid down a few ground rules. Everything would be confidential but there were to be no areas that were off limits to his questioning, and Noilly wasn't allowed to kill or deliberately injure anyone in front of him. At least not without Clive's prior agreement. That done he settled down into his comfy leather chair and began to do what he did best.

'Start where you like, where you feel comfortable.'

'Like I said before, I'm a cleaner and I clean up messes. The messes I clean up are discarded husbands, wives and business partners. Any mess involving rivals really, in love or business.'

Clive still needed clarification, as if he couldn't quite believe what he was hearing, which he couldn't.

'So you do kill people then?'

'Yes. It's the only thing I've ever been good at. I do whatever needs to be done for whoever is paying. Sometimes it's a kill, sometimes just damage limitation. It can be a complete termination, a simple maiming or a quiet disappearance.'

'Where do people quietly disappear to?'

'Usually under a new motorway.'

Clive studied his man carefully while he talked. He had eyes that could, when necessary, fix one with an unflinching stare that would make the headlights of an oncoming train look away in fear, but most of the time they flitted around like restless butterflies, landing on something and then immediately taking flight again. He was nervous but not out of a lack of self-esteem; Noilly was nervous in the sense that he had good reason to be. He had seen and done things that even the blackest of black hearts could barely imagine. Clive felt scared in Noilly's presence, not scared for himself – that he might be injured or killed – or even for all the pain and suffering the man had caused others, he was more scared *for* Noilly. This man had caused such terrible things that he must have suffered equally unpleasant things to be able to do what he did. If this man was cursed with a memory as reliable as Clive's then he was to be pitied.

'I don't know if I can carry on being the person I am.'

'I know. That's why you're here.' Clive smiled as he saw Noilly give him The Look. Clive saw this look in every client, not always straight away but it came eventually. It was a look that pleaded for pity, like a charity poster at Christmas, and it marked the point when the client gave up hiding behind the fabrication they had created and revealed the depths of their self-loathing. The Look said 'Help me'. Clive rubbed his hands together gleefully.

'Let's get to work.'

'Tell me about your mother.' As counselling questions went this was on a par with 'Are you or have your ever been a member of the Communist Party?' Or 'Does anyone gathered here know of any just impediment?' It was the sixty-four-thousand-dollar question of therapy, and frequently cost that much.

Noilly sniffed and then snorted and his hair fell forward like a mousy brown avalanche. Clive heard a sucking noise that could only mean that somewhere under that mess of hair a man was crying.

'I can't.'

'Too painful?'

'No, I just can't. I never knew her.'

'Lucky sod.' Clive tried to stop himself, but it was out there, like a stray fart in polite company. He had broken the first law of counselling. Empathise by all means, encourage with vague personal reminiscences yes, give examples drawn from professional experience of course, but never, ever, put forward an opinion based on one's own life. 'I'm sorry, that was uncalled for.'

'Don't you love your mother?' Noilly asked, turning the tables on Clive with another classic question.

'That's a question I've asked myself a lot lately. The truthful answer is I don't know how to.' He was being truthful with a client. That was rule two shattered. He only had to shag Noilly and he would have broken all

the major commandments of his profession in less than
ten minutes.

Twenty minutes later and he realised he was still talking
about Euterpe, and so by insinuation Christopher and
Julia and Disney and Grace and his kids, and he hadn't
left so much as a fag paper width of a pause for Noilly to
say anything.

'I'm sorry. Again. I shouldn't be talking about myself
here.'

'That's all right. It's nice to hear about someone else's
messy life. Like I said, we're alike you and me. We've
gone through different things but there's a connection.' As
if to prove his point Noilly began to sing. His voice was as
rough as sandpaper. It grabbed hold of Clive's open-car-
door ears and nearly wrenched them off with its grating
insistence. It was like heavy objects being thrown on to a
thin tin roof. It was completely without mercy.

> *'Apron Strings,*
> *Apron Strings,*
> *Love and hugs and all nice things.'*

Clive was worried. He had always kept his career as a
juvenile pop star secret from people, especially at work.
It had been something that had happened to him when
he was young that he'd had no control over, like chick-
enpox or teenage erections. He wasn't ashamed or
embarrassed about it, he just didn't want to relive it all
the time. Now he was scared that this dangerous man,
who claimed to have a lot in common with him, might
know even more about him.

'Why are you singing that?'

'"Mother Love" by The Family Affair? It's my favourite song. Got to number 2 in November 1967.'

'August,' Clive's methodical memory corrected Noilly before he could stop himself.

'Was it? I wouldn't know, I was only two months old. I just love the song. It's like a song that my mother would have sung to me, if she'd lived.' Noilly paused and Clive desperately tried to untangle the spaghetti logic of this statement. He had just about got there when Noilly went on. 'I always wanted to be in The Family Affair, not singing I mean, but actually a part of the family. To be their little brother. Little Noilly Griffin.'

Clive gave a secret sigh of relief. Noilly hadn't made the connection. Like every other unquestioning pop fan, he had assumed that the family name given to the members of the short-lived Family Affair, Griffin, was their real name and not just a stage persona. It was chosen because there was already a Wrigley family who were busy spinning plates on the northern working men's club circuit. The Talk of the Town wasn't big enough for the both of them.

'What about your father?' Clive asked.

'Didn't know him either. Apparently he wanted me to have everything he never had, you know, a liver, that kind of thing. So he shoved me straight into the Saint Martin's Children's Home, into the hands of vindictive priests. I guess I should thank them for helping to inspire my life of surreptitious violence. What about your father?' Noilly asked, not aware of the fourth law of counselling, which decreed that the client should never ask the questions.

'I don't really remember him,' Clive said. 'He died when I was three.'

'I'm sorry. What of?'

'A faulty Yale lock.'

'How did that kill him?'

'It locked him in the garage when the car engine was running.'

'Suicide?'

'I used to tell everyone at school that it was an accident. That he couldn't open the garage doors because of the broken lock. I think they believed me too. I was a convincing liar, runs in the family. He couldn't take any more, I suppose. Poor bastard.' Clive looked out his window at the butcher's shop where the day's pork pies lay cooling on trays ready to be filled with jelly.

'I think we need to look at closure,' Clive said, slipping seamlessly back into his professional role.

Noilly looked at his watch.

'No, I mean closure in the sense that you need to work through something and put it behind you. In this case the loss of your mother and the sense of guilt that you still carry around.'

'Is that why I kill people?'

No, that's because you are a sick psychopathic bastard, Clive thought, but was sensible enough not to say it. He may have believed in being honest and open with his clients but there was a limit to which you could take this with mad shits like Noilly.

Two hours and ten minutes later Noilly came out of Clive's office, his hair tucked behind his ears like elegant drapes on a spring morning, and his eyes ringed by sore red lines from constantly wiping away tears. He stepped into the reception area like a cinema goer stepping out into the remains of the daylight, and blinked as he acclimatised his eyes to a bright new world.

Larry wanted to laugh but even he was not stupid enough to dare. If he had, permanent sick leave might have been his for the taking. Great big poof, he thought. It was a very quiet thought, so quiet that it would have made a pin dropped on to a shag pile carpet sound like a busy day in a shipyard.

Noilly shook Clive's hand and nearly cracked every bone. 'Thank you. I feel fantastic. I really do.'

'I should warn you about the Healing Crisis.'

'I've told you, money is no object, I'll pay whatever it takes to retain your services.'

'That's not what I mean.' Clive tried to explain the symptoms of the Healing Crisis. 'Someone experiencing emotional healing for the first time can develop all kinds of symptoms: flu, a bad back, a migraine, or, and perhaps more dangerous, an intense rush of unbelievable goodwill, a feeling of being cured. You may even begin to think of me as some kind of miracle worker. It can be quite dangerous.'

'I can handle danger.'

'Sure. But you'll think I'm the best thing since sliced bread and it's important you remember that it was you who did the good work here today.'

'You're pretty good yourself, and I don't care what you say. I would do anything for you.' He gave him the wink that Clive had seen once too often already. It was the wink of death. The Healing Crisis had begun.

'Don't worry about me, I can take care of myself.

Expect me when you see me. Which will be soon,' Noilly said and then marched out of the office.

Clive looked over at Larry and shook his head as if deeply disappointed with what he saw, which he was.

'When he comes back, whatever I'm doing, interrupt me. He gets straight through, got it?'

'Yeah yeah,' Larry said derisively, as he concentrated on holding the Ctrl/Alt/Scroll Lock keys and hitting the up cursor to score the winning goal in his bootleg copy of World Cup Professional Foul.

Mandy interrupted Clive during his first session after lunch. 'Sorry, Mr Wrigley, but you have a visitor.'

Clive was going to ask what had happened to Larry but there didn't seem much point. Whenever Larry went home to lunch he rarely came back, especially when there was a good film on the telly. Even a mediocre film about a woman dying from cancer and choosing a new mother for her three special-needs children was often enough for him to cancel all immediate plans and remain prone on his brown velveteen three-seater.

'Mr Upchurch?' Clive asked expectantly.

'No, Mr Durkin.'

'Oh fuck,' Clive couldn't help saying.

'Never mind,' Mandy said, surprising him with a cheeky smile of collusion. Clive felt a nudging reminder in his trousers of his lust for her. It was just as quickly extinguished on the appearance of Amen Durkin in his doorway, leaning on his crutches.

'Hello, old chap. How's tricks?' He lingered on the last word, filling it with insinuation. Clive nodded, taking the fifth amendment.

'Thanks for seeing me, I know you must be busy.' About as busy as a brooch shop in a nudist colony was the suggestion in Durkin's tone.

'What can I do for you?'

'I want to share in your dreams.' Durkin waved a wooden crutch in the general direction of a wooden carving that appeared to be a pair of testicles wrapped around either side of the biggest marrow in the village show.

'What is it you want?' Clive bristled; that was his favourite carving and he was damned if he'd share it with anyone.

'I want us to be close. I want us to be partners. Of course, you'll only get point-nought-five of a per cent of the net and for that I want total control of your tin-pot business. I want you where I can keep an eye on you and if you don't play ball I'll be dropping heavy hints to Mr Plod about your plan to have me executed. That's what I want.'

It felt a bit like dying, except that instead of his life flashing before his eyes it was his illustrious career. It was about as rewarding as a season ticket to Leeds United.

'I don't know what you're talking about.' It was a pretty clichéd defence and all he hoped to achieve from deploying it was about twenty seconds to think up something better.

'I didn't expect you to be here.' Durkin sat heavily in the chair opposite. 'I rang your house and your mother answered. Lovely woman.' Durkin pressed the pause button to add to Clive's discomfort.

'Oh yes?'

'Luckily for me your mother was keen to talk. She told me all about the night I got shot.'

'Told you what?' Clive asked, already knowing the answer.

'About how you had a visit to Queen's Road. She doesn't like you much, does she?'

'How the hell did she know?' Clive asked.

'Search me.'

But Clive didn't have to search him. He remembered Christopher's visit to the office, which had coincided with Noilly's first session, and his interest in the bundle of money.

'It isn't how it looks.' When it came to clichéd defences this was almost as weak as Clive's earlier one.

'Glad to hear that, old chap, but I couldn't give a toss. It's what everyone else thinks that will matter. Mud sticks as well as shit and no one, particularly the police, can tell the difference. You'll never work again, if you're lucky. If not, you might be sharing a cell with a thirty-stone psychopath who feels in need of a cuddle. It happens.'

Clive should have known that this was what Durkin had in mind. The tell-tale signs had been there since he had seen him in hospital. The smiles and winks, the sarcastic comments, it was like a million pennies dropping in perfectly choreographed harmony. Durkin had always wanted revenge and he had known from the moment Clive had intervened in Noilly's murderous attack that he had found a way to achieve it. It wasn't just snatching his empire that sparked the greedy look in Durkin's red-tinted eyes, it was the prospect of beating Clive by owning him lock, stock and barrel. All thanks to the lock, stock and barrel of an assassin's gun.

'You won't lose everything. I fully intend you to play a relatively major role in my reshaped business.'

The key word in this sentence was 'relatively', which suggested that Clive would be responsible for his own mop and bucket, at best.

'I need time to think about this.'

'And . . .?' The And question. It was one of the most effective counselling techniques and here was Durkin using it against him. Like 'Tell me about your mother?', the 'And' question was guaranteed to unwind the truth from the most tangled web of lies. It hung in the air causing a vacuum in the office that sucked in every loose thought and emotion. Clive fought to avoid being pulled in but he couldn't stop himself.

'And . . . if I agree, how much involvement are we talking about me having over day-to-day decisions?'

'Day-to-day decisions? About the same as over long-term strategy.'

'Really?' Clive was almost enthusiastic.

'Sure.' Durkin was smiling demonically.

'That's none, isn't it?' Clive asked, his voice already waving a white flag.

Durkin didn't patronise him further by confirming the fact.

'There's no real value in Listen To You, even the office space is rented.' Clive was drowning somewhere between the devil and deep blue sea but he was going to give it one last kick.

'Do I look like someone who gives a fuck? You'll be at the Sheffield conference tomorrow.' Durkin's tone was full of pompous assumption. 'Make a final decision there.' From behind his red glasses he looked deep into

Clive's eyes, burning them out with vicious intent. 'One way or another.'

'I wasn't planning to go to Sheffield.'

'I don't think you'll want this to drag on too long. I noticed your sad, bearded pal sitting outside with his fat nose stuck in a book. You may not know it, but I think you're already helping the police with their enquiries. Until tomorrow then.' Durkin saluted and turned to leave. He stopped at the doorway and looked at the filing cabinet. On top was a green glass figure representing the role of the vagina in Zimbabwean mythology. 'Very nice,' he said, as he picked it up and put it in his jacket pocket.

Clive waited until Durkin had left and then searched in a top drawer for his A4 page-a-day diary. Inside on the next day's date he found the words 'Sheffield (provisional)' printed in Mandy's big round letters.

'Shit. That's it then,' he said resignedly, as he picked up his black cordless phone and rang through to Mandy on the internal line.

Eleven

Mandy was at her most demure and consequently most alluring. She wore a crisp white blouse through which Clive could see a pearl-coloured lacy bra. Her light grey pleated skirt swirled out at every move and gave teasing glimpses of white thighs and exotic underwear. This surprised Clive; he had always put Mandy down as a fan of the sensible stuff, the kind that the British Empire was built on, big, elastic and ribbed, built to keep all intruders at bay. What he was seeing now was more like Japanese art; what was exciting was what wasn't there.

'Having a hard time, Clive?' she asked with her usual innocence.

'You can say that again,' Clive said, hoping that his hard time was about to get harder.

'I know what will help,' she said, breathless as Marilyn Monroe in a room full of Kennedy brothers. She began to unbutton her blouse. It was an act that paralysed every part of Clive's body, with one notable exception. White button after white button jinked through the slit of the hole, like mice released from a laboratory cage, exposing the pearl bra beneath.

'I don't think we'll be needing this,' Mandy said, deftly moving her hands behind her back and returning with both ends of the bra strap in her grasp.

Her breasts pointed invitingly towards him.

'Come here,' she said, unzipping her skirt and letting gravity rip it swiftly away, putting Clive in mind of the Bucks Fizz Eurovision triumph (April 1981) 'Making Your Mind Up'. That about summed it up.

Clive felt the blood pounding in his penis, and then in his ears, and then all around him. The noise filled the room.

Knock knock knock, it went.

Knock knock knock. It went again. Only it wasn't Clive's bloodstream, it was the bathroom door which was being knocked almost off its hinges with the urgent banging.

'Hurry up, I want a piss. What are you up to in there? There's a terrible smell of kippers.' It was Euterpe. There was a slap as the thick mail-order catalogue fell off Clive's knees and landed on the linoleum. He wobbled dangerously on the loose mahogany-effect toilet seat, almost falling into the waiting arms of Anthea Turner.

'Fuck it,' he said to himself, hiding the catalogue in the dirty washing basket and tucking his crumpled penis back into his worn boxer shorts.

As he passed Euterpe on the stairs she put out a short fat arm to halt his escape.

'There's some costumes coming today, so you'll be needed for a fitting.'

'Costumes?'

'For The Family Affair reunion. There's a sparkling blue shirt with ruffs that I think might suit you.'

'There's a lead-lined coffin that I'm sure would suit you,' he whispered as he scampered down the stairs and out to the limited freedom that a drive to Sheffield offered.

Clive arrived early at the venue for the Sheffield conference but there was already a number of delegates cluttering up the foyer of the hotel demanding to know when the first coffee of the day would be available. Hotel staff in burgundy uniforms, with yellow stripes on the sleeves, presumably to indicate they were officers on the ship of bad taste, pretended to appear bothered and made Easter-egg-hollow promises that coffee would be served in five minutes. Happy with this, the early arrivals went off in search of colleagues they hadn't seen since the last major conference, two weeks previously.

The hotel was unashamedly 1970s Swiss Chalet style. It had lots of red and blue wood and sharp-pointed roofing modelled on a Toblerone packet. Clive wouldn't have been too surprised to have seen a one-hundred-foot cuckoo spring out the front and declare that it was fifteen minutes after eight. The hotel desperately hung on to the damp hillside above Sheffield, giving all the double rooms breathtaking views of the Meadowhall car parks far below.

Clive had been here before. There had been the

symposium 'Gender Blending in the 1990s – Is there a penis left to envy?', and the workshop on 'Non-Directive Counselling with the Elective Mute – The Silence Between Friends', amongst others. The hotel management knew that niche marketing was the only way to make a success of an ugly building in a terrible position and it had set about making the world of psychosis its own. Amongst the therapeutic fraternity it had become known as The Emmental Health Hotel.

Clive bought a paper and sat down in the cosy lounge to immerse himself in the world's problems. It made his feel somehow more manageable. He became so diverted that when he finally emerged from a dull tale of insider dealing he was amazed to find the place teeming with grey suits, all of whom sported badges announcing who they were. The more pompous had insisted on having their many qualifications listed after their names, and in one notable case having a separate badge to reflect a lifetime spent seeking out every professional certificate going. The more radical delegates, especially those who had recently qualified and were still on a mission to liven things up, had written things like 'Hi! I'm Jamie' and 'Talk to me, I want to listen' on their badges. These didn't wear ties or jewellery, or jackets that matched their trousers, or anything that had ever been within a stone's throw of a current fashion. Instead they wore denim. Neat, steam cleaned and well pressed, but still denim. Denim jeans, skirts, waistcoats, jackets and even hats, it was like a 1970s nostalgia convention. Almost without exception these people were ignored by their more traditional peers, for nothing shook the pillars of the establishment like youthful, iconoclastic Samsons.

They were too much of a reminder of where those establishment figures had come from themselves, a very long time ago.

Today's conference was entitled 'The Confederacy of the Mind – Unconscious Collusion in Familial Guilt'. But for Clive it was treble D Day. D for Decision day. D for Durkin. D for Death of his career. Clive felt trepidation flood his stomach, setting off an acidic chain reaction that took away what little remained of his appetite.

Just before they were called into the main hall for the opening remarks there was a commotion in the foyer. A non-grey-suited, non-denim-clad man, who was neither old guard nor new blood and who consequently stood out like a spare thumb on the offspring of first cousins, was arguing with the burgundy-clad staff.

'Get your bloody hands off me.'

A man with five yellow stripes on his sleeve, which probably made him an admiral, was holding on to the intruder as if his company pension depended on it.

'Call the police, Miss Harper. Tell them we have a drunk on the premises.'

'I am the fucking police,' DS Gerhardie whispered far too loudly for a man bent on top-secret surveillance.

Clive went over to the group.

'He's with me,' he wearily told the woman who wore a burgundy bowler hat for no apparent reason other than to make her look insane. She looked closely at Clive's badge for confirmation.

'Very well, Mr Wiggle, but I'll have to ask you to sign him in officially.' This done the two men walked towards the hall.

'Very kind of you, Mr Wrigley,' DS Gerhardie said, bitterly. He shook the last vestiges of burgundy staff from his fawn Daks windcheater.

Clive stopped and turned on his shadow. 'Or very foolish of me. Whichever it is, I'd prefer it if you didn't sit near me.'

'As long as I can keep both you and Mr Durkin in my sight at the same time you won't even know I'm here.' DS Gerhardie flicked a bit of that morning's toast from his beard.

'Somehow I find that hard to believe,' Clive said without humour.

In the hall the introductions were made and Clive and several hundred other professional agony aunts and uncles settled down to a day of doing what they all did so well, which was listening. The morning passed by pleasantly enough as Clive, along with a fair proportion of those in the auditorium, dozed through the lectures. At the mid-morning break he enjoyed a coffee and a fresh Danish, while one or two acquaintances came up and congratulated him on his heroic intervention in the assault on Durkin. If only they knew the truth, he thought. But many of them did know the truth.

'Consider it,' the whisper went around the auditorium. 'Two people who were known to hate one another happen to meet while one of them is in the middle of being assassinated by an unknown assailant? That's some coincidence.' As coincidences went it was of the no-smoke-without-fire variety. Clive was the man they all saw with the matches. 'Yes,' the many accusing looks told him, 'there's more to this story than is being told.'

Clive took his lunch out to the car in order to escape the accusing silence that his peers wrapped around him. After lunch he subjected himself to the tedium of a workshop called 'Wholesome and Home-made, The Recipe for Mama's Oedipal Pie', which involved the usual embarrassing role-play, then writing down on large pads of white paper how it felt, before 'feeding back' to the rest of the group. Clive noticed he was the only one in the room who looked even vaguely uncomfortable during these proceedings. When this torture was finished it was time for afternoon tea, which was followed by the final slot of the afternoon, a keynote lecture by Dr Amen Durkin.

Durkin hobbled up the steps to the stage on crutches and then paused to charismatically throw them down. He hopped the rest of the way to the podium. The house was brought down by this dramatic act; it felt as if the ground below Clive was opening up. The applause went on for five minutes. Everyone, it seemed, loved a hero, even if the hero was a pompous tosser like Durkin. He stood and soaked it all up like an egotistical sponge with a particularly selfish streak. He made no attempt to call the applause to a halt, he just put out his hands, palm up and gently encouraged the plaudits to continue. Eventually, when the skin on many of the delegates' hands was beginning to split from excessive wear and tear, the mood of the crowd decided it had paid due respect and it was time to call a halt. The applause ceased, almost as one.

'Wow!' Durkin said and the applause began again,

only a short reprise this time, but long enough to confirm that Durkin could do no wrong. He could spend the next hour reading out bus tickets and he would be lauded to the Swiss-style roof-tops for his breadth of vision.

'Friends. I am lucky to be standing before you today.'

Nods all round, some yelps of support and plenty of dark looks of disgust shot at Clive. Across the room, higher up, towards the back, Clive could see DS Gerhardie was also glaring at him.

'I had intended to talk about my area of special interest, 'The Challenge of Addiction', but in view of everything that's happened to me recently it seems enough just to be here in front of you.' A ripple of applause reciprocated the feeling. 'Anyway my book, *Combating the Enemy Within You*, will be available at all good bookshops next month.'

Clive saw the majority of the crowd make a mental note to put it on their shopping list.

'Instead I want to talk of healing, of hurt being mended. When I was in the hands of my own addictions, unable to break free of the iron-grip that was entirely of my own making, I had an experience.'

'Oh no,' Clive mumbled to himself, 'he's going to do his Dead Pets' Society again.' It reminded him of Grace.

'I had been drinking, lighter fluid, I think.' He smiled at the memory, recalling it through the double thickness of his rose-tinted spectacles. 'I woke up, sick in body as well as spirit. I was in complete darkness but was at least warm and comfortable. It was as if I was surrounded by a much-loved cuddly toy from childhood. I lay for what seemed like ages and then, as gradually as the creeping dawn, I noticed the smell. It was a smell that was both clean, or rather cleansing, and yet also foul, like death. I didn't know then that it was chloroform. I tried to move, to get up, but when I did I felt the thing that was comforting me move away, sliding stiffly out of reach. I was then visited by a feeling that was a mixture of fear and panic. I began to struggle and in so doing I found a trapdoor above me and pushed it upwards as hard as I could until it flew open. Bright sunlight poured in and scoured my eyes so I couldn't see where I was or what was in there with me. Eventually my eyes adjusted and what I witnessed was carnage. I was in a skip outside the local vets. I was knee-deep in other people's destroyed animals. Dead dogs, cats, litters of puppies, bags of kittens, hamsters, pigeons, rabbits. All of them put down by the vet and then 'taken care of'. At that moment all I could think was that I was as dead as those once-loved animals. That I had put myself down.' He paused and took a long drink of water, gripping the glass and swallowing deeply.

'That was the first time I came up close to death. The recent attack on me was the second time I have faced it. I have twice looked into universal emptiness of death and I know my place. Believe me, you have no choice but to know it.' He looked around the room like a searchlight seeking out enemy bombers. 'Which is why I want to make an announcement.'

Without anyone saying anything there was a buzz of expectation. It was a kind of collective inhalation of breath, a wondering of what could possibly follow

Durkin's story. Clive was pleased to hear one or two dis-
senting murmurs speculating if the smug old bastard
was finally going to retire.

'When you've seen what I've seen, then every day is a
big day, but today is a very big day indeed, isn't it?' he
asked.

To the hundreds of delegates in the hall it was obviously a rhetorical question. An evangelical call to arms.
Only Clive knew the truth. Durkin's gaze was fixed on
him and the question was directed straight at him. Clive
looked down at his black leather shoes and could see his
defeated expression reflected in their shine. He looked
up again and found Durkin was still watching him
closely. The auditorium was really buzzing now, excited
at the long pause, wondering if Durkin had stopped
talking and had no intention of ever starting again.

Clive had never been to an auction but the delicate,
almost unseen movement of his head acknowledging his
complete acquiescence would have served him well
from Smithfield to Sotheby's. This gentlest of gestures
shouted to Durkin 'It's a done deal, I'm all yours'. It also
managed to shout to DS Gerhardie, but something got
lost in the translation and he read it as 'I'm hungry'. But
that was enough for him.

Up on stage, under the gaze of a hundred of pairs of
eyes, Durkin gave one of his most winning smiles. He
was, after all, the winner.

'Good. Very good. Then I should like to call on my
friend . . .' He paused while his voice went into an
enforced pit-stop, changing his tone to one of italicised
triumphalism. '. . . *and future partner*, Clive Wrigley.
Clive, please come up.'

There were astonished gasps and even a few boos from here and there. Clive stood up and made the long walk to the stage and up to the podium. It was his winning walk towards the Golden Lobe again, only more humiliating, if that were possible. From the stage Durkin made encouraging noises to 'come on, give him your support', but even his prophet-like status with the crowd couldn't rally them. Clive finally made the centre of the stage, where he stood nervously, as if expecting to be hit by a missile, a Perrier bottle maybe, or worse, a crust from the wholefood buffet he had endured at lunchtime.

'I give you Clive Wrigley, my saviour.'

The only people clapping with any enthusiasm were Durkin and DS Gerhardie.

'Thanks to the bravery of this man I have been able to look at my life from a fresh perspective. We all know how near-death experiences can do that to a person.'

Everyone in the room nodded at Durkin's professional truism.

'So it is with great pride that I am announcing that Clive and myself are becoming partners once more. Clive is giving . . . merging all his business interests with Shrink-Fit, with immediate effect. I shall now offer the largest and best practice in the north of England. This marks a great day for our profession. Clive will be going on an immediate sabbatical to look at preventative strategies in suicide management at the Bergman Centre in Sweden.' There was warm applause at this news. Even Clive joined in. The audience figured that whether Clive was innocent or not, if Durkin had forgiven him then that was good enough for them.

Clive had to admit that Durkin's idea of exiling him to Sweden was a clever move, publicly committing him to clear out quickly. Durkin hugged Clive and made as if to kiss his new partner on the cheek. He turned them both away from the microphone in a smart imitation of the Tango, putting his mouth against Clive's ear as he did so.

'It's over. It's all mine now. And I want you out by Friday.'

Clive felt his ear filling up with little blobs of Durkin's phlegm. It was the least of his problems.

Soleil was carefully tending the walled garden at Nostrum Hall. Although it was still March outside, within the crumbling red-brick square it was summer. Plants burst forth early in the warm soil as if they too were hoping to move to America with the rest of the inhabitants. Soleil was hoeing well-rotted manure around the vines that somehow managed to cling to life, protected from the damp, breezy climes of the area by the wall. He had always hoped that the vines would one day create their own brand of English wine, Chateau Rajneesh, but these plans would have to be put aside. He wondered about starting the process again in Minnesota, having a go at creating a nice buttery Chardonnay to rival the Californians. He sniffed the manure on his fingers and felt Rajneesh was with him. He heard a click and turned around, half expecting it to be a religious vision and so was quite unperturbed when he saw the Angel of the Lord behind him.

'Hello,' he said warmly. He had spent much of his life preparing for such an eventuality and he wasn't going to blow it now it had happened. The Angel glowed in the late-afternoon sunset. He stood in front of the sinking sun, framed as a silhouette and yet giving off an incredible, sparkling white light. He said nothing. Soleil didn't feel it was his place to develop the conversation beyond 'Hello' but the ensuing silence was a bit embarrassing.

After a few moments he decided to risk another opening. 'Have you come to give me a message?'

The Angel appeared to look around, although Soleil found it hard to tell as the sunset behind the apparition was blinding.

'Your hoe looks loose. You should always look after tools,' the apparition said.

It wasn't exactly the kind of message Soleil expected from an angel, but it did fit in with his musings on producing fruits of the earth so maybe it was meant to be cryptic.

'Right. I'll fix it. The Brahmin shall provide. And God of course,' he added quickly.

The Angel swung his arm from behind his back and his silhouette took on a different, oddly threatening shape. Soleil still couldn't see the man clearly as his face was covered by what looked like a dark veil.

'Is there anything I can do for you?' Soleil asked, piously.

'No. But there is something I can do for you,' the man said.

'What's that?'

'You want to get closer to God, don't you?'

'Absolutely, friend. That's why I'm here, it's my greatest desire.'

'Then I can make it happen.'

The man held up his hand, which Soleil could now see had something solid, metal and long in it. Something a bit like a gun.

Twelve

Just when Clive didn't think things could go any further downhill, that whatever lay ahead in his life the gradient must surely have a modest upward incline away from disaster, he slept with Julia.

Clive had counselled a million errant husbands and as many betrayed wives. He knew all about man's lazy ability to slide into someone else's clean sheets and indulge in a little deceit. He was perfectly qualified to spot a classic case of adultery almost before the adulterer had innocently asked a third party if they fancied going back to his place for a quick coffee. Yet despite having this lifetime of experience available to him, he foolishly achieved an infidelity that was straight out of the adulterer's handbook. Filled with an overdose of raging hormones let loose in a man who had sunk as low as it was possible to sink, he blindly followed the well-worn path that a billion fools had already trodden. But then, given the perfect laboratory conditions of his messed-up life, it was perhaps surprising that it hadn't happened earlier.

Clive desperately hung on to the phrase 'slept with' as opposed to 'had sex with' or 'made love to' or even 'fucked the arse off'. This was because he had been so drunk he wasn't completely sure he'd done the full deed, and until he had incontrovertible proof that he had he was admitting nothing. The distinction was merely academic anyway, given that they had done most other things. Drunk or not he remembered that much. Her lips had offered succour to his lips and shortly afterwards to the rest of his body. At which point her lips had swapped succour for good old-fashioned suction. The next day it shamed him to think about how willingly he had gone along with everything she had offered. No matter how much he tried to shake his memory, dull it with alcohol or simply deny the accusations it levelled at him, he couldn't lose the picture of himself happily shoving parts of his anatomy into that greedy great cake hole of hers. Nor the tingling joy that surged through him when she turned on the high-powered vacuum cleaner of her mouth.

After selling out his business to Durkin or, to be more accurate, giving it away, he had gone into Bradworth and availed himself of the many delights that lay in wait for lost souls such as his. Wine bars that didn't waste time selling wine but concentrated instead on alcoholic Dandelion and Burdock; fake Irish pubs with sawdust on their floors that had been specially sterilised to meet the strict hygiene requirements of the conglomerate that owned the brewery; student bars full of watery half-price drinks and the smell of teenage vomit; Clive did them all. Then things went a bit blank but he assumed from the state of his best purple Katharine Hamnett 'denim' shirt, which now had an aroma of coriander soaked into the armpits and a pebbledash of dhansak sauce down the front, that he had gone to one of Bradworth's fine curry houses. He remembered a night-club with a very big penguin on steroids turning him away from the door. He must have convinced a bouncer somewhere that he was a decent and respectable piss artist because he remembered dancing like a mad thing to a repetitive dance song on which an under-employed female soul singer chanted 'Fill my hole with your pole'.

He was still singing this when he got home. He had paused in the hall to take a closer look at the tight spangled blue shirt with a foppish ruff down the front that was hanging there. It had a note written in his mother's handwriting, pinned to it, which said 'This is yours, Fatso'. It didn't occur to him that the label might be meant for anyone else. He put on the shirt and began to cha-cha around the coat stand. Then he went upstairs and got into his bed, having first stripped naked apart from the shirt.

In bed was a body he drunkenly assumed belonged to his wife. He claimed to himself afterwards that the drink had deadened his fantastic powers of recall and that he had forgotten Grace was no longer sharing his bed, or his life, or his planet if she got her wish. This was where his lies really began. It wasn't long before he realised the truth, that it wasn't Grace, but he swore he couldn't pinpoint the exact moment. He estimated it was about five minutes. But five minutes with Julia, who was obviously keen to fill her hole with his pole, was enough to take him well past the point of no return. When he did realise his mistake, or so his weak defence claimed at the trial that he ran over and over in his head, it was too late. Julia and he were tangled up in a heady bout of sexual athleticism and both were too turned on to turn it off.

The next morning he lay for ages pretending not to be awake. To admit to wakefulness would start the post-mortem. Julia would roll over and say something like 'Hey, look at us! Back together again!' And the rest would be history. So he didn't move a muscle, not a sinew, not a nerve ending. Instead he lay like a corpse and prayed that he would soon be one. If Grace had walked in at that moment he would have got his wish. Such was his luck it was hardly a surprise that the person who did walk in was Euterpe.

He couldn't pretend to be asleep any longer when she began her piercing scream. It was the kind of scream that large industrial complexes used to indicate work was about to begin and that the local workforce should get their arses into gear. It wasn't a scream of rage, or anger, or even shock, but of someone who has just got all the numbers up on a roll-over week.

'Stay there, you little love birds, I'll get you breakfast in bed. You'll need to keep you strength up. And other things, eh, Clive?'

'Can I have some of that garlic sausage?' Julia asked, the sheets wrapped around her body in a display of modesty that reminded Clive of unlocked stables and bolting horses.

'Sure. But first I want a piccy.' Euterpe, apparently from nowhere, pulled out a camera and with the well-practised skill of unprincipled paparazzi everywhere snapped at the scene in front of her. The flash dazzled Clive and provided a white backdrop in his mind, like a cine screen on which he could view the awfulness of his recent actions. He turned to Julia. The way she smiled made the pencil-thin moustache of dark bristles above her top lip curve into a broad 'U'. Clive felt the tidal pull of seven gin and tonics, four continental lagers, three American lagers, six Japanese lagers and a lamb tikka massala with a beef dhansak on the side, as they ebbed and flowed in the pit of his stomach. Without speaking to Julia or his mother he leaped out of bed and ran into the bathroom where he spent the rest of the morning lying perfectly still and concentrating on not throwing up.

Clive made his way to the Lard 2000 Diner just before lunchtime. He was shown to an empty table by a Sex Object who might have been the model on which the job description for all waitresses at the Lard 2000 was based. Leggy, blond, tits that came out like motorway cones and no moral objection to wearing revealingly tight clothes, it was a recipe for success and bugger equal opportunities.

The Diner was a converted mill set in the heart of the burgeoning financial sector of Bradworth. It had 'ambience', which meant it had opera played very loudly and food served in fashionably geometric patterns. The atmosphere of the place was a delicate blend of urgency, noise and casual elegance and the telephone-number prices flattered every customer's desire to feel successful.

The diners sat in the Wembley-sized floor space, coolly ignoring one another while furtively watching to see who was there and what they were wearing.

Lard 2000 also boasted the largest permanent exhibition of Bile Art in Europe. Milos Creilman, Bradworth's own *enfant terrible* of the modern art world (Clive felt the epithet was particularly appropriate as Milos's Bile Art was pretty terrible and it looked as though it was painted by a child) was a regular visitor. He would order the dish of the day, chew it, swallow it and then, in keeping with the bulimic times, throw the lot up on to canvas. This was specially treated so that every tooth mark, every drizzle of saliva, every partially digested tomato skin was preserved for posterity. Clive agreed that this was where it belonged; up Milos's posterior.

It was a very post-modern kind of sexism that was practised at the Lard 2000 Diner. The work of waiting on tables was done by sex-object women and the cooking was done by sex-object men. Clive had chosen it for two reasons. First, it was warm and comfortable and he was surrounded by leggy waitresses with pointy breasts, and second, it was the best place to hide if he didn't want anyone to find him.

'Clive!'

A clash of primary colours crashed towards his table and gave him a rush of vertigo.

'Disney. How the hell did you find me?'

'It took me all morning. I rang your office and got some cheeky sod who told me he was too busy to speak to me, something about a penalty shoot-out in which he had to beat the Germans, but that I could probably find you here. I think he said his name was Lance.'

'Larry. Lance is what I'm going to do to him, with a blunt, rusty pole.' Into his mind came the refrain 'Fill my hole with your pole' and he gave an involuntary shudder.

'I really need to talk. Something terrible has happened.'

'Don't tell me, Soleil has said you've got to go to Australia with mother,' Clive teased her gently.

'Worse. He's dead.'

For the first time Clive realised she had been crying. Buckets by the look of it.

'How?'

'Shot. Some maniac killer walked into Nostrum Hall and shot him point blank in the head.' Disney began to cry again. A few diners nearby shifted uncomfortably at this show of emotion.

'Shot in the head?' Clive didn't like what he was hearing, not so much because it was tragic but because it was familiar.

'Yes. The police have been on to me.'

'Did anyone see who did it?'

'I don't think so. Someone in the upper rooms reckoned they saw what looked like a snowman leaving over the fields. But she had been smoking grass all day.'

Clive shivered. It couldn't be? But what if it was? What were the odds on him knowing two completely separate people getting shot?

'The police are saying it's a professional job. They suspect someone from within the sect, one of our American brothers and sisters. After a bigger slice of heaven presumably.'

'That's families for you,' Clive said cryptically. 'Have they asked about me by any chance?'

Disney was nonplussed. 'Why would they ask about you?'

Clive explained, slowly and with some awkwardness, that before his recent stay in hospital he had witnessed the attempted assassination of Durkin.

'It's probably just a coincidence,' Disney said emptily. Her inability to grasp even the most obvious of concepts never ceased to amaze Clive.

'They didn't ask about you over the phone. Do you think they will?'

'Maybe. I don't see how there can be a connection, not really,' Clive said, more to convince himself than Disney, who already accepted this as fact. 'What will you do now?'

'Oh look, Creilman's.' Disney swiftly and inelegantly changed the subject. 'He's quite a favourite of Soleil's. Was. He bought a lot for the Brahmin's collection. He loved all that outpouring of inner turmoil.'

'That and the fact they increased in value by two hundred and fifty per cent last year,' Clive said, not meaning to be cruel but failing miserably.

Disney looked at the nearest example of modern art, entitled, *When Did You Last See Your Dinner?* 'I have to do what Mother wants.' She made it sound like it was somehow all his fault and Clive was starting to wonder if it was.

'Don't be daft. That's stupid. Give it some time, think about it some more.'

Disney didn't seem to hear him and was looking into the far distance as if she was already restocking her mother's medicine cabinet in the Outback.

'Disney?'

'Sorry. I think I need a faith lift. I haven't felt this pathetic since Doug died.'

Even with his inch-perfect memory Clive only vaguely remembered Doug. He was one of a hundred men Disney had attached herself to for no other apparent reason than to completely destroy any remnants of her self-esteem.

'Doug? Was he the one who drank aftershave?'

'No, that was Billy.'

'I thought he was the armed robber.'

'No. I can't remember his name,' Disney said wistfully. 'No, Doug was the man who died having sex.'

Surprisingly Clive didn't remember that bit. He decided that there was probably something Freudian behind this memory loss.

'God, that must have been awful for you.'

'Well, yes it was, although it was worse for the Spanish au pair. She was the one he was having sex with at the time.'

'I'm really sorry, Disney, but despite everything terrible that's happened to you I'm really going to have to laugh at that,' Clive said as a guilty laugh shook his shoulders and started him coughing.

Disney smiled vacantly, unsure whether to be hurt by this outburst. 'A smile is the curve that straightens most things out,' she said forgivingly. 'Soleil taught me that.'

The Sex Object came back with a large paper menu with a Bile Art design copied on to it (anchovies, scallops and salted fish curry – titled 'Surf's Up'). The dishes of the day were written across it in brown felt-tip.

'Y'all ready to order?' she drawled in an uncomfortable accent which attempted (and failed) to blend gritty

Northern Bradworth with faked Southern Belle. Desire was coming home and it was crunching up Clive's gravel path. The Sex Object gave him her patented smile.

'Get me the most expensive steak you can.'

'How would y'all like that, love?'

'Still twitching,' he ordered. The waitress showed her professionalism by allowing no emotion to cross her face, only a gorgeous pout.

'And charge it to Amen Durkin's account.'

Around him acolytes of modern art chewed on their salmon and soured-cream bagels, the familiars of the financial services industry licked their Mocha ice-cream and the Muslim businessmen toyed with their Tall, Skinny, No Fun Café Lattes. Clive sipped his double-fun double espresso, partly to try to clear the fug of his hangover but mostly in hope of encouraging a fatal heart attack by an overdose of caffeine.

'Mother was to blame for you and Julia,' Disney spoke after a long silence between them. Clive was shocked. How did Disney know about him and Julia? He briefly ran through the pathetic excuses stored in his head, excuses that would need some serious crash testing before he dared use them on Grace.

We're just good friends.

I was drunk and there was some silly, harmless business, but we've put it all behind us.

How dare you infer there is anything going on between us.

They were that pathetic.

'Don't panic.' Disney laid a soft hand across his clenched fists. 'I'm not going to judge you. If you want to sleep with Julia that's your business.'

In Clive's mind the last-resort excuses scrolled past,

excuses created in case the truth about last night ever leaked out.

You'll laugh at this but the funny thing is we went and had sex, all accidental like.

She pulled a gun and made me impregnate her with my seed.

I want to announce our engagement.

'I may have had sex with her, I can't actually remember. But that's not the worst of it.' Clive steeled himself for the replay of his mother's ecstatic face mooning over his desecrated marital bed that would inevitably fill his mind any second.

'I know.'

'You know about mother walking in on us?'

'No, I mean that's not the worst of it. Mother rang Grace on her mobile and told her. Then she sent her a photo for proof.'

The work of Milos Creilman, never the easiest example of modern art on the eye, suddenly began to race around Clive like horses on a Victorian fairground ride. Colourful combinations of sweetcorn, anchovies, red and yellow peppers, and warm green leaf salads waved at him as they passed, like excited children. Clive let his head fall forward in slow motion but it hit the hard mahogany table-top in fast forward. The thud echoed around the cavernous stone walls of the Lard 2000 Diner.

From his position hidden behind a large, leafy Amazonian shrub DS Gerhardie was watching Clive and Disney. Or that's what he was meant to be doing but his attention was momentarily distracted by the shrub. It had been specially chosen to emphasise both the enormous ceiling height and the Diner's commitment to things rainforesty. DS Gerhardie wondered about getting something similar, if considerably smaller, to do the same job for his loft conversion. He fingered the bark and leaf mould in the large pot looking for clues to its formal identification, such as a neat plastic label. He was concentrating on the task so intensely he didn't hear the waitress come up behind him. She had brought his coffee and bagel, which he'd ordered as 'expressed milk and cheese bar-jell', much to the smug amusement of the Diner staff.

'Y'all OK there, my ducks?' she enquired. He jumped backwards at the shock of being discovered up to his wrists in potting compost and knocked the tray clean out of her beautifully kept hands. The tray bounced across the floor and rang like a doomladen church bell solemnly announcing some terrible event. Clive and Disney along with everyone else in the room looked over to the scene of the disturbance where they saw DS Gerhardie standing exposed before them. If he could have smiled at them he would have done, but such a skill wasn't in his repertoire. Instead he gave them the opposite of a smile, a glum perhaps.

'What the hell is he doing here?' Disney asked. But Clive had a good idea of what DS Gerhardie was doing, even if he wasn't doing it very well.

Suddenly Disney raised her glass of organic sarsaparilla milkshake. 'Mother has made me an Oedipal wreck.'

'If I give her the wool, will she make me one?' Clive added the punchline. The next two minutes were like a scene from the *Exorcist* as they dissolved into maniacal, devilish laughter. Every so often they would both come up for air and Clive would grab his throat and growl, 'Motherfucker'.

Outside Clive put his arm around his sister.

'Go back to Nostrum Hall now, take care of things there. Whatever you do, don't worry about Mother. Take care of yourself; it's a dangerous world out there.'

'You take care too,' Disney said as she walked away in the direction of the railway station.

'I intend to,' Clive said to himself.

Thirteen

Since they had last met Noilly had obviously fallen under a lawnmower, or possibly a combine harvester, or at the very least joined a strange religious sect comprising entirely of disgraced hairdressers. His fringe was gone, torn away by some primeval force, and now the first thing Clive noticed about him was his forehead, which seemed to enter the room a good few seconds before the rest of him. Its shiny surface dazzled all before it like the explosions at the end of a heavy metal band's stage show. Its shape and size were reminiscent of the dome on St Paul's Cathedral.

That's what he's been hiding away all these years, Clive thought. But he was wrong, for the second thing Clive noticed was Noilly's eyes, which thanks to his newly shorn image were on permanent view to a discerning world. Clive felt uncomfortable exposed to their full madness. He'd had glimpses, but these had been no more the forked lick of a tame grass snake. This was a full-frontal attack by a hooded cobra who'd just had his favourite parking space nicked by a rusty Nissan full of mongooses. Clive wished for the return of the hair fringe to shield him from those eyes.

'Noilly,' Clive welcomed his client, the lush tonal quality of his honeyed voice instilling a feeling of warmth and well-being. It was like being in bed with Radio 2. 'New image?' He nodded at the remains of the badly razored fringe that peeked shyly over the edge of the world to the forehead way below.

'New beginnings. I want to look the world in the eye. Like that song.'

'What song?'

'Walk tall, walk straight and look the whole world in the eye.'

'Val Doonican, king of the cable-knit jumper. Highest chart position, number three; New Year 1965,' Clive said before he could stop himself.

'If you say so,' Noilly said without much interest in the discography of his muse.

Clive bristled, he wanted to tell him that he certainly did say so but Noilly's eyes proved a great leveller of his ego.

'Whatever, that's me from now on.'

Clive thought about Noilly walking tall, walking straight and looking the whole world in the eye. He felt a cold shiver wrap itself around his spine as if it were a silk scarf in the grip of the Boston Strangler. 'Nice idea,' he said.

'What are we going to do today?' Noilly began energetically. 'I've done what you asked at the end of the last session, and I've been spending time thinking about the things that have made me unhappy.'

'Good, but I'd like to start with something else.' Clive still couldn't believe he was going to ask Noilly what he was going to ask him. He shut his eyes, the truth was best viewed in the dark.

'I want to talk to you about your profession.'

From below the enormous moonscape of his forehead Noilly looked unsure, angry even. 'Profession?'

'What you do. Cleaning up messes. Something happened on Monday and it seems too much of a coincidence.'

There was a silence that spanned generations, a silence that torched villages and ethnically cleansed countries. It burned the earth and shattered the spirit. It told Clive he was treading on thin ice, the kind you'd expect to find at sea level in the equator. Worse, below this thin ice lurked a whole school of hungry sharks. It wasn't the kind of silence one could interrupt. Somewhere deep in Noilly's soul a shrug began which flooded through his body with the force of an epileptic seizure. Clive took this as permission to continue.

'Someone I know, well he was my sister's friend really. He got shot. In what seems a very professional way. I want to know who did it, and why,' Clive trailed off, letting his words lay where they fell.

'I don't talk about the details of what I do. Not here. This is a different place where things are said and done that don't belong to my other world.'

'I need to know if you were involved, and if not who was. If it was you I need to know who hired you.'

'If you want to find out more about using my services

then this is how you contact me.' He gave Clive a surprisingly neat and well-made business card with the address of the Muscle Club on it. 'And I'm only giving you this because I admire and respect you. But I won't answer those questions here, and if you push me too far I will shove back. Hard. Understand?'

Clive nodded, he understood. 'Thanks. Sorry to bring it up here.' Then he had a brainwave, a way of salvaging something from this bad start to the session, he'd give his client a treat. 'Tell you what, why don't you tell me all about your mother.'

'I never met her, I already told you that. She died when I was born.'

Clive looked at the empty and lonely man who sat in the chair opposite. 'I know, but what if she were here, sat on that couch over there. What do you think she'd say to you? Would she be proud of you?' Clive was throwing caution to the winds as if it were confetti. For a second he thought Noilly was going to throw something heavy at him, like himself, but then he saw his client's eyes moisten. This actually made them appear even more venomous than before. Finally he succumbed to a Noah's Flood of tears.

'Let it go, let it go,' Clive intoned with genuine sympathy. Noilly had his head down between his knees and was shedding enough tears to satisfy a Shirley Bassey audience. Clive took the opportunity to sneak a look at the card he had been given. Underneath the address of the Muscle Club, in ludicrously neat handwriting that must have been practised for hours before being committed to paper, it read: 'Play B7 on the jucebox and wate. If Im' their Ill' let you no.' Clive was glad Noilly had his head between his knees because if he had looked up he would have seen him trying and failing to stop giggling.

The following evening, Friday, Clive decided to spend some quality time with his family. For what seemed like many hours but was probably only two, Julia insisted on performing her Persil catechism, showing him every item of his dirty laundry and demanding a detailed explanation as to what had caused each suspicious mark. Only when she was satisfied with his replies did she move on to show him everything she had washed that day, insisting he examine them and confirm they were spotless.

'Digesters, that's the key. That stuff your Ex used wouldn't get Teflon clean, never mind a heavy hemp.'

'She's not my Ex.' Clive felt it only right to mention this fact, showing a sense of loyalty he hadn't managed to reproduce with his body parts during the night of lust with Julia.

'She soon will be,' Euterpe shouted from the sitting room and then bursting into a laugh that sounded like sheets of sandpaper being rubbed against each other.

As soon as Christopher returned from wherever he had been all day Clive grabbed him firmly.

'Fancy a drink?' he asked, as he pulled his older brother out the front door and into the dark cold night.

'What time do the boozers shut over here?' Christopher looked at his watch, which he had stolen off Clive's dressing-table earlier in the day.

'Boozers?' Clive marvelled at his brother's anachronistic terminology. Next thing he'd be wearing a chunky Starsky and Hutch cardigan and going down the disco.

'Do they still shut at ten thirty?' Christopher mocked as only a true exponent of It-Takes-One-To-Denounce-One can.

'We're at the heart of a modern Europe these days, Christopher. We have all-day opening now,' Clive bragged, aware too late that he was standing on the shifting sands that were the moral and cultural high ground.

'So when do they shut?' Christopher asked eagerly.

'Eleven.' Clive was already stomping off down the high street to stave off the brick of sarcasm that Christopher was about to lob in his direction.

The pub he chose was Brontë Bridge's finest, The Dreaming Sheep. Deserving the plaudits partly for its range of apparently authentic local beers and partly because it sometimes had lock-ins until as late as eleven forty-five. That would show Christopher, he thought. Clive bought his brother a pint without waiting. There was no point. He'd be an old and very thirsty man before Christopher went to the bar.

'What's so urgent?' Christopher asked after they had both drunk two-thirds of their drinks in one long, brotherly swig.

'I've got a scenario I want to share with you. I have a client who, not to be polite about it, kills people for money.'

'It's a living. Or maybe "it's a dying" would be more accurate,' Christopher laughed. Clive chose not to join him.

'I've seen him in action, much to my regret. It isn't funny.'

'I guess not,' Christopher said, still smiling at his joke.

'Then two days ago Soleil, who happens to be a close friend of our sister, gets shot in what looks like a professional hit.'

'Coincidence?'

'That's what I want to ask you.'

'Me? How the hell should I know?'

'Because you met him.'

'Pardon?' It was the only time Clive could remember Christopher being so polite.

'The other day. You met him in my reception. My client the hitman. He was leaving as you arrived.'

'And you think we stopped and chatted about the best ways to blow someone's brains out? I think you've been working too hard, or maybe all that physical exertion with Julia has sapped your mental strength.' Christopher laughed again, which made Clive grab his coat collar roughly and pull him close, face to face.

'You are a devious, slimy bastard and I've never trusted you. You're the only one who makes any kind of connection between the two. If anyone is behind this, it's you.'

'You're mad. I'm as sad about Soleil as anyone. Between you and me,' he gave Clive a brotherly wink, 'I had high hopes of doing some big business deals with old Sol.'

'Maybe that's it? He didn't come across with the big deal so you had him shot.'

'Don't be soft, I didn't have him shot. This is one terrible coincidence. I swear it on Daddy's grave. Now is there any danger of you getting another drink in before these archaic licensing laws force us out on to the streets.'

Clive made his way to the bar and ordered two more drinks. The barmaid was wearing the sort of short, tight clothes that up until a few days ago might have turned his head, but now, thanks to his guilt about what he had done with Julia, made him turn away. Over in the corner Ronnie George's blind and ancient springer spaniel, Grappler, started snarling. No one in the bar could remember a time when Grappler had ever growled. He was so old and infirm that the most vicious thing anyone could remember him doing was pissing himself while sleeping on Ronnie's lap. It was even more surprising when Grappler got up and started blindly snapping at random trouser legs and howling like a rabid wolf. Clive looked in the direction of where the trouser tearing was taking place. The man whose trousers were most ripped, and whose legs were bleeding, was beating at the blind old mutt with a copy of *Power Drill Monthly* in a desperate attempt to save his remaining limbs.

Clive added another pint and a bag of crisps to his order and directed the scantily clad barmaid to take them over to the battered and torn DS Gerhardie. Discovered undercover once again, DS Gerhardie glumly raised his drink in thanks, although he felt like smashing it on the table and using it to cut the bastard dog's bollocks off.

'How come you were doing deals with Soleil? He's hundreds of miles away.'

'You spend so much time dwelling on the inner self

you've lost touch with the wider world out there, bruv. The Brahmin Rajneesh has his own web site, as does, or did, Soleil. Then there's the phone, fax, e-mail and so on.'

'"And so on" meaning my Celica GT?'

'Sometimes I need to get out and press the flesh. Face to face is always the most beneficial in business dealings. But I don't have to tell you, you and Julia know all about that, don't you?'

Clive turned away from his brother and sipped his drink. 'Go home and leave me alone,' he said.

The next morning Clive woke early knowing he had a date with destiny. His sureness wasn't due to a premonition – since he'd started sleeping with Julia his nights had become matt black, devoid of anything that might lighten the gloom – but he still woke up knowing what it was he had to do. He slid out of bed so carefully that even the most sensitive rocker alarm wouldn't have detected it.

'Going out, lover?' The alarm industry would have done well to employ Julia as technical adviser.

'I've got some business to attend to.'

'You've got some business here if you want it.'

Clive turned back and saw the expanse of well-toned flesh that Julia flashed at him in what was supposed to be a provocative manner. It merely helped deflate his early-morning full-bladder erection, which had up until that moment always proved immune to any such reduction. He dressed in the safety of the locked bathroom and noticed with some satisfaction that he had lost three-quarters of a stone since the whole nightmare of his mother, Christopher, Grace and Julia had begun.

'Bugger Slim-Fast, get yourself a disastrous personal life and lose pounds,' he said to the bathroom mirror in the manner of a celebrity endorsement.

He crept down the stairs so as not to disturb the rest of his family and let himself out into the first fine day of the year. The sun was shining on the damp streets and, despite the cold wind from the Urals that always made a beeline across the flat lands of northern Europe directly for Halcyon Terrace, he could feel spring was somewhere out there, waiting to make its entrance before an adoring public.

Clive would have jumped into his car and set out on his date with destiny but for one small detail. His smart red sports car was not there, again. Christopher had borrowed it. In fact, though Clive didn't know it at that moment, Christopher had borrowed his car on a permanent basis and he would never see it again. Clive did a hopping, jigging dance that summed up the ultimate futility of the human condition and the fact that he would love to kick his brother's arse, should it ever again come within reach of his cultured right foot. Clive's last dribble of good fortune had just evaporated away into the ether and the only choice he had was a terrible one. He would have to get the bus.

'One pound twenty, please,' the bus driver insisted in much the same way a high-court judge handed out a mandatory life sentence. Clive paid up for the privilege of sitting on a dirty, stuffy bus. In fact he overpaid for the privilege, as he let two pound coins drop into what turned out to be a black hole of a coin slot.

'No change given,' the bus driver said pointing at the sign behind him which said exactly the same thing. He didn't bother to keep the king-size packet of glee out of his tone.

'What?'

'This machine don't give change, pal. Take your ticket and sit down.'

The bus driver was the consummate professional. He could thrash the gears so hard the noise made people's ears bleed, brake so hard the high-pitched screech rendered all the dogs on the route irreversible psychological damage, and he had graduated with BA honours as A Sullen Git, minoring in Sadistic Tendencies. Clive remembered what he hated about buses. Everything. He hated everything about buses from the miserable sod of a driver to the ever-present aroma of full ashtrays.

He tumbled down the aisle as the driver crashed from first to third gear in two seconds without bothering to reduce the revs, and fell into a seat in front of a man who kept blowing smoke over his shoulder for no obvious reason other than to piss him off. On the window next to him the exhaled mixture of barbecue-tarred lung and carbon dioxide had steamed up the glass around the red triangle that said 'Positively No Smoking'.

'Owyoubastard,' Clive yelled as he was painfully reminded of another reason why he hated buses. The seats had so little leg-room that even a short-arse like him got bruised knees and debilitating leg cramps from a four-stop journey.

'Give me a fag,' he demanded of the man behind

him, anger at the pain in his leg helping him find a hith-
erto unknown level of assertiveness. The man was so
surprised at his insistence that he gave him one (and one
for later) and lit it for him without argument. Clive let
the smoke sink into his lungs and do its worst while he
enjoyed watching the world go by, or at least the bit of
the world on the way to Monica's, where Grace was in
hiding with Dan and Hattie.

An unwelcome surprise awaited him, as Monica's open
book of a face revealed all.

'Clive, what are you doing here?' she said, quickly
filling the doorway with her slight frame to establish her
'You-shall-not-pass' intentions. Clive immediately knew
this action was a double-bluff; she appeared to be blocking the door to stop him getting access to his wife and
children, but she was actually blocking the way to an
empty house.

'Where are they?' he asked.

'Not here,' Monica said, hoping it would sound as if
she was lying, and that they were there, hiding upstairs
safe in the knowledge that Monica's six-stone body and
pipe-cleaner limbs would bar the way to all intruders.

'I can see that by the look on your face. Where is
she?'

Monica started to blush. She was no good at lying, it
was one thing about her that Clive found likeable. It was
also the only thing he liked about her. Everything else
about her was whining, selfish and miserable. Monica
hated all men especially her girlfriends' men, mainly
because they weren't her men. Even Grace struggled to
tolerate her, finding it impossible to see her as anything

more than a college acquaintance who could, on desperate occasions, be promoted to handy baby-sitter. In fact Clive had been surprised by his wife's choice of bolt-hole but he guessed any port would do in a storm, which made Monica the Harwich Container Port of irritating friends.

Monica wiped her reddened forehead and tried to look calm. 'I don't know.'

Oh yes you do! her face screamed back like a panto audience baying for the attention of the fairy.

Clive studied her face for more clues. Her twitching nose suggested there was something about this whole Grace situation that he wouldn't like. Another man maybe? The wrinkles around her eyes swirled like ripples in a muddy puddle. Someone from college maybe? She bit her bottom lip as if to stop the truth pouring forth from her mouth. Her personal tutor maybe?

'Ben bloody Hopkins!' he shouted.

Her whole head seemed to implode, her skin was being sucked in as if it were quicksand. Shit, how did you guess? it said. She had confessed all without saying a word.

'There's three quid, keep the fucking change.' Clive slammed the money on the little shelf that separated the bus driver from the great Bradworth public, took a swig from a nearly empty bottle of Jack Daniel's and marched down the aisle. Three teenage girls, who wore a frightening amount of blue make-up, started giggling. He stopped and walked back to where they were nudging one another.

'Give me a fag or else.'

The teenage girl nearest to him broke off from nudging her friends and passed him her packet of Silk Cut without a word.

'And you,' he said waving a finger under the nose of one of her blue-faced friends, 'light me.' Then he gave them a ten-pound note.

'Enjoy it, because one day, when you finally get all the money you ever wanted, you'll have no one to spend it on because they will have betrayed you.'

He sat at the back of the bus smoking his second cigarette of the day, and his third cigarette since he had given up fourteen years before.

Up in front the teenage girls held the ten-pound note reverentially. What time does McDonald's open? was the thought that passed none of their ultramarine lips.

Clive was angry but he was also ashamed about what he had done at Monica's. He had never liked Monica but that was no excuse for pushing past her, bounding upstairs to her bedroom, searching her dresser drawer for an address book, and when he found it, hidden amongst underwear and a sizeable collection of battery-operated sexual toys, tearing it to pieces to get Ben Hopkins' address. Pausing only to tell her that she was an uptight cow who would never get a boyfriend while she insisted on wearing a pearl necklace with jeans, he left for Ben Hopkins' house.

He didn't know why he was going there, because if Grace saw him like this then his pain and humiliation would surely get worse. In his muddled mind Ben Hopkins evened the score, balancing out his indiscretions with Julia. In this Jack Daniel's-driven euphoria

Clive began to quite like Ben. Good old Ben. He was almost a mate. As the bus rocked him back and forth into drunken daydream land he even began to imagine scenes where they all went on holiday together, or shared a table at one of Clive's dinner parties, or stood on the terraces at a football match thumping one another affectionately on the arm, and all the time warmly reminiscing about when they had been rivals in love. Of course none of this could begin until he had gone round and beaten the pug-ugly smart-arse intellectual to a pulp.

The house looked unprepossessing from the outside. It was new, built on an upmarket executive estate. The surrounding lawn was open plan and offered no resistance to his march up to the front door. He hit it hard enough to put his fist through anything thin or substandard, but this was the Versailles Show Home at the top end of the European Palace Range, and the genuine oak door altered Clive's knuckles permanently.

Clive was ready for violence, indeed he would have welcomed it. He expected a real sticks 'n' stones trade-off. What he didn't expect, what he wasn't ready for was Ben Hopkins being calm, rational and, God help him, kind.

'Hello there, Clive, Monica said you might be calling. Come in, I've just brewed up.'

Clive found himself padding in meekly, noting the quality of the hall carpet and the tasteful prints on the walls in the sitting room. He also noticed with some pride the felt pen marks on the wall behind the sofa, done in the unmistakable hand of Dan and Hattie.

'Please sit down,' Ben suggested quietly. He had studied the Management of Aggression well; an angry man who is seated is rarely a violent man. Ben sat down as well, a seated man rarely being a good target for a punching man.

'I know this must be hard for you, losing your wife and family.' He knew a lot about Clive, it seemed. He knew this was a difficult time for him, he knew how confused he must feel, and how easily the thing with Julia must have happened. He knew Clive must feel hurt, and he was sorry about that.

'I don't make a habit of sleeping with my students, you know,' Ben said in an attempt at an explanation.

Clive looked up. 'You're sleeping with her?' In his mind he made a mental note to cancel the holiday, rescind the invite to his dinner party and start supporting another football team. This bastard had slept with his wife and he could never forgive him.

That was how it started. He repeated the phrase about bastards sleeping with wives several dozen times. Ben merely stated that this was no big deal given that Clive had slept with an ex-girlfriend within days of Grace moving out. Clive leaped to his feet, keen to get on with the gratuitous violence, which was when Ben dropped his Management of Aggression techniques in favour of something more practical. He reached behind his carefully placed chair and pulled out a well-kept, high-quality, stainless-steel spade, which he had brought in from the shed the moment he had got off the phone from Monica.

'Get out or I'll double dig your face,' he said in a calming monotone.

Clive stood defeated on the Chinese rug, which had additional Ribena stains courtesy of Dan and Hattie. Defeated emotionally, sexually and now physically.

'You'd better look after my children,' he said, managing a glimpse of dignity before he went out, slamming the front door behind him and, having waited a few moments to make sure Ben wasn't following, pissed through the letter box.

Physically satisfied at least, Clive pulled his zip up, turned around and forced a quick smile at Grace, Dan and Hattie, who were on the front drive and had witnessed his performance with interest.

'Hello, love,' he said, in a badly faked fancy-seeing-you-here-do-you-get-out-this-way-often tone. 'Fancy seeing you here.'

'Mummy, Daddy done a wee wee,' Hattie pointed out helpfully.

'Through the door,' Dan added, a note of deep admiration in his voice.

'Funny he should choose our door, eh, kids?' Grace said, dryer than a James Bond Martini.

'How are you?' Clive asked, not being specific about who he was directing the question to.

'We're fine, Daddy. We've got a new Daddy. He's called Daddy Ben and he makes Mummy play bears in the morning,' Hattie said happily.

'Bears?'

'Yes,' Dan joined in eagerly. 'Every morning we hear Mummy playing bears with Daddy Ben. "Oh Oh Oh," she says, "Yes Yes Yes," she says.'

'Then she goes "Grrrowlll". She sounds ever so funny.'

'And that's playing bears, is it?' He looked straight at Grace this time.

'A girl's got to fill her day somehow,' Grace said. She was smiling sheepishly, or was it bearishly?

'Are you coming home?' Clive asked with a similar mutton look around his chops.

'Yes, can we, Mummmeeee?' both children demanded.

'*Live and Kicking* is on. I'll be along in a minute.'

'Great, *Live and Kicking*,' Dan said to Hattie and they set off to race for control of the TV remote.

Clive and Grace walked until they were out of earshot of the executive houses and their executive occupants. They sat on a green iron-work bench surrounded by shrubs that had been carefully placed as a 'feature', which meant that it wasn't intended for sitting on. Clive worked this out pretty quickly. The seat cut into the back of his legs and gave him pins and needles within thirty seconds while the backrest banged into his vertebrae with the ferocity of a wildly swung cricket bat. They sat for several painful minutes in silence, the bench causing their bloodstreams and nervous systems to adopt an unofficial go-slow . Clive was the first one to crack.

'Come back, Grace.'

She looked at him as if it was the only thing in the world she wanted to do.

'That's the last thing in the world I want to do.'

'This Ben thing. Has it been going on long?'

'God no. He was just there when you weren't, you know. When I needed someone to be on my side. I looked around and you had your barmy family and were fucking the world's most hideous woman. What else could I do? Ben is very kind, very sensitive and quite a good fuck too, all things considered.'

'What things?' Clive asked, hoping the chink of light he saw at the end of the tunnel wasn't the 3.45 from Kings Cross.

'Things like the fact that he's a university tutor, which means he's about as much fun as a wet afternoon in Wigan . . .' she stopped and gave this a bit more thought before adding, 'on half-day closing.'

'So come back. We can work this out.' Clive was already looking forward to the entirely new range of sulks he could try out, ranging from the 'you-moved-in-with-another-man' seven-day silence to the fully extended one-month-long 'you played bears with another man every morning'.

'No. Your family make the Borgias look like the Von Trapps. Your mother invites your ex-girlfriend over, she makes false allegations to Social Services about our children. She is one hundred per cent pure evil.'

'Actually those are some of the nicer things she's done.' Clive saw the questioning look on Grace's features. 'I'll tell you later. Meanwhile I'm going to sort it all out. That's a promise.'

'Fine. You sort them out; meanwhile I'll get on with the rest of my life.'

'But I want you back when it's done.' He would have gone on one knee at this point to dramatically underline his commitment to her but he could no longer feel his knees and he wasn't sure they would bear his weight.

'Whatever you do, I'll be gone. It's time to move on. I'll be in touch about a settlement soon.'

'A settlement?'

'Fair access to the kids, fifty per cent of your business. That sort of stuff. Don't panic, I'm not greedy.'

'I know,' Clive said. 'Just one slight problem. There isn't a lot left to take fifty per cent of. Durkin's taken the lot. You see there's this hitman that I kind of got involved with.' Clive explained the whole sorry mess, ending with Durkin's blackmail. 'I've lost everything. You, the kids, my business. It makes the average nightmare look like an enjoyable wet dream.'

'You should know about them.' Grace gave him a severe look. 'So Durkin's taking the bread out of my children's mouths, is he? Phoney bastard.' Grace was screwing up her eyes and staring menacingly into the far distance.

'Don't do anything rash,' Clive begged.

'Would I?' she asked, sounding like the Big Bad Wolf applying for a job in childcare.

She stood up and began to bang her foot on the ground to try to rid it of cramp. Clive took the opportunity to do the same. They both stood in the shrubbery jumping up and down on dead legs.

'Grace?' Clive pleaded for the last time, hopping as he did so.

'Don't ask me to come back again, Clive. I just can't,' Grace said, jumping down hard on her throbbing leg. With that she turned and hobbled away, back into the heart of executive darkness.

'Don't Walk Away' ran through Clive's mind. Several different songs sharing the same title, by the Four Tops, Electric Light Orchestra, Pat Benatar and Toni Childs. Whatever the individual quality of these songs, any one of them could have provided the perfect soundtrack for the tears rolling down his cheeks. When he could stand the sadness no longer and could at least stand up straight, he hopped off in the opposite direction to Grace. His tears were quickly jolted aside as he triple jumped back into town.

Clive walked around the not-so-clean streets of Bradworth for the rest of the day. The city was enjoying the first kiss of sun; jackets were discarded, shirt sleeves were rolled up and forearms appeared everywhere. Clive was oblivious to all this thanks to his sadness and Jack Daniel's. He didn't even pay much attention to the first mini-skirts of the year, but wandered around in a self-absorbed daze, not connecting with anyone or anything.

It got dark and Clive bought a pink paper to look up the football results, something he only ever did when he was in town on a Saturday evening, which was hardly ever. He was sure the last time this had happened Accrington Stanley had been challenging for major honours. He read his paper in a cheap coffee house, which smelt far too much like a bus for comfort. He went to the phone booth next to the counter, with its fat sound-proofed walls of padded plastic leatherette, and rang home.

'Yes?'

'It's me.'

'Oh.' Christopher sounded disappointed.

'Where's my fucking car?'

'Funny you should ask that. It's a bit of a long story.' Meaning Christopher needed a bit of a long time to think up an excuse.

'Don't bother. Listen, I want you to meet me for a drink, tonight.'

'Bit awkward that, bruv.'

'I'm paying.'

'Maybe a swift half.'

'I'll meet you in Little Italy, at a place called the Muscle Club. Do you know it?' There was a guilty silence.

'Of course not.'

Against his better judgement, and only because taxis wouldn't venture into the no-go area of Little Italy at night, Clive found himself on another smelly bus an hour later. The bus took the same route he had taken on that fateful day when he obeyed Noilly's instructions and headed for Queen's Road. In the area of deserted mills and warehouses lurked the Muscle Club and Clive's destiny, if not the destiny of the whole Wrigley family.

He got off the bus and wandered down the first dark alleyway he came to. Once he was out of the glare of the orange street-lamps he began to feel very alone and vulnerable, which was exactly the way the Muscle Club regulars wanted people who had wandered into their territory unbidden to feel.

It was a typical Saturday night in the Anabolic Arms, a few shadowy figures laying low in the comfort of their natural habitat, nonchalantly served by a barman with a long-term memory of about eight seconds. Christopher was already there when Clive arrived.

'What do you want to drink?'

'I think I might have a Mouton Cadet spritzer,' Christopher said seriously.

'I don't think so,' Clive laughed, jabbing his thumb behind him at the bar, which stocked beer, spirits and a bottle of Liebfraumilch that had been opened on Christmas Eve 1991. 'But you already knew that, didn't you?'

'What?'

Clive looked at his brother. In the darkened room he looked strangely pale and was clearly uncomfortable with their surroundings. He was frightened of being discovered. 'You already knew because you've been here before. How did you work it out?'

Christopher looked as if he was about to try and put another story together, but then it occurred to him that it might be too much bother, so he sighed and broke the habit of a lifetime by telling the truth.

'That day in your office, I did see Noilly. I've hung out with enough bad lots to know a really rotten guy when I see one. I decided to join in with your rendezvous, in secret. I saw him shoot Durkin. I figured it could be useful to know a man like that so I followed him afterwards. He came back here. I thought it was dead cool that you were involved in all that.'

'But I wasn't. That's the point. It was all a silly mistake.'

'Whatever. I didn't intend to do anything about it, just store the information away for a rainy day . . .'

'But?' The But question if used in the right circumstances was almost as effective a counselling tool as the And question. So it proved.

'But I kind of mentioned it to Ma.'

'Mother? What the hell has she got to do with this . . . Oh no.' Clive had suddenly seen the whole thing mapped out before him, and his memory was already beginning to navigate through it with the ruthlessness of Columbus.

Euterpe had seen it as a perfect solution to making her final wish for Disney come true. She had told Christopher to go back to the Anabolic Arms and commission Noilly to kill Soleil. Christopher had argued, mainly because Soleil was showing interest in importing Liebfraumilch from the Bluebell Valley, but he had done what Euterpe had asked because it wasn't in his genes to disagree with her.

'She had Soleil killed,' Clive repeated the explanation matter of factly.

'To be fair it was me who did the deal,' Christopher said, seeking to place credit where he felt it was due.

'Come outside for a minute,' Clive asked in a friendly manner. 'There's something else you should know.'

Christopher walked behind Clive as they made their way out on to the dark street, wondering excitedly what it was all about.

'What is it?' he asked when they got outside.

'First. Where's my car?'

'I've sold it. Don't worry, bruv, it's given me the collateral to set up a deal and pretty soon you'll be thanking me.'

'Who did you sell it to?'

'The Brahmin Rajneesh. He fancies a nice anonymous run-about. It's the right colour too, although he's going to have the insides done out in green leather. The car's going to be shipped over to Minnesota next week along with everything else from Nostrum Hall.' Christopher blithely began rummaging inside his coat pocket and then pulled out a paper that Clive had last seen in the private, locked cabinet in his study at home. 'In the meantime I need you to sign this.'

Clive signed the proffered DVLA log book without comment, handed it back to Christopher and then sweetly knocked his brother's teeth so far down his throat he could have used his arse as a bottle opener. Christopher lay in the gutter spitting out the bits of teeth he didn't think he'd need again.

'You should be more grateful. I've a good mind not to tell you the rest.' Christopher regretted this rash statement as soon as it left his swollen, bleeding lips.

'The rest of what?' Clive stood over his brother, fists poised and ready for round two.

'The rest of the contract with Noilly. After Grace ran out with the kids Ma wanted to make sure she never came back. She told me to pay Noilly to remove them.'

Seeing that honour had not, in fact, been fully satisfied, Clive gave the prone figure of Christopher a right good kicking until he heard the gratifying sound of blood being vomited down the nearest drain cover. He then stopped, wiped the blood and vomit from his shoes and on to Christopher's coat sleeves (a Paul Smith wool coat he had stolen from Clive) and went back inside the Muscle Club.

It was over an hour before he saw Noilly arrive, still sweating from a workout in the gym. He went and sat in a dark corner on the other side of the room from Clive. Clive waited a few moments and then followed the instructions, word for misspelt word, on the business card Noilly had given him.

The Anabolic Arms had a state-of-the-art switch box that cut in on the radio whenever the jukebox was activated, which wasn't very often. But it did its job efficiently now and allowed B7 to shut up 100 Best-Loved Weepy Favourites. To Clive's surprise B7 was 'Mother Love'. His mood deepened at yet another ominous coincidence. He remembered that it was Noilly's favourite song, acting as a kind of sentimental cipher for his own long-lost mother, but that it was also the introduction to his bloody business activities was more chilling than an early-morning dip in the Baltic.

Clive sipped his lager and pretended to be interested in the details of the song typed on the ancient square of card that was stuffed in a small frame under the perspex lid of the jukebox. He noted with his usual inescapable pedantry that the song was wrongly ascribed to the pen of E. Griffin (Euterpe grabbing the glory – as well as the royalties – again), when he knew that it was actually written by Gerry 'Gerbil' Williams.

> *The loving way you kissed and pleased us,*
> *We're sad you're gone but happy for Jesus.*
> *You've got your wings and learned to fly,*
> *God above is one lucky guy.*

Clive became aware of something standing close behind him; something big, strong and Noilly shaped. He turned around very slowly.

'Hello, Noilly.' The words were still rolling around in his dry mouth as a big, hard-skinned hand clamped across his lips and locked them tighter than Tutankhamun's tomb, sealing his breath in as it did so.

'ABSOLUTELY NO FUCKING NAMES.' Noilly whispered in a way that was calm, quiet and yet had capital-letter impact. This wasn't Noilly. Not the big, shambling, almost-shy lump that came to Clive's office and poured out his heart and cried out his eyes over every bad thing that had ever happened to him. This was a different Noilly. It was Noilly on duty, Noilly at work, Noilly the killing machine. On the top ten chart of total bastards he was Number One, with a bullet. Noilly as a bad person who wanted penitence made Clive feel uncomfortable, so it made sense that Noilly as mad, unrepentant widow-maker should have scared him shitless. But the area of his temporal lobe that controlled the scared-shitless bit had apparently developed a malfunction.

'Don't threaten me, Noilly Upchurch.' Clive stated his client's name slowly, deliberately and quite loudly.

'Sorry.' Noilly couldn't remember ever having used that word before. It felt very strange.

'Noilly,' Clive said his name almost warmly, as if greeting a very old and dear friend. 'You've come to feel like one of the family, but that's probably because you're working for half my family and trying to kill the other half.' Clive then did something quite extraordinary. He slapped Noilly around the face. He expected that such an action would bring instant reprisals of the sort that would leave him still and serene on a marble slab. But the reprisals didn't follow. Instead Noilly turned back to the jukebox and put B7 on again.

'I do the job I'm paid to do, no questions.'

'You were going to kill my wife and kids?'

'No.'

'Don't lie, my brother has, with gentle persuasion, told me everything.'

'You said I was going to kill your wife and kids and I'm saying that's wrong.'

Clive softened. There was some humanity in this monster after all.

'I *am* going to. The deal still stands. Sorry.' Noilly said the 'S' word again and it felt even odder this time, like he actually meant it.

Clive listened to the rest of the song and remembered his time as a juvenile pop star. Long days in a coach, hard nights working on stage, never a break, never any toys or regular school or fun of any kind. All the time his mother driving them on, manipulating them, forcing them to be the perfect family. He started to cry at the same moment as Noilly.

'The bit about the angel's wings always gets me too,' Noilly said.

'What if I paid you to kill the person who hired you to kill my wife. What would that cost?'

'A grand. In cash.'

'And then you'd call off the hit on my wife?'

'No. That goes ahead whatever happens. People who hire me have to know they can trust me to finish the job. Otherwise people would pay me not to kill people. It'd be anarchy.'

'Your sense of order is very reassuring.'

'Do you still want me to kill the person who hired me?'

'A grand?' Whichever way Clive looked at it, at that moment it seemed like value for money.

*

He crashed through his front door and into the darkness of the hall. He made noisy progress through the house without bothering to put on the lights. He wanted her to hear him coming. Coming to get her. He stomped up the stairs to the room where Euterpe slept. He kicked open the door, went in and grabbed her.

'What are you doing?' she screamed, fighting to remove his hands from her throat.

'Is it true? Did you get Christopher to pay a hitman to kill Grace and my children?'

'Is that all this is about? I thought something important must have happened.' Euterpe's voice was calm despite the threat of imminent strangulation.

'You don't deny it then?'

'No. I'm proud of it.'

'What about killing Soleil?' Clive's voice was imitating the high-pitched whine of a formula one Grand Prix.

'It was necessary. I had to overcome the inconvenience of Disney always doing what that religious nutter told her.'

'Inconvenience? We're talking murder here, you evil cow.' Clive took his hands from around her throat, sat back on the bed and looked at her from a safe distance.

'We're talking about losers who don't deserve a second chance. All my life they've been getting in my way and ruining things. Like Gerry the Gerbil fucking up my big chance with The Family Affair.'

'Gerry? Don't tell me you had him killed.'

'Of course not. But when he tied us down to a rubbish record deal I had to do something.'

'What exactly did you do?' Clive asked, his ears were tuned like CNN satellite dishes, sensing more bad news.

'I took him out on the town. The silly bastard always liked to show off by drinking too much. "I always drive better when I've had a few," he said. Not after three bottles of sweet sherry he didn't. Bang! Straight into a tree, stupid twat.'

Clive would need to put in an order for more horror and revulsion as all the reserves in his stomach had been used up.

'Don't look so disapproving. If I hadn't we'd never have got out of that contractual mess, you'd still be on stage now, wearing shorts, lisping and pretending you were cute. I was lucky to walk away with as much as I did.'

Clive's mouth was impersonating the entrance to the Mersey Tunnel as Euterpe's boasting confessional took its toll.

'I don't believe I'm hearing this. Is there anyone else I should know about? Thank God Father killed himself before you could get to him.'

'Oh yes, your father. He always got so drowsy on those anti-depressants. Sleep through anything. Even a car engine running at full revs in a locked garage.'

'This is definitely not happening.' Clive gave himself one of Euterpe's Coco Chanel pinches on his forearm to test if this could actually be the arse end of a bad acid trip. Sadly it wasn't.

'The police were pig thick in those days, too. Never thought to look beyond the obvious.'

'What have I done to deserve this?' Clive asked himself. The obsessed librarian in his head was already researching a million pointless details about the late-1980s anthem of the same name by gay icons the Pet Shop Boys and Dusty Springfield. Another song by the Pet Shop Boys sprang into his mind, the librarian cross-referencing for topicality. 'It's A Sin'. And then some.

Fourteen

The Listen To You office was normally very quiet on a Sunday, it being a day when therapists of all shades and styles preferred to stay at home and ignore the problems of the world. But this Sunday was different because Amen Durkin was making himself at home in his new surroundings. As excited as a child with a new toy he was full of ideas for improvement.

'The sooner I close this place down and put everyone out on to the street the better.' He sat back in Clive's prized leather chair and the quality hide gave a squeak of pain. Reassured he closed his eyes and began to dream of future empires. His eyes were still closed when he heard the front door being unlocked. He opened one eye and listened intently, following the progress of the intruder as they made their way quietly through reception to the outer door of Clive's – now his – office. The door opened slowly.

'You came.'

'You sound surprised.'

'A pleasant surprise, my dear. As it was when you rang and asked to meet.'

'Why here?'

'I thought this place would be more . . . apt.' Durkin chuckled as he looked around his new kingdom.

'It's this place I need to see you about. Half of it's mine.'

'I'm sorry, Grace my dear, but my deal was with your husband. If there's any marital sharing to be done, that's his problem.'

'He says you got it for next to nothing.' Grace fixed Durkin with a scrutinising look, checking for the faintest hint of deceit in his reply.

'I negotiated a very reasonable settlement.'

'Reasonable for you.'

Durkin gave a slight nod, acknowledging this fact.

'I could be persuaded to re-open negotiations.' He gave Grace his best I-may-be-old-but-I've-still-got-some-booty-to-shake look.

'You sad, dirty old bastard,' Grace said, astutely.

'Oh come on. You'd get your rightful share and have a nice time into the bargain. What else is there to do on a dull Sunday morning?'

Grace looked around at the room full of phallic trinkets that she knew so well. She thought for an all too brief moment and then shrugged.

'All right. Where do you want me?'

The black leather chair gave a farting squeak as Durkin slid down it in surprise.

'What, really?'

'Sure. Name your fantasy. Of course the more perverted it is the bigger the percentage share I'll want in return.'

'Give me a minute to think.' Durkin sat up and tried to find some saliva to rinse out his bone-dry mouth. This was perfect. He had beaten his rival in love as well as business. He looked at the big desk in front of him; that was it. He was going to take his rival's wife away, even if it was just for a few sweaty minutes, on the altar of Clive's business world.

'The desk. I want you on the desk.' He was panting now.

Grace nodded and gave her tight-lipped smile. She opened her coat and lifted the black and white checked skirt to reveal the upper echelons of black woolly tights.

Durkin got up and walked round to the front of the desk. By the time he got there Grace had rolled the thick tights down to her knees and he could see her big black knickers with 'Sloggi' writ large across the waistband. They reminded him of the shorts on a heavyweight boxer. It was an image he unwisely chose to ignore.

'You are one sexy lady. I had no idea you could be so . . .'

'What?' Grace asked as she pulled Durkin's leather belt from around his waistband and stood back to avoid the subsequent avalanche of fat that was suddenly freed from captivity.

'So gentle. You always struck me as, forgive this crudity, my dear, a vindictive little bitch.'

'Why, thank you, kind sir,' Grace said in her cutest voice before sinking to her knees to help ease Durkin's trousers on their journey south.

'Oh my goodness.'

Trousers and pants successfully lowered Grace stood up and twisted herself and Durkin around in one movement so that she was sitting on the desk and he was between her thighs, ready for the fun to begin.

Clive had an appointment with a safe. More importantly he had a date with over one thousand pounds in cash that was inside it. He went to let himself into the Listen To You offices only to find the door already unlocked.

'Durkin. I forgot about him.' He hadn't really forgotten about Durkin, ripping off his business and blackmailing him into a partnership that was going to leave him with less than nothing, but he had managed to block him from his mind thanks to the ongoing drama of his mother. He crept into reception and could hear muffled voices coming from his office. He slipped behind Larry's desk where the safe was kept. With luck Durkin wouldn't have had time to check it yet. He fed in the code (Freud's birthday, which psychologists always used for the important things, such as lock combinations, pin codes and their weekly lottery numbers) and opened the metal door. It was still full of cash. For a brief moment at least he had got one over on Durkin.

In the background the voices had changed. They were

no longer exchanging words but grunts and moans. Clive looked at the calendar above Larry's desk. It was official Pamela Anderson merchandise and the pose, wet swimsuit, pout and big tits, appeared to have little to do with the month of March.

'Unless it's the March wind that's making her nipples stick out like chapel hat pegs,' Clive exclaimed, quietly. He checked the day, Sunday. The seductive moaning couldn't be Marilyn Barker doing her Exploration of Self exercises, but if it was he was going to send off an application form; it sounded a lot of fun. He smiled to himself and went quietly over to the door. The couple in the office were making so much noise he could have stomped over in steel toe-capped boots and they wouldn't have heard him. He pushed the door open far enough to see Durkin's fat hairy arse, which he noticed had the same silver hairs swept across it as on his head. With the same nap too. Wrapped around Durkin's fat arse was a pair of rather fine legs, tangled up in what looked like a pair of badly stretched woolly tights. Legs that were somehow familiar. Clive bit his lip until it bled and crept quietly away.

'Oh my goodness,' Durkin said again, mainly to take his mind off the possibility, indeed probability, of premature ejaculation. He felt Grace's hands lifting his shirt and massaging his bare flesh. Her long fingers were kneading down to his buttocks and seemingly playing noughts and crosses on them with her talon-like fingernails. He tried to remember the Leeds United team that played in the disastrous Coca-Cola Cup final of 1996, which he had watched from an exclusive box thanks to a computer magnate who was addicted to wetting himself for pleasure. He had only got as far as the back four when those nails pricked him mercilessly back into hyper consciousness.

'Oh my . . .' Durkin didn't get to the end of the sentence as the pain of an extremely sharp nail digging deeply into his right buttock took his mind off all things sexual much more effectively than the worst cup-final performance in history.

'What the hell are you doing?' He pushed Grace away. As she stood back from him she raised her right hand, as if she was going to swear allegiance to some country other than his.

'What's that?' he asked, pointing fearfully at the syringe in her hand.

'Biata Dama.'

'Pardon?'

'Polish vodka. It means 'white lady'. Quite apt that. Oh, and it's ninety per cent proof. There's about enough in here for a three-day hangover, or rather there was. It's now in your blood stream. Whoosh!' Grace opened her eyes wide as she spoke.

'Whaaa . . .?' Durkin could feel the rush starting. A rush that would carry on and on and wouldn't stop until he was once more in a skip with a hangover, a burial mound of dead animals and a dangerously overspent Visa account.

'You remember I used to be a nurse? Years ago now. But I can still do intravenous injections. You draw a cross on the right buttock and stick the needle in the upper part of the north-east quadrant. Or is it North West?'

'What about infection?'

'Where you're going that's the least of your worries.'

'Why me?' Durkin sat back on the desk, defeated, then quickly stood up prompted by the still-smarting wound.

'Clive helped save you last time and what did you do? You took all the credit. You took his business and you tried to take me.' Grace popped the syringe back in her handbag, rolled her woolly tights back up, and smoothed down her skirt. 'Well this time he's not around, so let's see how you get on alone. I'll leave you to enjoy your aperitif. Bye bye.' She smiled and left the office.

Durkin tried to remain standing while the room started to spin gently around his head. He felt like the spindle of a spinning top. After a few seconds he realised he couldn't stay upright much longer and made for the black leather couch. He lay on the side that hadn't been injected, closed his eyes and tried to remember the whereabouts of the nearest all-day casino with a decent bar.

Clive had run for longer than he remembered ever running before. A man with shit for lungs like Clive rarely ran to the front door, let alone any further, but he had managed a very creditable two miles in his desire to be far away from the scene of his worst nightmare. A nightmare that his perfect memory was going to torture him with for ever and ever, Amen.

That night Clive went back to the Anabolic Arms. He tried to look nonchalant as the underlying scent of stale gymnasium stuck like a wishbone in the back of his throat. He ordered a bottle of lager from the barman and didn't complain when he sipped it and found it was luke-warm. He had already tried to make small talk and found that even the smallest of words were far too big for the barman to grapple with.

Clive recognised the shiny domed forehead signalling to him from a dark cubicle. He didn't acknowledge Noilly; he knew that wasn't how it was done. To B7 or not to B7. As Shakespearean tragedies go there was no option really. B7 it was.

This was the moment of truth, although perhaps 'moment of deceit' would have been a more apposite term. There were plenty of people in Clive's firmament that he would gladly see taught a lesson, Durkin for example, but there was only one person who resolutely dominated his night sky and who he wished would disappear over the horizon for ever. His mother. Clive played with the word, trying to change the intonation so that it didn't come out sounding like an indictment of his own wickedness. But play as he liked, the word 'Mother' could come out only one way.

'This is like that thing,' he said, for want of saying the one thing he had come to say.

'What thing?' Noilly asked.

'That thing you find on the road to Damascus.'

'A Little Chef?' Noilly guessed, failing to understand why Clive was laughing, albeit nervously.

'No. Not that. The other thing. A revelation. A dawning realisation. A vision of what must be done. That thing.'

'Oh that thing,' Noilly said. He would have been far

more comfortable with a roadside café. 'Isn't that three things?'

Clive decided to start again.

'It's Mother. My mother. She's behind all of this. I've got a new commission for you,' Clive said, feeling a guilty relief that the words, the desire, the festering hatred were spoken at last.

Noilly didn't blink, under the artificial ski slope of his forehead his eyes continued to burn like the core of a failing nuclear reactor. If Clive expected something from Noilly it might have been disbelief, shock, maybe even violence at the terrible suggestion he had just made. Instead what he got was business as usual.

'What's in the bag?' Noilly asked. Clive had been fiddling with a green plastic bag between his knees. He didn't say anything, he just handed the bag over. In delivering the bag to Noilly the decision had been confirmed, ratified, signed, sealed and delivered.

Noilly rummaged in the bag and took out Euterpe's Australian passport, a paper label containing Clive's address which was tied with meat string to a spare door key that Clive had spent most of Sunday scouring Yorkshire to get cut, and a bundle of twenty-pound notes with a total value of one thousand pounds. Noilly looked at each item carefully as if he was on a jury and these were exhibits for the prosecution, proving Clive's guilt, which in a way they were.

'Anything else you need to know?' Clive asked worriedly.

'Just two things.'

'Which are?' Clive prompted, uncomfortable that his ordeal wasn't over yet.

'When?' Noilly asked.

'When's good for you?' Clive sounded as if he was arranging to meet for afternoon tea.

'No, when's good for you. It's your alibi.'

'Right.' Clive thought about his alibi and told Noilly a suitable time.

'What was the second thing you needed to know?'

Noilly pointed a bitten fingernail at the address label.

'What's this say?'

'Halcyon. Halcyon Terrace. It's my address.'

Noilly nodded, satisfied with this information. Clive tried not to think how he might have pronounced it, as to do so would have set him off giggling nervously again, which could have proved terminal in the vicinity of Noilly.

'How do you feel about doing this?'

'Feel?' Noilly didn't seem to recognise the word.

'I need to know how you feel about doing this to my mother.'

'I don't feel anything. That's what I tried to tell you last night. It's not personal, it can't be. Business must be business, or it won't work. I dare say you have your reasons and even if you don't it's nothing to do with me.' Noilly's stare certainly showed no sign of disapproval, twisted madness maybe, but nothing else.

'And my wife and children?'

'I don't know where they've gone. If I find out they'll disappear again, permanently. It's my job.'

'You're a proper Paul Daniels, aren't you?'

'If you know where they are I may need to speak to

you about it later.' It was a promise and a threat, in that order.

'I don't know and right now I don't much care,' Clive said honestly.

Noilly nodded. 'I believe you.'

That night Clive indulged in some light petting with Julia. He figured that his life couldn't get any more complicated than it already was, so what the hell? It was only light petting after all. Light petting, that is, if wet, sticky and not-quite-penetrative sex counts as light. He stopped short of full penetration only because he was scared it might burst her pumped-up body and she'd spend the rest of the night flying around the room like a pricked balloon blowing raspberries. Penetration or not it wasn't a particularly pleasing experience, which was why he did it. He wanted to punish himself. He knew that sex with someone he didn't respect would be cold and loveless and ultimately unrewarding, especially if he was sober. Clive remained stone-cold sober so that every aspect of the sexual act was recorded with perfect clarity in his memory to be replayed for his discomfort in perpetuity. It was his own version of purgatory, the knowledge that he had swapped Grace, who was probably playing bears with Ben, or being taken over his desk by Durkin, for Julia. Look at it any way, it still seemed a poor deal.

He woke up and found himself in a wet patch. He knew it couldn't be from having sex with Julia as his pathetic efforts wouldn't have produced so much as a single drop of dampness. This was a wet patch that had been caused by sweat, the sort that only guilt and regret can cause. Across his mind a phrase kept repeating itself, like one of those old ticker tape-machines sending through details of the latest scoop to the waiting journalists.

'What have I done?' it read. What he had done was terrible and unforgivable. He looked at Julia, who was on her back and snoring with the contentment that only a bucket full of orgasms can inspire.

He got out of bed carefully and crept over to the window. He wrapped the curtain around his cold, naked body and looked out through the crack of glass that his robing had created. From just down the street came a noise, like a baby crying, or a child in great distress. Clive went back to the bed and gently shook one of Julia's enormous biceps. It felt like a dead pig, full of growth hormones and flavour enhancers.

'You wanna go again, mate?' she slurred, only half awake.

'What are you doing today?' he asked.

'What?' She wiped the crust of sleep that had formed like a rind over her eyes, mouth and nose. 'I was thinking of going over to Cromer to take a look at the theatre. Maybe get some ideas for the reunion show.'

'Good. Go. But don't come back, it's too dangerous. Get a job backstage or something.' Like propping up heavy scenery, he thought. Having done his duty and delivered his warning, he quickly dressed, picked up his shoes like a guilty husband in a dumb farce, and crept downstairs.

Outside he looked for the cause of the wailing and found that it was a cat in search of another cat, preferably of the opposite sex. Clive shooed it and it begrudgingly sloped off underneath a nearby car, where it intended to stay until the mad human with no shoes on buggered off. The car it had chosen for a hiding-place was a green Vauxhall Vectra.

'Clever puss,' Clive said.

DS Gerhardie was half asleep at the wheel. It wasn't a bad way to earn time and a half but he still wished he could be at home in his newly converted loft, with his wife asleep next to him while he looked out of the velux windows at the distant stars and dreamed of better things. He started when Clive tried the door handle, which was locked. DS Gerhardie looked around, anxious that he was being set upon by enemies old and new. When he saw Clive he grumbled to himself.

'What's that bugger want?' He leaned across and unlocked the door. Without further explanation Clive got in.

'Take me to the station, I've got something to tell you.'

'What?' DS Gerhardie was already looking for a catch and had no intention of falling for it, whatever it was.

'To the station, I have information.'

'Sorry, sir, it doesn't work like that. We go to the station when I have something on you.'

'Very well, take me to the station, I want to confess.'

DS Gerhardie was sure that this must be another of those disappointing dreams, like the one where it's Christmas and you've got all you desired, and then you wake up and find it's Boxing Day and all you have is a soap-on-a-rope and twenty hankies. Despite these doubts he realised he had little choice but to go along with his chief suspect. He started the car, swung it around dangerously in the confined space of Halcyon Terrace and drove through the quiet streets of Brontë Bridge. Once they were on the main trunk road he put his foot down with an unexpected lack of concern for the speed limit and headed for Bradworth Central police station, and Clive's confession.

Fifteen

The duty sergeant looked up from filling in yet another form (one recording details of the phone call he had just taken – from someone wanting Polite Pizza Delivery, a common mistake) and his attention, which had been on a life-support machine for most of the night-shift, was now stretching and yawning at the prospect of some excitement.

'If it isn't our esteemed Detective Sergeant Gerhardie, and with a villain in tow, if my eyes are not mistaken.'

'Suspect,' DS Gerhardie corrected, somewhat pompously.

'No, he's right, I'm a villain. I'm guilty as hell.' Clive was starting to enjoy riding the tidal wave of total honesty that was washing through him.

'Shut up until I get a tape in the machine and everything is rolling,' DS Gerhardie said firmly. Too many times he'd found singing canaries turned into tone-deaf fowl once they tasted the gaseous air of an interview room.

Clive shut up. He looked at the duty sergeant while DS Gerhardie signed them both in. The officer had a face that lay in the permanent shadow of early-morning stubble. On the counter was a notice that read 'Your Customer Care Officer Today is . . .' and in the blank white space had been written in permanent red felt tip 'Sgt Freemantle'. Clive looked around at the grim reception area. The dull ache in his head was the sort one got when there was nothing left in life to fuck up.

DS Gerhardie took a gentle yet Superglue-firm grip of Clive's arm and steered him towards the side door.

'This way, sir,' he said, as if Clive had a choice. 'We'll use interview room two,' he shouted at Sergeant Freemantle.

'You mean the Van Gogh Suite,' Sergeant Freemantle said without obvious irony. He then switched off his interest and went back to ticking boxes in the Self-Assessment Customer Evaluation Record. It asked questions like 'Would you describe your telephone manner with the customer as: 1) Warm 2) Cold 3) Neutral'. He had already filled in enough forms to keep him going for the next eight days of erroneous pizza orders.

Having completed the niceties of establishing that Clive didn't want legal representation, DS Gerhardie switched on the tape recorder and began. His complete change of personality took Clive by surprise.

'Clive,' he said warmly, and just in case Clive had

missed it he tossed in a friendly smile, a thing that was rarer than chocolate buttons inside a Fabergé egg, 'tell me what all this fuss is about.'

Clive was thrown, which was the whole idea. DS Gerhardie, the man with the human face, the caring copper, the competent copper; it was enough to make the most hardened villain pour out his heart. It certainly made Clive want to throw up.

'I need to use the bathroom.'

'You want a bath?' DS Gerhardie's bushy eyebrows collapsed towards each other, accentuating his complete confusion.

'No, I want to be sick.'

'Oh for fuck's sake.' It wasn't a bad effort considering. After a lifetime of being a hard, miserable bastard, it was inevitable that DS Gerhardie's attempt to be a nice guy would founder after only a short while. This being so it was quite an achievement that it had lasted a full eight seconds.

'Really I do.' Clive's mouth started to leak what looked like tinned mixed vegetables and DS Gerhardie knew it was only a matter of seconds before this tiny, hot interview room was filled with the acrid smell of vomit. He threw Clive into the adjacent toilet and listened for ten minutes to the plaintive lament down the wastepipe. Eventually Clive emerged looking as white as a sheet that had been washed in industrial-strength bleach.

'Sorry about that.'

'Can't be helped,' DS Gerhardie said, in such a way as to imply that if there was any way it could be helped, such as through unprovoked violence, then he was the man to help it. 'Can I get you anything?' he asked, intending it to be a rhetorical offer.

'A pork pie.'

'What?' DS Gerhardie was making fists in his pockets, fists that he dearly hoped would soon see some action.

'I want a pork pie.'

'You've just spent ten minutes throwing your ring up and you want a pie?' DS Gerhardie was more full of disbelief than a twelve-year-old being dragged into Selfridges and made to sit on Father Christmas's knee.

'No, not a pie, a pork pie. I haven't had one for the best part of two decades and now I want one.'

'It's . . .' DS Gerhardie looked at his watch more for reassurance than anything, 'five thirty on a Monday morning and I can't get a pork pie.'

But Clive was resolute, possibly for the first time in his life. He wanted a pork pie and he wanted it now. 'You'll get nothing out of me until I get one.'

'Jesus.' DS Gerhardie had turned a certain victory into a five–nil defeat, and even he wasn't sure how. He stormed out of the interview room.

'Make sure it's a Melton Mowbray. I can't stand those pink efforts,' Clive shouted after him.

Noilly was up early and preparing to go to work. He sat cross-legged in the middle of his small lounge. The room was completely empty except for a dated music centre and a pile of records, all of them vinyl. He had put on an album called *Mother's Day*, which had a bunch of daffodils on the cover. The album brought together every schmaltzy ballad and country-picking waffle on the subject of maternal love into one soul-destroying circle of black plastic. While it mawkishly wailed its way through side one Noilly sat cross-legged, wearing only a white waxed-paper suit, his eyes closed and his hands in his lap. He wasn't meditating or exercising, although his position did mirror a correct yogic body shape taught to him by his instructor in the Territorial Army. Instead of concentrating on a single thing, a shape or a colour, in order to reach the state of nothingness that was every devotee's nirvana, he was singing along with the record at the top of his utterly tuneless voice.

'Mother of Mine' by Neil Reid, 'Mama' by Dave Berry, 'Mama' by David Whitfield and, just to introduce a note of originality into the proceedings, 'Mama' by Connie Francis. On side two, to give a more upbeat feel to things, was 'Mama' by Genesis and 'Mama' by Kim Wilde. This bizarre, some would say excruciatingly awful collection finished with the unorthodox 'Mama Weer All Crazee Now' by Slade, which Noilly took to be the proper spelling.

On the floor in front of him was a bottle of bittersweet smelling liquid and a pad of cotton wool. Once he had finished his morning's devotions he went into the kitchen, which other than a kettle had few of the usual trappings of inhabitancy, like food or drink or crockery or furniture. He made himself a cup of black decaffeinated coffee and drank it standing up, partly because he had been told that it aided digestion and partly because his flat had no table or chairs.

Duty Sergeant Freemantle kept his head down and pretended to be filling in forms but DS Gerhardie knew he was laughing at him. They all laughed at him in this place. He was an incompetent fool who never consulted his colleagues, worked all hours, never joined in with the station gossip and was an uncomfortable reminder of what dedication to the job involved. Even if that dedication was always fruitless. As station pariah he needed only a bell to fulfil the role completely. DS Gerhardie ignored the stifled sniggers of the duty sergeant and stomped back towards the interview room.

He went into the Van Gogh Suite, as the pretentious chair of the Police Committee had insisted on renaming it, and threw the pie at Clive, who was sleeping upright in the plastic chair. He woke up just in time to stop the pie hitting him hard in the eye, employing a catch that was so good it deserved a slow-motion replay. He looked at the pastry missile.

'Melton Mowbray, too. Thanks.' Clive noticed that DS Gerhardie had the distinct aroma of bacon and eggs about him. There were some things that DS Gerhardie could do well, it was just a shade unfortunate for him that none of them had anything to do with police work.

'Had them in the canteen. Now get on with it.'

'Is there any mustard?' Clive asked, not realising he was meant to be getting on with his confession, not the pie.

When he had finished eating he rolled the wrapper up into a ball and threw it at the bin in the corner. To his surprise it went in and he had the urge to pretend to be an enthusiastic audience cheering the shot, but wisely scrapped the idea when he saw the murderous look in DS Gerhardie's eyes.

'All right, this is what I want to say. I'm caught in a circle of violence and evil. There are all sorts of terrible things happening, some have already happened, but the one you need to know about is yet to happen. Someone is trying to kill practically all my family.'

'What?' DS Gerhardie had heard the words but had been following a different plot. He had been expecting something to do with drug smuggling, or terrorism, or phials of piss. 'Who is?'

'He's this man I've been working with, who's been hired to kill my wife and children, if he can find them.'

'You've hired someone you work with to kill your wife and children?' DS Gerhardie had seen some terrible things in his career, his arrest rate for instance, but this was one of the worst.

'You're not listening to me. I didn't hire him. I just met him through my work. But he's going to kill my wife and kids if we don't stop him. If *you* don't stop him.'

'So who did hire him?'

Clive could see that DS Gerhardie was the Plods' plod. He was methodical, thorough and so slow he was going to make a stalagmite look hasty.

'My mother. She hired this hitman. I haven't an address for him but I do know where he works from. Do you want the details?' Clive handed him the Muscle Club card.

'Hold on a minute.' DS Gerhardie waved his hands and chased the card away. 'Does this have anything to do with the attack on Mr Durkin?'

Clive didn't want to admit to this, not from fear of implicating himself but because he knew it would slow DS Gerhardie's investigations further.

'Look. There's this hitman I've been counselling and

he's out there now looking for my wife and children. But I know where you can find him.'

'Where does the drug smuggling fit in to all this?'

'Christ almighty. There is no drug smuggling. My brother works in the wine trade and he was doing a test run with the refrigeration unit.' Clive saw the look on DS Gerhardie's face. 'Yes, I reckon it's all bollocks too, for what it's worth. But that's not what's important here.'

DS Gerhardie could see what was important. He had to hang on to the thread of his case, which was that Clive Wrigley was somewhere in the centre of a drug-smuggling ring. All this nonsense about hitmen was a diversionary tactic, as was the urgent confession in the middle of the night, it was a smokescreen intended to obscure whatever was going on in his shifty family.

'Stop fucking me around and tell me what you and your devious family are up to or I'll lock you up for what's left of the night.'

Noilly found Halcyon Terrace basking in a sunny break between cloud bursts. The Victorian stone face of the street was an elaborate mixture of styles originally designed to fool the occupants that they were no longer working class but had crossed that invisible divide into prosperity and were now middle class. Nowadays it had the opposite effect, disguising the fact that the occupants were solidly and successfully middle class behind a screen of rustic working-class romanticism. 'Cottage' was the word that one thought of when first seeing Halcyon Terrace. The gardens, kitchens, bedrooms, sculleries, bathrooms, all of them demanded that prefix. Cottage gardens full of well-tended yet wild flowers, cottage kitchens full of ancient cooking implements and heavy, cast-iron stoves, cottage interiors everywhere, dark and intimate, draping around the occupants like something out of a mutual wet dream conjured up by Laura Ashley and William Morris.

Noilly didn't know his prefix from his elbow, his verbs from his vertebra or his adjectives from his arsehole, so he didn't ascribe the term cottage to any of what he saw. To him they were just old houses and old houses were full of dust. Noilly hated dust; he hated dirt of any kind. Even looking at the houses in Halcyon Terrace made him want to wash his hands obsessively. The thought of going into one of them and actually touching things filled him with an itchy foreboding. He was thankful to be wearing his white paper suit, knowing that when the deed was done he could disrobe in one movement and be rid of dirt, dust and any extraneous body fluids.

He opened the green gate, which creaked in a reassuringly cottage-garden manner, and stepped through. The daffodils stood to attention in the small front garden, shyly turning away from him as he passed. He padded silently up to the front door, turned to look back to the street to see if there were any unwelcome witnesses and then, sure that he was unseen, bent down and opened the flap of the letterbox. He studied the quiet front room through this widescreen format. When he was happy that there was no one waiting in ambush he put Clive's spare key into the mortise lock and let himself into the house.

'We haven't got all day you know.' Clive looked at his watch. It was nine a.m. 'I've arranged to meet him at ten at my house. You've got to set up an ambush, organise the armed police squad, all that sort of stuff.'

DS Gerhardie had his arms folded across his barrel chest where they had lain like Christmas hams for the best part of an hour. He soaked up Clive's increasingly desperate attempts to get him to arrest Noilly. It was clear that the more Clive protested the less he was being believed.

DS Gerhardie thought about everything he'd heard in the last few hours. It was an intelligently argued explanation of events that made perfect sense, and yet it didn't quite hold true. There was something about it that wasn't right, even with his few remaining investigative instincts he knew that much. What was Wrigley hiding? What did he want? Every minute he was there being interviewed gave him a water tight alibi for any nefarious activity that might be happening. Maybe he should kick him out and see what he did.

'That's it, I've decided. You can fuck off.'

Clive sat up and rubbed at his chubby cheeks in nervous disbelief. 'What?'

'You can fuck off out of here, just as soon as I've done the paperwork.'

'But you can't. My family is in danger. They won't be safe out there with Noilly on the loose.'

'Tough, I'm not risking my career for a lying shithead like you.' DS Gerhardie felt a little guilty at using the word 'career' to describe his natural disaster of a job.

Noilly stood in the hall and absorbed every sound in the house. The cat asleep and purring on the dining-room table in the next room; the fridge juddering away in the kitchen as it obeyed its own microchips and set about defrosting itself; the rumbling of the washing machine, the big stainless-steel drum gently massaging Julia's well-soiled lingerie. Above this homely drum and bass rhythm section was the melody line of Euterpe Wrigley singing like a banshee in the shower upstairs.

He took the bottle out of his pocket and eased the top off with his teeth. It looked like he was gently kissing it. He then took out the cotton swab and set off slowly but surely up the stairs. As he moved upwards he smoothly transferred his weight from one foot to the other, a perfect counterbalance against even the faintest creak or groan of wood. In this way he reached the top of the stairs without making a single sound.

He held the cotton in his hand and filled it with the contents of the bottle. The chloroform odour drifted back into his face and irritated his nostrils.

Satisfied that his equipment was properly primed he continued his journey along the landing to the bathroom, the door of which was slightly ajar. It was a curious fact he'd noted during his career that people invariably relaxed their approach to personal security when alone in their house. They would take baths, empty their bowels, even indulge in solo sex without it ever occurring to them that they should lock the door behind them. Yet if there was someone else in the house these same people would lock the bathroom door with the dedication of the Fort Knox night-shift. This curious lapse in human nature made life for Noilly a lot easier, and death for them easier still.

The banshee wail was reaching a high-pitched

crescendo. Downstairs the cat was woken from its slumbers and began to stretch and yawn and wonder what it was that its subconscious sixth sense had picked up. Breakfast? A hormonal tom-cat in the neighbourhood? No, it was just death paying a call.

Noilly began to creep forward on his perfectly balanced way towards the unlocked bathroom door, the cotton swab in his hands lifted to the height of an average little old lady's nose.

DS Gerhardie threw the forms back at sergeant Freemantle.

'Done,' he said, with some feeling.

'You have been,' the sergeant said, his light joviality coming up close but never daring to cross the border into unfettered sarcasm.

DS Gerhardie looked back at Clive. 'Now fuck off back to your crooked relatives and don't waste any more of my fucking time.'

'For God's sake, I'm trying to prevent murder here. Listen you,' he turned to the sergeant, 'there's a killer after my family and this idiot won't believe me.' If he had thought that Sergeant Freemantle might take his side against DS Gerhardie he hadn't reckoned on the loyalty of uniform. Take any profession, no matter how high or low – lawyer, doctor, road sweeper, bingo caller – pick on one of them and all their colleagues instantly become your sworn enemy.

'Who are you calling "idiot", bollock breath?' the sergeant asked.

Clive recognised a brick wall when he saw one, and banging his head against it was going to be futile as well as painful. He looked at his watch, rescued from Christopher's clutches; it was nine thirty. He'd just have to go home and protect his family himself.

The shower was hissing and spitting its warm jets on to the short yet extremely round figure of Euterpe Wrigley. Noilly could just make out the shape of a body through the plastic shower curtain, which provided a veil of modesty for his victim. Her singing was torturing his ears and he was looking forward to seeing her off gracefully into the next world, or anywhere that was out of earshot.

He looked around the room. To the left of the shower was a group of mirrored tiles, misted over but still giving a picture of something unusual glittering on the wall behind him. He turned to look at it.

Suddenly the plastic shower curtain flashed open and a short, fat naked woman jumped out and began to tear at Noilly with flabby wet hands.

'You bastard pervert, I'll show you, you dirty-minded shit,' she spat at him.

Noilly could have put the cotton to her face quite easily, despite her anger and the surprise of her attack. It is a common fallacy that someone whose life is in danger can fight with the strength of two; all that happens is that they fight without care or attention, which makes the job of a professional like Noilly even easier. So he let her hit him, scratch his face and neck and drag him down to the floor, knowing that each blow she landed only drained her strength. When she had collapsed, tired and without any more fight in her, he took the big blue towel from the pine rack and wrapped it carefully around her shoulders to protect her modesty and prevent her catching a chill.

'Who are you, you bumfucker?' Euterpe asked, shivering with both cold and fear.

'I work for your son.'

'What are you, some kind of window cleaner?' she said, looking directly at the cotton swab that had been discarded on to the wet bathroom floor.

'No. I'm here to kill you,' Noilly said, as if telling a joke.

'My son Christopher sent you?' she asked, brightening slightly.

'No, not this time. The other one.'

'Clive? Are you sure?' Euterpe's brightness had vanished and been replaced with astonishment.

Noilly nodded.

'Who'd have thought it. The little shit has some spunk in him after all.'

Clive tore home as quickly as a 647 bus would allow, which wasn't so much a tear as a gentle origami fold.

'Come on, man,' he yelled at the bus driver from his front-row seat. 'Can't this thing go any faster?'

The bus driver readjusted his rear-view mirror to see if the mad passenger was for real.

'This is the steepest public road in Yorkshire, this bus is twenty years old and the frequency of engine servicing has dropped off dramatically since deregulation. What do you expect, buster?'

'I could bloody run faster than this.'

The bus pulled away from the bus stop and left Clive

swearing at the driver and bringing down a million curses on his family. It was the first time he had ever been ejected from a bus. He wasn't sure he'd even met anyone who had met anyone who had suffered such a humiliating fate. There was nothing for it but to walk the last two miles. It started raining.

'So what happens now?' Euterpe asked, knowing when she was beaten.

'I'm going to cover your mouth and nose with this pad and you'll go into a nice sleep.'

'And then?'

'A pillow over your face.'

'And then?'

'A midnight burial in a quiet spot somewhere in the country. It will be very tasteful, I promise.'

'You'd better get on with it then.'

Clive staggered up Halcyon Terrace, his hot lungs bursting from the effort of pushing his overweight body along. It was after ten and as he reached the front door he knew he was too late; it swung loosely on its hinges, open and unlocked, mocking him.

'Mother?' he called into the house and received a sonar echo that told him it contained no living beings whatever. Unsurprisingly there was no answer. 'Mother?' he tried again, hope already scraping the bottom of the barrel.

Clive walked in quietly, which in comparison to Noilly's entrance was more like a herd of pissed elephants in search of a late-night curry house.

'Mother!' he shouted once more, mainly for comfort

in the silence than from any expectation of finding her alive.

Downstairs was empty. Upstairs was empty. But the bathroom was where it had happened, he could tell. There were damp towels tossed aside, water was lying on the cushion flooring in a million small lakes. It was like Finland viewed from the air. The room still dripped but it wasn't the warm foggy air of a recently used shower, it was cold and wet, and said that the excitement had happened some time before.

'I'm too late,' he said, flatly. 'He's got away.' Clive slowly slipped down the wet wall and fell into a heap on the floor.

Sixteen

There was a number of questions unanswered, hanging around like the smell of chloroform in Clive's bathroom. What had happened at Halcyon Terrace and where was Noilly now? After several hours drip-drying in the damp bathroom Clive got up and went in search of the cordless phone. The first number he rang was Ben Hopkins', then Grace's mobile, but there was no reply from either, so he rang Nostrum Hall.

'Disney? How did the funeral go?'

'It was beautiful, I've never seen such a colourful ceremony.'

'I can imagine,' Clive said, blanching as he did so. 'Something's happened up here. It's all getting a bit complicated. Can I come down and stay with you for a while, and bring Grace and the kids too?'

'Sure, but I was going to come back tomorrow to take Mother to Australia.'

'I wouldn't bother.'

'Why.'

'I paid someone to kill her and he's just fulfilled his contractual duties.'

Clive tried to pack, which he soon found was the hardest part of fleeing. If he took too much he might be dangerously weighed down. But if he didn't take enough he might not have the necessary equipment to cope with the long haul. As a minimum he would need his passport, warm clothes, cool clothes, clothes that could disguise him, toiletries, food, money (cash only and lots of it) and a comfortable pair of shoes. In Clive's case a pair of over-priced loafers by Patrick Cox.

He sneaked out of the house and caught the last bus into Bradworth. He felt a great sadness as he left the place that had been his home for so many years and yet which had so quickly become tainted with bad memories. But by the time he reached the city centre he was starting to feel a lessening of the weight that had been pressing down on his chest for the last couple of weeks. Then he remembered his inhalers, which were still in the kitchen at home.

'I'll manage,' he said, with some conviction.

The next morning, after a night of dodging imaginary assailants he imagined were pursuing him, Clive arrived at Nostrum Hall to find the beautiful stately home in a bit of a state. All the hi-tech equipment had long gone, shipped in special containers to Minnesota, and all that was left were a few bits of furniture covered in red and green sheets.

'Looks like someone died. From colour blindness,' Clive said.

It was Tuesday morning and oddly quiet as most of the devotees of the Brahmin had followed their computer terminals and gone West. Clive stood around in the hallway humming the Village People's minor hit from 1979 'Go West' (later covered by the Pet Shop Boys) while waiting for a sign of life to emerge from the clashing ghostly sheets. A couple of verses in he spotted a familiar figure approaching.

'Disney. How are you?' He hugged her tightly.

'When Soleil died I thought I was being penalised for being bad. But coming back here I realise that when it comes to penalties, the Brahmin always saves. I feel complete again.'

Completely nuts, Clive thought. He felt uncertain about revealing all that had happened since she'd left Bradworth, if anything was going to make her feel incomplete again it was that. He decided to begin gently.

'Any news on Christopher?' He hadn't seen him since he'd attacked him and left him for dead the previous Saturday night.

'Christopher is now in America. He's responsible for developing the import and export strategy for Rajneesh Holdings Inc.'

'Is he taking the piss again?'

Disney looked blanker than a self-employed builder's VAT return. 'He's taking urine out of the country, if that's what you mean.'

'I don't understand. Why urine, why not Liebfraumilch?' Clive asked.

'Liebfraumilch? I don't know anything about that. All I know is it's not ordinary urine he's carrying, it's the urine of celibate women.'

'What?'

'It's to do with test-tube babies, apparently.' Disney sounded vague. In a deep, dark vault of Clive's memory a light went on.

'Test-tube babies. Of course. In-vitro fertilisation treatment. Drugs are injected into women to increase egg production in the womb. They're made from urine. The urine of women who never have sex. They usually use nuns' urine.'

'That's right. He said that. He also said that the major drug companies have tied up long-term deals with most of the European convents.'

'I remember Grace telling me all about it when we went through IVF, before we adopted Dan and Hattie. It made me feel weird, the thought that nuns' piss was being injected into her. I was worried in case she developed an unhealthy interest in *The Sound of Music*.'

'I had no idea that you went through all that,' Disney said tenderly.

Clive brushed her sympathy aside. 'So our smart-arse brother realised he could use this religious community to provide the basic raw ingredient for the Bluebell Valley's other business interest, fertility treatment.'

'He set up the deal with Soleil.'

'But I guess Soleil didn't fancy the idea of going celibate.'

'I wouldn't have thought so. Not Soleil,' Disney

sighed, as if wishing she could have her time with her mentor again.

'Which meant that Christopher was quite happy to go along with having him killed. That would leave him free to deal direct with the main man. The real top banana,' Clive mused.

'Christopher was behind his death?' Disney was horrified at this news.

'Sorry. I seem to have been waist-deep in death for so long I forget how little everyone knows. It's worse than that, I'm afraid. The idea for the hit came from Mother. Christopher was just a willing go-between.'

He took Disney's hand and squeezed. 'There's more, can you take it?'

Disney gave him an anxious look. Reluctantly she nodded.

'The man who did it, who killed Soleil, I know him. It's kind of through me they got in touch with him.' Clive explained how Christopher had witnessed the abortive attack on Durkin. 'The other night I went to see this man. I paid him to kill Mother. The idea was I'd go to the police and tell them. Then they'd go to the house in time and arrest him. Trouble was I went to DS Gerhardie who wouldn't believe anything I said. By the time I got to the house the deed had been done.'

'That was brave of you, Clive, if a bit dim.'

Clive gave her a forced smile. He could see she was shaken, so it didn't seem a good time to mention that although he had told the police to arrive at Halcyon Terrace at ten a.m to make the arrest, he had arranged for Noilly to make the hit on their mother at nine thirty. His hope was that Euterpe would already be dead and

Noilly would be caught making his escape. He would then implacably deny anything Noilly said and take his chances in court.

He told Disney about the other contract that Euterpe had ordered, the one on Grace and the children. 'He's out there now, I was hoping to bring her here but I've no idea where she and the children are.'

'That's easy. They're here,' Disney said matter of factly. Clive felt oddly muted rather than excited by this news.

'Great,' he said, as if he'd just been told he had something terminal.

'She arrived last night and asked if she could claim sanctuary here. I told her "When you feel you're about to burst, you can safely pop in here." That was one of Soleil's favourites, bless him.'

Clive felt hot and bothered. He wasn't sure what he would say to Grace after what he saw her doing with Durkin, or what he had done again with Julia. But when Disney took him to her and he saw her sitting in a sparsely furnished room playing with the children, he knew instinctively what to say.

'Sorry.'

But it was never going to be that simple.

'Love is never having to use a pathetically inadequate word to cover up your heinous crimes against womankind.' She had obviously been rehearsing.

'Does that mean I'm forgiven?'

Grace stuck her knee deep into his testicles. 'What do you think?'

*

After a few days of having no one to keep under surveillance DS Gerhardie started to worry. He was confronted with a vision of his own failings and it filled a worryingly large canvas. He felt redundant having no one to follow. What was worse, he knew that when his seniors heard the truth about all the cock-ups he probably would be redundant.

His reports to DI Corby diminished in credibility daily as he tried to hide the fact that Clive had told him about potential crimes, had not been believed and so had been thrown out, and then, along with every other suspect in the case, had disappeared.

'Pardon?' DI Corby said in disbelief at what he had just heard. DS Gerhardie had decided to adopt the oldest police adage 'Honesty is the best policy'. DI Corby adopted the same approach and the next ten minutes were a detailed breakdown of where DS Gerhardie's career was headed for the remainder of his working life. It appeared to include a range of new challenges that included giving the police dogs their early-morning feed, and a secondment to the supplies stores as junior assistant stock-control officer. It also pointed out, with a frankness beloved of DI Corby, that DS Gerhardie was a useless cunt, had always been a useless cunt, and always would be a useless cunt. From now on, thanks to the skill match that modern policing required for its staff, he would be a useless cunt in a useless cunt of job.

After the initial shock of this assessment DS Gerhardie started to relax. He saw a dawning future of regular hours, no responsibility, weekends at home with his DIY manuals and pet projects. He could even detect the faintest whiff of early retirement wafting over the horizon towards his crusty nostrils. He started to feel almost cheerful. At this rate he might be able to manage a smile in time for his disciplinary hearing.

Seventeen

They stayed on at Nostrum Hall after all the acolytes had left. Disney arranged for some frugal supplies to be left behind to enable them to stay indoors and keep a low profile. Frugal as in seven chest-freezers full of food, a walled garden with spring vegetables coming to fruit and a well-stocked wine cellar with a passable Liebfraumilch specially imported to please the palates of the godly. The police were still nosing around looking for clues about the death of Soleil, but a man, woman and two children wearing red and green robes were much like any of the other religious nuts, so no one thought to ask too many awkward questions. After a while the search moved on to Payback Falls and they were left alone.

Clive and Grace spent the time trying to put their lives back together. Clive made Grace tell him over and over again about the details leading up to Durkin's alcoholic injection. Not only because he was insanely jealous, but also because he enjoyed hearing it so much. Grace enjoyed hearing about Julia too, but for different reasons. The more she committed Clive's embarrassed confessions to memory the longer she would be able to hold it over him and ensure his eternal contriteness. Then he told her of the contract taken out on her and the children, and of his own terrible revenge on his mother.

'I thought men wanted to fuck their mums, not kill them,' Grace asked mischievously.

'Sex and death, it's pretty much the same thing.'

'It certainly was with Ben Hopkins.'

'Was it?' Clive tried hard to sound nonchalant but it still came out sounding like 'Please tell me more'.

'There's something about having sex with a man who, out of choice, wears corduroy jackets with leather patches on the elbows,' Grace explained. 'It was a constant reminder of how low I had sunk.'

That was good enough for Clive. The idea of corduroy alone was enough to remove Ben Hopkins as a symbol of sexual potency.

'That's how I felt about Julia, too,' Clive agreed, seeing an opportunity to defuse the thorny issue of his indiscretions with Julia for ever.

'Don't push it, mate,' Grace said, with some ferocity.

As time passed, Clive made a few careful phone calls to see how the land lay. If he expected it to be bumpy he was as surprised as anyone to find that things had actually reached a stable plateau. The police investigation had first stalled and then completely failed its MOT, and had now been taken off the road altogether. No body, no evidence, no ideas; that seemed to be the progress made so far.

'Thanks to DS Gerhardie it sounds like there's nothing left to investigate,' Clive reported back to Grace after a crafty phone call to Mandy at the Listen To You offices. There was another bit of good news: Durkin had disappeared on a private journey into the long dark night of his soul. He had last been seen standing around a flaming brazier under the railway arches, shouting obscenities at nobody in particular and clutching a jug of anti-freeze.

'He's finally got what he deserves,' Grace said without remorse.

Listen To You was running along nicely in Durkin's absence. After a few weeks of expensive inactivity Clive's lawyers were happy to inform him that the official papers signing it over to Durkin had never been successfully delivered. Technically it was still his, if he wanted it. Then Marilyn told him that Headline Television, who produced Durkin's daily show *Amen in the Confessional*, was urgently looking for a temporary replacement for its errant star. Clive's name had been mentioned by several people, probably because of his infamy rather than any talent as a therapist; it was day-time TV after all. He let it be known on the grapevine that the only way they'd get him to do it would be over his dead body.

It was twelve weeks later, one night after the children had gone to bed and Grace and Clive were opening their fifth bottle of Liebfraumilch, that Noilly broke into Nostrum Hall. The door opened silently as they were laughing at the sort of joke only newly acquainted lovers find funny. Grace noticed the shadowy figure first, standing on the other side of the large room.

'Jesus.'

'No, it's Noilly,' Noilly said.

'Hello,' Clive waved drunkenly, as if to an old friend. Noilly had grown his fringe again, although it had been thinned out so that his features could be seen, like an ageing film star being viewed through a Vaseline-coated lens.

'Oh shit.' Grace's legendary courage was burning its draft card and making for the Canadian border. 'What do you want?' she asked, already knowing exactly what Noilly wanted.

'We want what you want.' It was another voice, deeper than Noilly's. From behind him a small round figure entered the room. She had turquoise hair and was dressed in a blue-and-white two-piece suit that looked like Earth viewed from space. Only bigger.

'Mommie Dearest!' Clive's laugh was maniacal now.

'I'm not your mother any more. I'm his mother now.'

'She's Euterpe Upchurch. Changed her name by dead poll,' Noilly said, proudly, wrapping a protective arm around Euterpe.

'Deed poll, I think you mean. So the rumours of your demise were just that, unfortunately.'

'I'm not dead, in fact I fully intend to live happily ever after. That's why we are here. I want to live with Noilly, my loving son, without any intervention from the authorities.'

'What's that got to do with us?' Grace asked nervously.

'Everything. If you keep quiet then we get our dream. If you tell people about us and what we do then we don't. But in that scenario neither do you.' Euterpe looked at Noilly who, on cue, drew a finger across his throat and then flicked it in the direction of upstairs, where Dan and Hattie were sleeping. Grace instinctively knew he had already been up there to check.

'Why don't you just kill us all now and make sure?' Clive asked, smiling madly. Grace gave him a look that said that, if they ever got out of this, she was going to kill him anyway.

'I would have done, once upon a time. But I have to admit to being impressed by you. For the one and only time in my life. You showed spirit, and some intelligence too. I didn't think you had it in you. I don't love you, I can't stand you in fact. Never could, but now I do at least admire you. For that you get one favour. You get to live. As long as you are a good boy.'

Clive looked at Noilly. 'What happened? I thought you carried out orders whatever. "Business must be business" and all that.'

'There's always one person you can't kill,' he replied.

'And it only took one look at your bathroom wall and he knew that was me,' Euterpe's tone was sarcastic. 'He'd drugged me and was about to finish me off when he noticed the gold disc.'

It was one of the few things that Noilly could read with ease, he'd read it so many times. The label of the long-defunct Tonic Bender Records, on gold-painted plastic, which recognised one million sales of the song

'Mother Love' by The Family Affair. It was the only thing Clive had ever received in payment for his small part in making the record and he had hung it in the bathroom intending the gesture to be ironic. He'd never expected it to act as a heavenly visitation for The Family Affair's most ardent fan.

'It was a golden vision. It took me a while to work it out but I got there in the end. The woman asleep in my arms was the mother who inspired "Mother Love". I couldn't kill her. She's my moose.'

'She makes you horny?' Clive sniggered.

'He means muse,' Euterpe said coldly.

'Yeah, that's what I meant. Muse. The mother who inspired "Mother Love" was the mother I always wanted.'

Euterpe started singing.

> *'Apron strings, apron strings,*
> *The joy that my love brings.*
> *Mother love, Mother love,*
> *I was sent by God above.'*

Noilly took her hand and kissed it. 'I love you, Mum.'

'He's just a poor, lonely, lovely boy who would do anything for me. Which, lucky for me, includes not topping me.'

'What about your suspicious nodule? Isn't that going to top you?' Clive asked hopefully. Grace shoved him, trying to cause as much pain as she could.

'Lump of benign fatty tissue. The doc whipped it out. I've got it in a jar at home.'

'Which is where?'

'You don't want to know, not if you know what's good for you. We shan't be there long anyway. We're going to Cromer. I have a fancy that Julia and my boy here will have a lot in common.' She gave Noilly a dirty look and he turned away shyly. 'She's playing the Giant in next season's panto, you know. We could even do The Family Affair reunion, without the original members of course.'

'Julia's slept with two of the original members, that's more than most sixties reunions can manage.' Clive laughed and swigged from the bottle of Liebfraumilch.

'Then maybe we'll go on to Australia. I'd like to show Noilly the Bluebell Valley. Anyway we shan't be in touch again, unless you choose to make it a necessity.' She gave them a knowing look.

'We won't.' Clive saluted and then fell backwards in a drunken heap.

'Come on, darling, let's go and leave these pathetic creatures to their dull lives.'

'Mother.' Clive's tone ordered Euterpe to stop and listen. He sat up. 'I want you to know that I hope you can be happy.'

'Don't start pretending you love me, I know it's not true.'

'I'm not. I don't love you. After all you've done I probably hate you as much as you hate me. But that doesn't matter. Just because we're related it doesn't mean we have to love each other, and while I wish you untold harm I also hope you can be happy. I really do.'

'Whatever.' With that Euterpe walked out of Clive's life for ever, he hoped.

Noilly covered her exit with a vicious stare and only

when he was sure she was safely away did he sweep out after her without a word.

They sat in silence for ages, until somewhere across the fields from down by the main road they heard a motorcycle engine start up and chug away into the night.

'You idiotic bastard.' Grace slapped Clive hard across the head.

'Ouch. What's the matter with you?'

'What were you trying to do, get us killed? He would have shot us for the slightest remark and what did you do? Take the piss.'

'It runs in the family.' Clive started to laugh.

'Stupid drunk bastard.' Grace slapped him again to release tension.

'We were quite safe.'

'How do you know that, Mister Perfect Psychologist?'

'Quite simple. He was wearing a tweed jacket and jeans.'

'An awful combination I agree but no real guarantee of safety.'

'Maybe not, but they weren't white. He didn't have his paper suit on. Mad tossers like him are so anal they can't deviate from their conditioning even if they want to. He couldn't have laid a finger on us without that suit. Fear of dirt. People like him won't go within half a mile of a Hoover bag,' Clive said, pleased with his fulsome psychological profile.

'I'm going to check on the kids.' Grace went out to the stairs.

After ten minutes she hadn't come back and Clive

started to worry that Noilly might have gone back on his word. He went in search of her. She wasn't upstairs, where Dan and Hattie were sleeping peacefully enough. He went down again and found her in the kitchen staring at the table and shaking gently.

'What is it?' he asked. Grace pointed at the table without speaking. Neatly laid out there was a white waxed-paper suit. It was a warning. He had brought it, ready for use in the event of Euterpe sending him to work.

Clive put his arm around Grace. She looked at him.

'Bloody therapists, what do you know?' She slapped him hard on the head for the last time and then kissed him.

When they finally pulled apart Clive had a distant expression, as if enlightenment had struck him like a thunderbolt.

'I've just had another of my premonitions.'

'What did you see?'

'I saw myself dead.'

'What does that tell you?'

'It tells me to give up counselling. Listening to what people say is too dangerous. I see my future in daytime television; I'll never have to listen to anyone again.'

'Do you wanna touch me?' Grace asked him and winked.

Clive had a vague feeling he should know this one. Was it Slade, or T Rex, or maybe even Mud? He could have recalled every detail if he'd tried, but why bother? Life was too short.

'Yeah!' he replied eagerly.

Grace struck her best Gary Glitter pose, hands on

curvaceous hips, chest thrust out, groin describing concentric circles.

'Where?' As if she needed to ask.

They burned the white suit on the open fire and watched the little black ashes float up the chimney while sipping an Australian sparkling wine from the special-reserve rack in the cellar. As the embers died away Clive looked at the rug on which they lay. It was an animal fur that had been dyed red and green. That or it had been experimenting with hallucinogenic drugs when it was shot.

'I've got a fancy to play bears,' Clive suggested huskily.

Grace smiled and enthusiastically set about showing him how.

SPITTING DISTANCE

Jon Wright

A story of sex, drugs, rock'n'roll and the care of the elderly.

In the punk rock explosion of 1976 Billy forms a band to beat the system with Kirk St John, an almost mythical figure from the shadowy world of catering. Together they go out to set the world on fire, but only manage to singe a Triumph Vitesse.

After a disastrous American tour and the fact that Kirk has had sex with Billy's girlfriend, they go their separate ways, but their feud is set to continue over the next twenty years. Kirk becomes a renowned chef, restaurateur, and TV celebrity – a friend of the rich and famous, whose girlfriends he still can't help shagging. Billy achieves the dizzy heights of nursing assistant (temporary) in an old people's home. In the final confrontation between good and evil, this is a battle between saucepans and bedpans …

Will Kirk ever get his come-uppance? Does Billy ever get his revenge? And most of all, can an old (and recently deceased) ex-punk rocker ever regain his anarchic soul?

'Richly entertaining … his touch is deft, and frequently spot-on … Wright earns full marks for making something genuinely funny from the grim truth that we pull the trigger on the slow death of middle age somewhere around the age of 24'
The Times

TIME FOR BED

David Baddiel

'Very, very funny'
Roddy Doyle

Gabriel Jacoby can't get to sleep. In fact, he can't get anywhere at all, either in his Triumph Dolomite or his life. Everything around him, from his large collection of coffee-machines to his balding Bradford-born flatmate, is breaking down. Not that Gabriel is bothered; he's too busy being in love with his intensely happily married brother's wife. Which is why Gabriel chooses to waste all his time – because he knows that whatever else he might achieve, it won't be happiness. There's no way there, when you're in love with your brother's wife.

Unless you suddenly remember your brother's wife has a sister …

'One of the best things I have ever read about the nature of mad, obsessive love … funny, sad and horribly, painfully true'
Tony Parsons

'… a richly observant and blisteringly funny, fabulously well-executed novel'
Kate Saunders, *Sunday Express*

'Sharp, funny and hugely entertaining'
Helen Fielding, author of *Bridget Jones' Diary*

GRIDLOCK

Ben Elton

Gridlock is when a city dies.

Killed in the name of freedom. Killed in the name of oil and steel. Choked on carbon monoxide and strangled with a pair of fluffy dice.

How did it come to this? How did the ultimate freedom machine end up paralysing us all? How did we end up driving to our own funeral, in somebody else's gravy train?

Deborah and Geoffrey know, but they have transport problems of their own, and anyway, whoever it was that murdered the city can just as easily murder them.

'Brilliant ... the comedy sometimes achieves Tom Sharpe levels of outrage and the thrills sometimes match Alfred Hitchcock for malign invention ... somewhere under the stage suit there may be a Booker candidate'
Richard Heller, *Mail on Sunday*

Other bestselling Warner titles available by mail:

☐ Spitting Distance	Jon Wright	£6.99
☐ Time For Bed	David Baddiel	£5.99
☐ Gridlock	Ben Elton	£5.99

The prices shown above are correct at time of going to press. However, the publishers reserve the right to increase prices on covers from those previously advertised without prior notice.